SHE IS GONE

Jack Anderson Book 3

Ben Cheetham

Cover designed by stuartbache.co.uk

This book is a work of fiction. Names, characters, places, and incidents either are products of the author's imagination or are used fictitiously. Any resemblance to actual persons, living or dead, events, or locales is entirely coincidental.

Visit my website at bencheetham.com

Printed in the United Kingdom

First Printing: June 2019

ISBN-13 978-10750026-9-4

PROLOGUE

30th July 1998

Marcus drew aside the net curtains to peer out of the window. The little cluster of picnic tables in front of the inn was unoccupied. Across the mini-roundabout where three roads converged at the centre of the village, The Lion and Lamb Hotel's beer garden was also deserted. The sky was grey with the threat of rain. Light showers had been sweeping in from the coast all day, driven by a stiff westerly. For the past half-an-hour the rain had held off. The sun was winking between the clouds, teasing the possibility of a sunny afternoon. Marcus turned to his wife and two young daughters.

Andrea was sleeping off a hearty lunch of Cumberland sausage and mash washed down with several halves of bitter. Despite the unsettled weather of the past week, her cheeks were flushed from the days they'd spent exploring the paths around Windermere and Coniston Water. The previous day, they'd relocated from Bowness-on-Windermere to Gosforth to do some walking in Wasdale. But as was so often the case even in July, the good old, crappy English weather had thrown a spanner in the works.

Not that Charlie and Tracy seemed particularly bothered. The sisters were quite content to lounge around the cramped room the four of them were sharing. They were stretched out on fold-down beds that flanked a double bed. As usual, Charlie's head was buried in one of the horror novels she'd come to love since hitting her teens. Tracy was busy chewing gum and staring into the Game Boy that Santa had brought her last Christmas. Not that she believed in Santa. In fact, Marcus couldn't recall a time when she hadn't doubted Santa's existence.

1

Tracy had asked the same old questions as all kids – how can such a fat man fit down a chimney? How can he deliver presents to every child in the world in one night?

And Marcus had countered her logic with the same answer he'd given Charlie – magic.

But unlike Charlie, Tracy hadn't believed him. Not for a second. Marcus smiled to himself. She was a sharp one, that's for sure. She drove her mum – and him too for that matter – to distraction asking questions. Why this? Why that? Why the other? Nothing escaped her keen brown eyes. She had a way of looking at you that made you feel as if she was rummaging around in your mind for the answers she wanted. No vampires and werewolves for her. She preferred to read the newspapers. He would often find her poring over stories of death and destruction from around the world – a woman strangled to death by her husband in London, twenty dead in a mass shooting in Texas, hundreds dead in conflicts across the Middle East and Africa. Even aged eleven, Tracy knew where the real monsters were to be found.

"So who fancies a walk?" asked Marcus.

The question drew an indifferent response. Andrea gave out a soft snore. Tracy shrugged without glancing up from her Game Boy. Charlie peered at her dad from between the curtains of curly brown hair she'd inherited from her mum. "My legs are aching," she grumbled.

"Oh don't give me that," said Marcus. "You're thirteen. You're as fit as a lop. Besides, we don't have to walk far. I only want to see Wasdale."

Andrea stirred, her eyes blinking open. "Was what?" she asked, yawning. There were dark smudges under her eyes. Four nights sharing a bedroom with two kids had left her more tired than before the holiday started.

"W-a-s-d-a-l-e," Marcus spelled out, pedantically emphasising each letter.

A deep crease between Andrea's eyebrows warned him that her patience was wearing thin. "What about it?"

2

"The weather looks like it's clearing up. I thought we could check out Low Lonning."

"What's a lonning?" asked Charlie.

"Lonning is a Cumbrian word for a lane," put in Tracy.

Charlie pushed her lower lip out as if to say, *Boring!*

Tracy sighed as if dealing with her sister required infinite amounts of patience.

"The views are supposed to be amazing," said Marcus, vainly trying to whip up some enthusiasm.

"Why don't you just go on your own?" said Charlie.

Marcus frowned as if hurt by the suggestion. "This is our first holiday since last summer. I want to spend time with my girls."

"And we want to spend time with you too," said Andrea. "But we've been out hiking every day this week."

"I thought you enjoyed walking."

"I do, Marcus, but I'm knackered. And the girls want to see the coast."

"Perhaps I've pushed you all a bit too hard," conceded Marcus. "But it's only because we spend so much time cooped up in offices and classrooms. Charlie was starting to look like one of the vampires in her books."

"She wishes," Tracy quipped with her usual dry humour.

Charlie stuck her tongue out at her. Tracy arched an eyebrow as if to say, *Is that the best you can do?* Charlie may have been two years the elder, but when it came to verbal sparring she was no match for Tracy, and both of them knew it.

Marcus's smile returned. He reached to ruffle Tracy's unruly mane of hair, whose auburn colour fell somewhere between Andrea's chestnut brown and his own vibrant ginger. "Leave your sister alone."

"How about this?" said Andrea. "We'll go for a walk with you if–" She was interrupted by a loud groan from Charlie. Andrea threw her a silencing glance. *"If* we can go to Whitehaven tomorrow. I'd like to have a look around the shops."

"Me too! Me too!" Charlie enthusiastically seconded.

"How does that sound to you?" Andrea asked Tracy.

Tracy responded with another shrug. Shopping was no more her thing than hiking. She would have rather curled up in some quiet place with a stack of newspapers and a packet of her favourite strawberry flavoured Hubba Bubba.

"It's a deal," said Marcus. "Now come on. Let's get going before the rain comes back."

He hustled his daughters into their jackets and trainers. The four of them tramped down a gloomy stairway to a cosy barroom – flagstone floor polished by countless feet, sooty stone fireplace, dark wood tables and chairs, dusty sash-windows. The air was hazy with cigarette smoke. The landlord Len – a man whose beetroot face and nine-months-pregnant belly suggested he spent too much time sampling his own wares – was pulling pints for three men at the bar. The men didn't look like tourists. Two had on the navy blue overalls and mud spattered wellies of farm workers. Their burly shoulders were made for tossing around bales of hay. The third wore heavy duty boots, blue jeans, a wax jacket and flat cap. He was as thin as a polecat and tall enough that he had to stoop to avoid the ceiling beams.

The trio were talking loudly, but they fell silent as the Ridleys entered the barroom. The men in overalls cast the family uninterested glances. The tall man surveyed them with hooded, sunken eyes. A cigarette dangled from his thin-lipped mouth.

Len stated the obvious. "You're off out."

"We're going for a walk on that lane you mentioned last night – Low Lonning," said Marcus.

The tall man exhaled a stream of smoke towards him and spoke through his cigarette. "You got a dog?" His tone was flat – not unfriendly, but not exactly friendly either.

Marcus gave him a thin smile. "No."

"What's it got to do with you whether we've got a dog?" asked Tracy, returning the man's narrow stare.

His companions burst into laughter. "Yeah, Phil, what's it got to do with you?" taunted one of them.

"Tracy, don't be so rude," said Andrea.

"I'm not being rude," countered Tracy. "I just asked a question. Why is that rude?"

Phil stooped towards her. His tanned, leathery skin pulled tight over sharp cheekbones as he pushed out his chin. "Because little girls should be seen and not heard. Didn't your parents ever teach you that?" His voice was the same raspy monotone, but there was a gleam of annoyance in his eyes.

Tracy didn't flinch from his gaze. She fought not to choke or even wrinkle her nose at the stench of beer and cigarettes that emanated from him. "Why would they teach me something as stupid as that?"

Another gale of laughter erupted from Phil's companions.

"Tracy!" reprimanded Andrea. "Say sorry, right now."

Tracy's eyebrows knitted together. "What for?"

"Just do as I say."

Tracy pursed her lips obstinately.

"Right, no more Game Boy for the rest of the holiday."

A glimmer of tears sprang into Tracy's eyes at the threat, but she held her silence. Phil drew away from her, a smile crawling up one side of his face as if he took pleasure from what he saw. "No need for apologies," he said. "The woods around Low Lonning are stocked with pheasants. That's why I asked if you have a dog."

"Phil's a gamekeeper," Len added by way of explanation.

"Well you've no need to worry," said Marcus, maintaining a strained smile. "We won't disturb your pheasants." He ushered his daughters towards the front door.

"Enjoy your walk," Len called after them.

Phil's gaze followed Tracy out of the door. She threw him a final defiant glance as the door swung shut.

"What was that guy's problem?" asked Charlie as they headed for the pub's carpark. "Did you see the way he looked at Tracy? He gave me the creeps."

"He didn't scare me," said Tracy, swiping the tears from her eyes as if irritated by them.

"Alright, that's enough," said Marcus.

"You know, Tracy, one of these days you'll get yourself into big trouble talking to people like that," Andrea said as they piled into a Ford Escort estate that had seen better days. "Not everyone is nice."

"Yeah, I know," Tracy responded. "There were over a thousand murders in the UK last year."

"How do you know that?" asked Charlie.

"There are these things called newspapers," Tracy said acerbically. "You should try reading one instead of those crappy books."

"I said *enough*," Marcus interjected as Charlie opened her mouth to make a retort. He darted a warning glance at Tracy. "And you watch your language."

Crossing her arms, Charlie subsided into pouting silence. Tracy held her dad's eyes for just long enough to let him know she considered herself to be in the right, before returning her gaze to the pub. She stared at it with an oddly intense look in her eyes, almost as if she was hoping to see Phil again. Marcus gave a despairing shake of his head. He knew that look only too well. He'd been subjected to it many times himself. It was a look she reserved for people who'd drawn some sign of weakness from her. It said as clear as crystal, *You may have got the better of me this time, but next time things will be different.*

Marcus puffed his cheeks as he accelerated out of the carpark. "You girls will be the death of me."

Andrea turned the radio on. The Spice Girls came through the speakers. Tracy rolled her eyes as Charlie sang along in an out-of-tune warble.

Rows of quaint white cottages gave way to sheep-grazed fields. A narrow river ran alongside the road, bubbling gently over a stony bed.

They passed through a hamlet signposted 'Wellington' and crossed the river on a little stone bridge. The road rose steeply, hemmed in by thick hedges. After a few hundred metres it briefly flattened out before beginning to descend steadily between fields and stretches of trees. Occasional farmhouses nestled in amongst the rolling landscape. Several miles to the east clouds clustered above the blunt brown peaks of Wasdale. Wast Water remained hidden from view in a deep valley.

"Looks like rain," commented Andrea.

"It'll hold off," said Marcus.

Andrea cocked a doubtful eye at him.

He pulled over at a crossroads. A stony lane with a strip of grass at its centre branched off to either side of the main road. A wooden sign identified it as a 'Public Bridleway'. "I think this is Low Lonning."

"Which way are we walking?" asked Tracy.

Marcus pointed north. "Len says that's where you get the best views." He inhaled a deep breath of cool air as he got out of the car. "Smells wonderful, doesn't it?"

Charlie wrinkled her nose. "Smells like sheep poo."

"One day you'll thank me for this. I'm teaching you to love the countryside."

"Charlie doesn't like to be taught anything," Tracy said dryly. "Just ask her teachers."

Marcus laughed. "I don't need to ask. I've read her school report."

Pulling an annoyed face, Charlie shoved at him. He dodged away, and she turned to grab Tracy. The sisters locked hands, striving to push each other off balance. Charlie was two or three inches taller and more heavily built than Tracy. Even so, Tracy often came out on top in scraps through sheer determination and intense competitiveness. If there was one thing she hated more than anything else, it was losing. She seemed able to draw on deep wells of strength that belied her scrawny frame.

For a second the sisters' hands quivered between them, poised in deadlock. Andrea stepped in and broke them apart. "No more wind ups," she said with a pointed glance at Marcus.

"Sorry," he mouthed. He shot a cheeky wink at Charlie and Tracy. They stifled giggles. Sighing, Andrea turned away and started walking. Marcus hurried after her and caught hold of her hand. Birch and oak trees overhung the left-hand side of the bridleway. The other side was hemmed in by a hedge through which glimpses of distant scree-strewn slopes were visible.

"Wow, what a view," exclaimed Marcus. "What do you think girls?"

"Not bad," Charlie begrudgingly admitted.

The sun nudged out from behind the clouds, dappling the lane. Andrea raised her face to it. The pale golden light shimmered in her thick hair and highlighted her sun-kissed cheeks.

"You're not too bad either," said Marcus.

Andrea smiled and blew a kiss in his direction.

"Bleurgh!" Tracy said with a nauseated expression.

Marcus and Andrea exchanged a knowing glance. Tracy still looked away when actors kissed on-screen. To her, boys were an entirely different and unpleasant species. It wouldn't be long, though, before puberty kicked in and reversed her outlook. Marcus and Andrea were looking forwards to the prospect with mixed emotions. It was wonderful to see your child developing into a confident individual, but adolescence brought a whole

8

load of new issues to deal with. Top of the list with Charlie was boys. They were already drawn to her pretty face and budding curves like moths to a flame. Marcus and Andrea sensed there would be different problems with Tracy. Her refusal to let anyone get the upper hand had been seen as an endearing trait, but the older she got the more it brought her into conflict with people. What would have been laughed off coming from a young child would be met with anger and hostility coming from a teenager. Encounters such as the one in the bar of The Rose & Crown were becoming increasingly frequent occurrences.

As the lane arrowed northeast, the trees clustered thicker, dousing the Ridleys in deep shadows. Tracy stopped abruptly, staring into the woods, a vertical cleft between her eyebrows.

"What is it?" asked Marcus.

"I saw something moving."

"What? An animal?"

"I dunno." Tracy darted out a finger. "There." She couldn't be sure, but she'd seemed to glimpse a dark shape flitting between the trees.

"I don't see anything."

"Neither do I," said Charlie.

"Are there deer in these woods?" asked Tracy.

"No idea," said Marcus. "They're a rare breed of blind deer." He chuckled. "Do you get it? No-i-dea."

Tracy rolled her eyes, unamused.

"Your jokes are getting worse," said Andrea.

"No idea," repeated Charlie, her face creasing in confusion. "How is that even a jo–" She broke off with a flinch.

There *was* something in amongst the trees. Or rather, someone. A tall – maybe 6' or 6'1 – figure stepped into view a few metres from the lane. A sweaty chequered shirt clung to the figure's skinny male torso. Baggy blue jeans hung from his hips. A hessian bag dangled from a loop of twine on his shoulder. But it wasn't these things that had thrown Charlie into silence. It was the second hessian bag that masked the figure's face and, above all else, the shotgun he was aiming at the family.

Charlie's lungs loosened enough to let out a delayed scream as the sinister figure advanced into the lane. Andrea caught hold of her, drawing her protectively away from him. Marcus stepped in front of Tracy, putting up his hands, palms out. "Wha...What is..." he stammered, his words catching in his throat.

A man's croaky voice with a Cumbrian accent came through the bag. "Do as I say and I won't hurt you." There was a tremor in it as if whoever was behind the mask was almost as nervous as his victims. Dark eyes darted around like panicked fish in the shadows of roughly cut eyeholes. "I just want your money and car keys."

"We don't have much money," said Andrea, swallowing hard between words.

Marcus reached into his jacket pocket and took out his wallet and keys. They trembled in his hand.

"Throw them to me," said the man.

Marcus tossed the wallet and keys to the ground at the man's booted feet. The man took one hand off the shotgun to withdraw a bundle of heavy duty twine from the bag on his shoulder. He threw it to Marcus and instructed him, "Tie your family up."

Until that moment Tracy hadn't made a sound. She'd simply stood there studying the shotgun-wielding figure with eyes like drill bits, as if she was trying to bore through the mask and see the face behind it. But now she asked without a trace of fear, "Why?"

The man stared back at her as if unsure he'd heard correctly. "Why what?"

"Why do–"

"Shh, Tracy," cut in Marcus.

But she persisted, "Why do we need to be tied up? If you just want our money and keys, then take them and go away."

"You might come after me," said the man.

"We won't," Marcus assured him.

"We're not stupid enough to do that," added Tracy.

"You might phone the police."

She raised her hands to indicate the surrounding sweep of fields and trees. "How? I don't see a phone box."

"I don't know how." The man's voice swayed between bemusement and irritation.

"So why–"

The shotgun jerked towards Tracy. "Listen, you'd better shut your gob or I'll shut if for you."

Charlie gave out another half-choked scream and burst into tears. Andrea pulled her closer, hissing at Tracy, "Do as he says."

Charlie's sobs grew louder as the gun swung in her direction. "Stop crying!" demanded the man.

"You're scaring her," retorted Andrea, given courage by her motherly instincts.

The man softened his tone. "You needn't be scared," he told Charlie. "I'm not going to hurt you."

Tracy made a doubtful *hmph* that drew the shotgun back to her. She stared defiantly at its wielder as if daring him to pull the trigger. She'd already cried once today. She wasn't about to do so again. The eyes blinked within the shadows of the mask.

Tracy flinched as her dad caught hold of her hands. She tried to pull away as he wrapped twine around her wrists. "Please, Tracy," he said, his eyes wide with pleading. "The quicker you let me do this, the quicker he'll go away."

Tracy shook her head and squirmed around, but it wasn't enough to prevent Marcus from binding her wrists and ankles. His eyes begged for forgiveness as he gently laid her flat on the ground. She glared back at him with clench-toothed fury, feeling the residue of the recent rainfall seep through her clothes.

Marcus turned to Andrea and Charlie. They held still as he tied them up. "It'll be over soon," he sought to reassure Charlie, stroking her hair as she quivered and sniffled.

"Move away from her." The masked figure motioned with the shotgun where he wanted Marcus to go.

Marcus moved to the spot a few metres from his wife and daughters.

"Tie your ankles."

Again, Marcus complied.

"Now throw me the string and lie down on your face with your hands behind your back."

Marcus lowered himself to the ground. His breath whistled between his teeth as a thick-soled boot pressed heavily on the small of his back. The gun's muzzle came to rest against his skull. Keeping the shotgun wedged between his shoulder and Marcus's head, the man reached down with clammy hands to tie Marcus's wrists.

"Dad." Tracy's voice was an urgent whisper.

Marcus knew what she wanted – she wanted him to make a grab for the gun. There wouldn't be another chance. His muscles quivered at the knowledge. A doubting inner voice jabbed at him, *What if he's lying? What if he intends to hurt us?*

But even as he asked himself the questions the chance was passing. The twine bit into his wrists. The man's hands returned to the shotgun. "Please just take what you want and go," pleaded Marcus.

In response, the man reached into his hessian bag again. He withdrew a matching bag and stooped to pull it down over Marcus's face.

12

"Wait, what are you–" Marcus broke off as the muzzle was pushed painfully into the back of his head. The man kept it there for a second before moving on to Andrea and Charlie. Charlie started sobbing again as a bag plunged her into darkness.

"It's OK, Charlie. It's OK, I'm here," soothed Andrea as a bag was yanked over her face too.

The man turned his attention to Tracy. Lips compressed into a bloodless line, she stared up at him. A single word was written large in her eyes – *Liar!*

She kicked out at him. Dodging around her feet, he thrust a boot into her stomach. The breath whooshed from her lungs.

"What's going on?" cried Marcus, futilely struggling to shake the bag off his head.

"She made me kick her," the man replied with a petulant twist in his voice, like a schoolboy protesting his innocence after being caught fighting. "Tell her to lie still or I'll do it again."

"For Christ's sake, Tracy, lie still."

Ignoring her dad, Tracy contorted her body like a snake pinned by a stick. It made no difference. Within seconds, a veil of rough hessian blocked the sky from view. As if shut down by her sudden blindness, she became still. There was a crunch of boots on stones as the man moved away. The hessian inflated and deflated in time to her rapid breaths. It had a musty animal stink. There was a moment of silence, broken only by Charlie's sobs. Had their would-be robber taken what he claimed to want and gone?

Then came another male voice. This one also had a local accent, but there was no nervous tremor. The voice was deeper and harsher. "Are they tied up nice and tight?"

"Yes," replied the first man.

"Who… Who's that?" Marcus piped up, panic sucking at his voice.

"None of your fucking business," growled the newcomer.

"Why didn't you help me?" grumbled his accomplice.

"This is your party, not mine. Besides, I didn't think in a million years you'd actually go through with it."

"Well you were wrong."

"Oh yeah," the new arrival said with a chuckle that sent prickles down Marcus's spine. "I have to hand it to you, you proved me wrong big time."

"Mum, I can't breathe," Charlie gasped.

"Yes you can," said Andrea, sounding as if she herself was clinging to calm by her fingertips. "Try to breathe slowly." To their assailants, she added in a tone that somehow managed to be both hostile and pleading, "You've got what you want. Now leave us alone!"

"Who says I've got what I want?" asked the harsh-voiced newcomer.

"My bank card is in my wallet," Marcus blurted out. "There's several thousand pounds in my account. I'll tell you the pin number if you leave us alone." It was a lie – there was barely enough money in the account to cover the cost of the holiday – but it was all he could think to say.

The chuckle came again, louder, as if its maker was relishing the effect he was having. "Keep your money."

Marcus's bladder twitched at the reply. He felt a sudden almost overwhelming need to release its contents. *Tracy was right*, his mind screamed. *Oh Christ, she was right!*

"What does that mean?" asked the first man. "I thought we were just after their money."

"Bollocks you did," retorted his accomplice. "You knew this was never about money."

"Help!" Andrea cried out. "Help! Someone–"

She was silenced by a foot thundering into her midriff. Charlie screamed as hands pried her and Andrea apart. A sharp blow to the head silenced the teenager too.

"What are you doing?" Marcus yelled as fury finally got the better of his fear. "You bastards! Touch my family and I'll kill you!" He jerked up onto his knees. The butt of the shotgun crashed into his skull, throwing him back to the ground. He kicked out blindly. A second blow caught him flush in the face. He felt the cartilage in his nose give way under its crushing force. Hot blood exploded against the inside of the hessian bag. He coughed and spluttered as he inhaled the salty, metallic-tasting liquid. He lay on the brink of unconsciousness, his mind swirling desperately for a way out of the horrific predicament. There wasn't one. His bonds were tight enough to cut off the blood flow. Even if he screamed himself hoarse, no one lived near enough to hear. Fear overwhelmed his anger again. "Please," he whimpered. "Please don't hurt them."

"Look at him," chuckled the pitiless voice. "It makes you want to puke."

"What now?" asked the first man. There was something new in his voice – a strange thickness.

"You know what now. You've told me what you want to do enough times. So go on, do it."

"Shall I? Shall I really?"

"Yes you shall."

Both assailants were momentarily silent. Marcus's breath gurgled against the blood-soaked bag. Charlie was making a pained, breathless mewling. As if in slow-motion, Andrea uncurled her winded body and groped about in search of her eldest daughter. Tracy lay as seemingly motionless as an animal that knew its best chance of survival was to play dead, but behind her back her hands were working to and fro against the twine. Perhaps deliberately or maybe because she'd struggled, her dad hadn't bound her wrists all that tightly. Now, millimetre by millimetre, she was manoeuvring the twine over her hands. She could feel slivers of skin curling on the backs of her hands, but the pain hardly registered. She barely even noticed what was going on around her. Her entire being was focused on freeing her hands. For a sickening second she didn't think she would be able to get the twine past her knuckles. With a final little wrench, it came loose. Her hands were free! But what now?

"Well what are you waiting for, a fucking invitation?" growled the second man. "We can't stand around here all day. Give me the gun and get on with it. Or are you going to prove me right after all?"

"I'll show you who's right," retorted his accomplice, almost hoarse with anticipation.

Tracy heard footsteps beside her. She tensed, ready to move the instant hands touched her. The bonds on her ankles were even looser than those on her wrists had been. She was fairly certain that, if need be, she could be up and running in a flash. But she also knew she wouldn't be able to outrun a shotgun. She had to wait for the right moment. What's more, in order to know when that moment was, she had to get a peek from under the bag. When both men's attention was focused elsewhere, *that* would be the moment.

Charlie's tremulous voice rang out as hands took hold of her instead. "Get off me! Dad! Dad!"

Her cries yanked Marcus back to full consciousness. "Don't you touch her!" he yelled, his voice cracking with helpless rage.

Charlie's molester let out a shuddering moan in which pain and pleasure seemed to vie for ascendancy.

"No," sobbed Charlie. "No."

"Oh you bastards," croaked Marcus. "You dirty, filthy…" He trailed off in agony.

"Is that it?" the second man asked with a boom of laughter. "You only put your hands on her tits."

"Shut up," shot back his accomplice, his voice a toxic brew of anger and embarrassment.

"You didn't even have time to get your cock out. Ten seconds and you blew your wad."

An echoing boom tore apart the air. Tracy pitched sideways as if the earth had shifted beneath her feet. Her slight frame bounced off a tree trunk and slammed into the ground. She lay stunned for an instant, inhaling the fusty scent of dead leaves and wondering if she'd been shot. She anxiously ran her hands over her clothes and hair. There was no blood. The only pain was where her shoulder had hit the tree. Scrambling upright, she forced her jelly-legs to run again. The ground rose steadily into the soft gloom of the woods. Tufts of grass and exposed roots strove to trip her up. The trees seemed to thrust their branches at her.

One of the men's voices echoed through the woods, jumping from baritone to falsetto. "Run, run as fast as you can!" There was nothing taunting in its tone. It sounded absolutely sincere.

Tracy's lungs were burning. Her heart was going like a jackhammer. But she didn't slacken her pace or glance over her shoulder. She did as her pursuer said, concentrating every ounce of her strength on driving her legs as fast as they would go.

The voice called out again, contradicting its previous words. "Stop! We want to eat you."

It was noticeably fainter. She risked a look over her shoulder. There was nothing to see except trees. *Stop! We want to eat you.* The words seemed to echo in her ears. Did her pursuers really want to eat her? Is that what they intended to do to her mum, dad and Charlie – kill and eat them? The thought was almost enough to bring her to a stop. *You have to go back and help them,* she said to herself. But another part of her – the cold, analytical part that had facilitated her escape in the first place – said, *What can you do? If you go back, they'll kill you too. You have to find help.*

But where could she find help? She tried to remember what houses she'd seen on the drive out to Low Lonning. There had been a farmhouse away to the right of the crossroads, but that would mean doubling back. Besides, she

21

wasn't even sure which direction the crossroads was in. She'd been running in a blind panic. But now her mind was clearing.

She had to find her way to the hamlet down by the river. She reckoned it was only about half a mile away, maybe less considering how far she'd already run. The problem was, she wasn't sure in which direction she was going. She knew from movies that people always ended up walking in circles when they were lost in the woods. The thing to do was to use the sun to orientate yourself. She looked skywards. The sun was vaguely visible through a pall of cloud. She remembered it warming her back as she'd walked along Low Lonning. It was on her left-hand side now. That meant she was heading in roughly the right direction, didn't it? If she kept the sun on her left, then she would at least ensure she continued in a straight line.

Laughter echoed in the air, wild and high, ricocheting off the trees, scattering her thoughts like leaves in a gust of wind. She whirled around. She couldn't see anyone. But that didn't mean her pursuers couldn't see her. Were they taunting her? Perhaps it amused them to watch her run. Well if that was the case, they'd picked the wrong girl to play with. She'd show them how fast she could run. Although her breathing was ragged, she put on a burst of speed, saying to herself with grim determination, *They won't eat me.*

The ground continued to climb. She had no concept of how long she'd been running. Five, ten, twenty minutes? Surely it couldn't be much further before she reached the other side of the woods. Moments later she was proved right. She emerged from the trees at a broad grassy clearing enclosed by a barbed wire fence and tumbledown drystone wall. At the centre of clearing were a slate-roofed stone barn and white farmhouse. A tractor with a trailer of hay bales hooked up to it was parked in a muddy yard.

Tracy would have wept with relief if she'd had any breath spare. It took all of her strength to haul herself over the drystone wall. She winced as the barbed wire gouged her trailing ankle. She staggered across a patch of grass sprinkled with sheep droppings. A black and white Border Collie emerged from the barn and ran barking towards her. The farmhouse's inhabitants were nowhere to be seen.

Picking up on Tracy's distress, the dog circled her warily. *Help,* she mouthed at it.

As if it understood, the collie turned tail and sprinted to the farmhouse's green front door. It nosed the door open and disappeared into the house. Seconds later Tracy too was at the door. She pushed it fully open, staggering to her knees on a flagstone floor. A pair of big dirt-ingrained hands caught her and set her back on her feet. Through sweat and tears, she looked up into strikingly blue eyes set in a weather-beaten face.

"What happened to you?" asked the man. "Are you hurt?"

Tracy's mouth worked rapidly, but she couldn't find her voice.

A woman stepped into view behind the man. She had dark bobbed hair and a broad, smiling red face. The smile disappeared at the sight of Tracy. "What have we got here?" she said, creases of concern spreading from the corners of her eyes.

Blood beat in frustration against Tracy's temples as, once again, her lips moved without producing any words.

"There, there," soothed the woman. "Whatever's happened, you're safe now. You just catch your breath and tell us all about it."

Tracy sucked in a shuddering breath and when she exhaled her voice finally came out. The man and woman took on matching bemused expressions as Tracy gasped, "You have to help. They're going to eat them!"

CHAPTER 1

2018

Butterfly followed Charlie around the room, ready to catch him lest he should fall. He reached a chubby hand towards a glass of water on a bedside table. A set of false teeth were submerged in the water. "Ah, ah, no you don't," said Butterfly, scooping him into her arms. He let out a shrill cry, arching his back in an attempt to escape. His annoyance turned to a gummy chuckle as she nuzzled his fine blonde hair saying, "Who's Mummy's cheeky little monkey?"

Keeping hold of Charlie, Butterfly dropped wearily into a high-backed chair at the side of a hospital-style trolley bed. He was only ten-months-old, but he was already like lightning on his feet. In the span of a few weeks, he'd graduated from using the furniture to prop himself up to charging around with kamikaze recklessness. It had been exhausting enough trying to prevent him from wrecking the joint when he was restricted to crawling, but now it was ten times worse. Finding his feet had brought all sorts of interesting new objects within reach. Anything was fair game – ornaments, mugs of scolding hot tea, the cutlery drawer.

A sunken-cheeked woman in a white nightie was propped up on a mound of pillows on the bed. She had wavy, shoulder-length hair like Butterfly, only hers was silver-grey not auburn. Her bony, liver-spotted hands lay at her sides. She was staring into space with an oddly blank expression. She showed no sign of having heard as Butterfly said, "Charlie's getting faster on his feet every day, Grandma. I think he's going to be a hundred-metre runner."

Butterfly picked up a hairbrush. "Are you going to help me brush Grandma Shirley's hair?" she asked Charlie. Careful not to let him jerk the brush around, she combed the old woman's hair.

Shirley didn't blink. Her gaze remained fixed on the ceiling. Or maybe she was seeing past the ceiling into some other place where her imagination could roam free. Perhaps she was with her husband William in that place, young and happy once again. That was what Butterfly liked to think. Not that she knew whether her grandparents had been happy together. She could no more remember her long-since-dead granddad than Shirley could remember what she'd had for breakfast.

Butterfly put down the hairbrush and lifted her hand to a circular red indent just below her hairline. Day by day, almost imperceptibly – like Charlie – the wound was changing. The redness was fading, the skin was growing smoother, the indent was becoming less pronounced. She couldn't say the same of the pain. It seemed to follow no logical pattern – sometimes receding to a barely noticeable deep throb, other times striking her as fast as… well, as fast as the bullet that was still embedded in her brain.

Charlie tried to pull Butterfly's hand back to the hairbrush. When she resisted, he gave out a warbling cry. The sound lanced through her skull. She felt it like a physical thing pushing into her brain, touching the bullet, nudging it even deeper into the soft grey matter. The pain was so intense that she too almost cried out.

Her voice grated between clenched teeth. "No, Charlie."

His hand became entangled in her hair and he yanked at it, his cries growing more insistent.

"No," Butterfly repeated, her tone shifting from irritation to anger. The pale August light seeping through the bedroom window suddenly seemed blindingly bright. She closed her eyes, clutching her hand to her head. Lights flashed like fireworks behind her eyelids. The bullet *was* moving. She felt certain of it. The blunt inch long cylinder was worming its way towards the centre of her brain. Once it got there, the pain would stop. But so would everything else. Her world would come to an end. No more visiting Shirley. No more chasing Charlie around. No more anything.

Charlie's crying ratcheted up even louder. This time Butterfly did scream, "Stop it! Stop crying you little shit!"

Her eyes snapped open, bloodshot with rage. Such white hot rage! It burned through her like a forest fire. Barely aware of what she was doing, she curled her fingers into a fist. Her pale knuckles quivered over Charlie's tear-streaked face for an instant, then she blinked and her hand dropped to her side. A horrified sob forced its way up her throat at the realisation of what she'd almost done. Her voice racked with shame, she said, "I'm sorry, Charlie. Mummy's sorry."

Butterfly held Charlie close, rocking him until his crying subsided. She rose to her feet somewhat unsteadily. The floor seemed to shudder beneath her as she stooped to kiss Shirley's forehead. "Bye, Grandma. I'll see you soon." In a whisper, she added, "Please don't remember this."

Shirley continued to stare into that other place. Butterfly's plea was needless. The chances of her grandma remembering what had happened were zero. Even on her best days Shirley didn't recognise her granddaughter. The only thing that tended to draw any sort of response from her was Charlie. Sometimes she would smile and coo at him whilst stroking his hands. But it had been weeks since even Charlie was able to work his magic on her. The Alzheimer's was progressing rapidly, destroying the neurons that transmitted information between her brain and body, severing her last tenuous links to the world. The doctors were reluctant to say how long she had left to live, but it obviously wasn't long.

Butterfly retrieved the bulging bag of nappies, dummies, teething rings and other baby paraphernalia that she lugged everywhere. The pain was fading now almost fast as it had arisen. She felt steadier on her feet as she left the room. She headed for the exit, hoping she didn't bump into any of the nurses who cared for her grandma. She didn't want to have to field any awkward questions about why she'd shouted.

She was almost at the front door when a nurse appeared and asked, "Have you signed out?"

Butterfly pushed out a smile. "Sorry, I almost forgot."

As she signed the visitors' book, she could feel the nurse's eyes on her face – more specifically, on the tattoo that flared outwards from her right eye like one half of a masquerade mask. The tattoo's centre comprised of three concentric circles of white, black, white. Then came a larger rusty red area with a slender band of brown along its outer edge. The edge itself was frayed like a butterfly's damaged wing. When she met people for the first time they invariably reacted in one of two ways. Some acted as if the tattoo didn't exist. Others were fixated by it. Occasionally they asked about it. How long had she had it? Where did she get it done? What had made her want to tattoo her face? She gave the same answer to all their questions – *I've no idea*. Which of course prompted more questions. *What do you mean, you've no idea? How is that possible?*

If Butterfly liked the person asking, she might answer politely, *I have amnesia,* before trying to change the subject. If she didn't like them, she would simply ignore their questions. And if she *really* didn't like them, she would let rip with the full story.

This particular nurse was new to the nursing home. She was a prim-looking woman with an unsmiling face. She'd made Butterfly uncomfortable on the way in by ogling her as if she was an exhibit in a Victorian freak show. Now Butterfly could almost hear the question on the tip of the nurse's tongue. *Don't go there,* she silently warned her. She could feel that same rage bubbling just below the surface, ready to erupt at the slightest provocation.

"I have to ask," began the nurse.

Before she could say anything else, Butterfly treated her to such a withering glare that she took a step backwards. "The answer is, I haven't got a fucking clue," retorted Butterfly. "You see, a pair of psychopathic pricks destroyed my memory." With a kind of perverse enjoyment, she watched the nurse squirm as she continued, "But they got what was coming to them. One of them's dead. The other's serving a life sentence."

"Oh… right," stammered the nurse, her eyes dancing around as if she didn't know where to put them.

"Have a lovely day."

The nurse smiled uneasily. "You too."

Another, less intense, twinge of shame passed through Butterfly as she stepped outside. *What the hell's the matter with you?* she asked herself. *Did that woman really deserve that?*

The answer to the second question was most definitely no. The first question was harder to answer. The bullet was part of it for sure, but there was more to it than that.

Butterfly opened the front passenger door of the lumbering people carrier Jack had insisted on buying her. He'd chosen it because it was supposedly the safest family car on the market. It certainly looked as if it could withstand a nuclear blast and there was more than enough room for Charlie's clobber, but that didn't stop her from hating the sight of it. Sometimes she would look at it and think, *Is this really who I am? Would the sort of person who had their face tattooed with a butterfly wing have been seen dead driving around in this glorified tank?*

She strapped Charlie into his baby seat and gave him his dummy in the forlorn hope that he would content himself with sucking it rather than scream his lungs out on the journey to Manchester. He spat it out and his cries reverberated painfully in her ears.

"What's wrong, Charlie? Are you hungry?" Butterfly tried to give him his bottle, but he pushed it away. She checked his nappy. Clean. She closed her eyes. The throbbing was building behind her forehead again. She started the engine. The drive home might do the trick. Charlie often fell asleep in the car.

As she pulled out of the carpark, she popped a couple of painkillers from a blister strip and dry-swallowed them, knowing they would make little difference. Doctor Summers, her neurologist, had prescribed a rainbow of medication – anti-nausea, anti-migraine, anti-depressants – but all the tablets seemed to do was make her constipated and lethargic. She slammed on the brakes hard enough to jolt herself against her seatbelt. If possible, Charlie's crying grew even louder.

"What the hell are you doing?" she yelled, hammering the horn at a car that had materialised from nowhere. Her bumper had come to a stop centimetres from its driver side door. The car was a sleek black sporty number with mirrored windows. Butterfly waited for it to either continue on its way or for the driver to lower the window and offer an apology. Instead the car merely sat there.

Butterfly's rage-inducing headache was back in full flow. The world seemed to be contracting and expanding ever so slightly in front of her eyes. What was this idiot's problem? She just barely resisted a temptation to put her foot on the accelerator and push the car out of her way. That was one time when the people carrier's bulk would come in handy.

She hit the horn again. With a screech, the car accelerated away like a sprinter bursting from the starting blocks. "Moron," Butterfly muttered as she turned in the opposite direction. As Doctor Summers had taught her, she focused on breathing slowly, counting her breaths – breathing in through her nose for a count of seven and out through her mouth for a count of eleven. The pain didn't lessen, but the anger died down. Charlie's crying died down too. Soon, lulled by the car's motion, his eyelids mercifully drifted shut.

She headed south out of Rochdale and got on the M62. To her relief, the mid-afternoon traffic was moving at a steady pace. If she was forced to stop for more than a minute, there was a good chance Charlie would wake up. The motorway took her around the western outskirts of Manchester, passing light industrial estates, shopping centres and suburban housing estates that languished under a grey late August sky. Heavy clouds were sweeping in from the Irish Sea, preparing to dump their rain on Manchester before crossing the Pennines.

She left the motorway behind for the dreary urban landscape of Stretford, passing rows of tightly packed terraced houses shadowed by tower blocks. The streets became leafier as she headed into the more affluent surrounds of Chorlton-cum-Hardy. She arrived at Naomi's school just in time. Children and parents were streaming out of the gates. Butterfly spotted Naomi chatting to her friends. Slowing the car to a standstill, she waved and called to her. Breaking into her usual toothy smile, Naomi ran to the car. Her raven black hair streamed across her pale, delicate face. She swept it aside as she ducked into the front passenger seat.

"Hi Mum."

Butterfly's heart gave a squeeze of pleasure. Naomi had only recently started calling her mum. Butterfly had always made it clear that she wasn't trying to replace Rebecca. She simply wanted them to be friends. But one day a few weeks ago, during the normal course of conversation, Naomi had called her mum. There had been a little silence afterwards as if neither of them were quite sure what to say next. Then, with a sheepish look in her big blue eyes, Naomi had asked, "Is it OK to call you Mum?"

Butterfly had smiled and replied, "Of course."

From then on Naomi had seemed to relish calling her it every chance she got. It was as if in the three or so years since Rebecca's death, she'd been storing up a surplus of the word ready for use. No one had ever called Butterfly mum before. It was still taking a little getting used to. Mostly it gave her a deep warm feeling to know she was loved and needed. But behind that there lurked something else – a queasy mixture of fear and uncertainty. Fear because at any given moment the bullet lodged in her brain might shift position and finish the job it had started. She wasn't so much afraid for herself – she'd come to terms with living in the shadow of that possibility – she was more afraid what effect it would have on Naomi to lose another mother. The uncertainty was a more nebulous thing. In the space of ten months she'd gained not only a new identity, but a family. She had no real sense of who she'd been before the bullet erased her memories. Nor did she have a firm grasp on who she was right now. At first, she'd been swept along on a wave of circumstance with hardly a moment to consider where she'd come from or where she was going. But now the wave was slowing, she was left with the feeling of being adrift in a strange sea, not knowing which direction to swim in.

On the way home, Naomi chatted about her day. Butterfly was content to listen. It was far preferable to thinking about what had happened at the nursing home. By the time they pulled into the driveway of a modest semi-detached house, her headache had once again receded to a nagging ache. Charlie woke up as he was lifted out of the car. A smile lit up his rosy-cheeked face at the sight of Naomi. He stretched his hands towards her. Butterfly unhesitatingly handed him over. It took a lot for her to trust people with Charlie, but Naomi had proved herself more than capable of looking after him. She was a dab hand at feeding him his bottle, changing his nappy and rocking him off to sleep. She would sit with him for hours, playing, reading to him, watching Cbeebies. Butterfly had remarked many times that she wasn't sure how she'd cope without her.

Holding Charlie's hands, Naomi walked him into the house. The pair of them went into the living-room. Butterfly smiled at the sound of them playing. She headed for the kitchen and set about preparing a meal. Jack had been called into the office early that morning. It wouldn't be long before he was home.

CHAPTER 2

Jack slung his laptop bag over his shoulder and all but dashed for the exit. It had been a long day. He'd been called out to a fatal stabbing in the city centre at 5 AM. A student walking home from a night out had made the mistake of resisting a mugger. His reward had been multiple stab wounds to the neck and chest. He was dead long before the paramedics got to him. The mugger had been caught on CCTV near the scene of the attack. Facial recognition software had identified him as one Darren McNeill, a well-known local scumbag with a history of petty criminal activity as long as Jack's arm. By midday, McNeill had been picked up at home out of his skull on Spice, the synthetic drug that was taking Manchester by storm, leaving its users slumped semi-conscious or making them hyper-aggressive. McNeill fell into the latter category. He'd ferociously resisted the officers who rammed their way into his Rusholme flat, punching, kicking and biting until they finally subdued him. The dead man's wallet and phone were subsequently found in his bedroom. By mid-afternoon he'd been charged with murder and the case was all but wrapped up. A criminal mastermind he was not.

Steve followed Jack out of the door. "Another delightful day at the office," he said sarcastically. "Don't you just love meeting so many wonderful people?"

Jack barely cracked a smile at the comment.

"What's up with you?" asked Steve as they got into a lift.

"I'm knackered that's what."

"Yeah well, babies will do that to you."

Now a smile slid across Jack's lips. "How many months gone is Laura?"

Steve's handsomely grizzled face contracted into a grimace. "Fuck you, Jack. You know exactly how far gone she is."

Jack broke into a laugh. "Sorry mate." He gave Steve a commiserating pat on the back. "I still can't believe I'm going to be an uncle. I was starting to think it would never happen."

"Yeah, that's what I thought too." Steve shook his head. "I'm still not sure how it *did* happen."

"Well it's a bit like getting inoculated. All it takes is a little prick."

"Fuck you, Jack," repeated Steve.

Jack laughed louder, dodging out of the lift as Steve made as if to take a swing at him. They made their way along a corridor buzzing with colleagues coming off and going on duty. A glass door led them to a large carpark enclosed by a tall wire-mesh fence.

Steve took a deep breath of the rain-scented air. "God, I'm gagging for a pint." His phone pinged. He glanced at it. "Your sister wants me to pick up some pickled onions on the way home. She's been eating a jar of the sodding things a day." His nose wrinkled. "I used to like them, but now the smell makes me want to puke."

Jack gave him a more serious look. "How are things going between the two of you?"

Steve shrugged. "Pretty good, all things considered. I mean five months ago we were both living on our own, not looking for anything more than a good time. Now we're living together, expecting a flippin' baby."

Jack resisted the temptation to raise an eyebrow. *Not looking for anything more than a good time.* That might have been the case for Steve, but Laura had long been hankering for something more serious. She was heading into her forties. Her biological clock was ticking down. A fact of which she'd been acutely aware. She'd contented herself with looking after Naomi whilst Jack was working, but Butterfly's arrival had lifted that responsibility from her shoulders.

Jack wasn't blind. He'd seen the half-happy, half-sad way Laura looked at Charlie. That was why he hadn't been blown off his feet when she

33

announced that she was pregnant. That's not to say he wasn't surprised. Steve was in his late forties with a failed marriage and two kids in the rearview mirror. He loved to get his hands on Charlie, but he loved to hand him back too. He took great pleasure in ribbing Jack over the bags under his eyes and the baby sick on his tie. He saw his own teenage son and daughter once in a blue moon. He was at his happiest chucking back pints in the pub. The idea that he would willingly plunge back into the crucible of parenthood was as absurd as it was irresponsible. But nature had taken its course and, despite taking the usual precautions, it looked like it was going to happen. Laura had tearfully confessed to Jack that it felt like some kind of miracle. Steve had drunkenly told Jack that he sometimes wondered if he was being punished for sins from a past life.

As if reading Jack's expression, Steve said, "I know what you think of me, Jack."

"I think you're a good bloke."

Steve smiled lopsidedly. "Yeah, a good bloke to have a laugh with down the pub. But not the sort of bloke you want knocking up your sister, eh?" He held up his hands, palms out, as Jack frowned. "I'm not having a go. I agree with you. I'm not father material. I never was. I royally fucked up my marriage and my kids are paying for it. But I'm going to do things differently this time. I'm going to be there to change the nappies and feed the little blighter. I'm going to be there for Laura too, no matter how many jars of stinking pickled onions she stuffs down her throat. I promise you that."

"You don't have to promise me anything, Steve."

"I know but I want to. And if I don't keep my word you've got my permission to kick my arse."

Jack's smile returned. "I'll look forward to that."

"Yeah, I bet. Right, I'd better get to the supermarket." A cheeky twinkle came into Steve's eyes. "But first things first, I'm going to grab that pint. I deserve it after the day we've had."

Jack glanced at the ultra-modern glass and concrete facade of Greater Manchester Police HQ where Darren McNeill was effectively beginning a minimum twenty-five-year sentence. He thought about McNeill's victim – a nineteen-year-old student. One life cut short before it had really begun. Another destined to rot in prison. McNeill deserved every one of those twenty-five-years, but still… what a waste. He sighed. "Makes you wonder, doesn't it?"

Steve nodded. He knew exactly what Jack was getting at – *should anyone even be bringing another life into this shitty world?*

"See you tomorrow, mate," said Jack. "Say hello to Laura for me."

"Will do."

As Steve headed for his car, Jack called after him, "Oh and don't forget the pickled onions."

Steve flipped him the finger in reply.

Chuckling, Jack ducked into his car. As he drove across Manchester, he brought down a mental shutter on the last ten hours. After Rebecca's death, he'd made himself a promise not to bring his job home. It wasn't easy, especially on days like today when the job rested on his shoulders like a slab of concrete, but he was determined not to burden his family with that weight. He skirted the city centre, heading south through Hulme and Moss Side. The nearer he got to home, the lighter he felt inside. He knew it was selfish, but he hoped Charlie hadn't gone down for his afternoon nap. A few minutes spent playing with him was all he needed to wash away any lingering traces of his day.

When he pulled into the driveway, Naomi came to the front door. She was carrying Charlie in her arms. The smiles they gave him made everything – getting up at 5 AM, spending half the day in an interrogation room with McNeill – worthwhile. "Hello you two," he said, smiling back.

"Hi Dad," said Naomi.

Charlie burbled, excitedly flapping his hands. Jack lifted him from Naomi's arms and nuzzled his soft cheeks. Jack's smile faltered as Butterfly emerged from the kitchen. She looked washed out, but she summoned up a small smile for him. He stooped to kiss her, then drew back giving her a concerned look. "How did it go with your grandma?"

"She was having one of her bad days. Even Charlie couldn't get a smile out of her."

"And how about you? How are you feeling?" As Jack spoke, his gaze rose to the round red indent on Butterfly's forehead.

"Tired," she admitted, somewhat self-consciously lifting a hand to sweep her hair down over the scar.

"Any more headaches?"

Butterfly glanced meaningfully at Naomi. "We'll talk later."

Jack went into the living-room with Naomi and Charlie, picking his way across a jumble of building blocks and soft toys. Peppa Pig blared from the television. A half-eaten rusk was encrusted to the sofa. Jack peeled it off before lying down and hoisting Charlie overhead. Charlie screamed with delight as Jack manoeuvred him around making aeroplane noises.

"I'll go see if Mum needs any help," said Naomi.

Jack smiled at her. Butterfly didn't like to talk about her headaches in front of Naomi, but that didn't stop Naomi from picking up on what was going on. She had Jack's eye for reading people, coupled with an acute sensitivity to their needs. If Butterfly was struggling, Naomi would instinctively recognise it and do what she could to help out. Her mother had been the same. In the end that sensitivity had become too much for Rebecca to cope with, pushing her over a cliff's edge. Jack was constantly watching for signs that Naomi was going down the same path, but she didn't seem to suffer in the same way her mum had. She'd apparently also inherited her dad's capacity to endure and survive.

After a while, Naomi returned to tell Jack tea was ready. They went into the kitchen and Jack strapped Charlie into a highchair. As they ate, they chatted about light topics – the changing weather, a new tooth Charlie was cutting, Naomi's homework. Jack divided his time between feeding himself and spooning a whizzed-up vegetable concoction into Charlie's mouth – much of which the ten-month-old spat straight back out. Jack cast an occasional worried look at Butterfly. She was smiling and chatting along, but he knew she was in pain. There was a telltale tightness to her face.

By the end of the meal Charlie's highchair looked like a crime scene. "I'll bath Charlie and put him to bed," said Jack.

Butterfly gave him a grateful smile. He took Charlie upstairs, leaving her and Naomi to clean up the carnage. He ran a shallow bath. Charlie splashed about delightedly in the water. Afterwards, Jack powdered him with talc and put him in a clean nappy and baby-grow. The routine was comfortingly familiar. When Naomi was a baby, Jack had made a point of putting her to bed every night no matter how exhausted he was from work. Partly circumstance had obliged him to do so – Rebecca's post-natal depression had often left her wiped out by the end of the day – but mainly it was because those moments spent watching Naomi playing in the bath or drifting off to sleep as he sang to her were the ones he treasured most.

Jack fed Charlie his bottle, before laying him down in his cot and reading to him softly from the 'Hungry Caterpillar' book that had been Naomi's favourite. Charlie's eyelids slid shut. Jack closed the book and crept from the room, leaving the door ajar.

"Is he asleep?" Butterfly asked as he entered the living-room. She blew out her cheeks in relief when he nodded.

"Where's Naomi?"

"Doing her homework in the kitchen."

Jack started to tidy away the toys, but thought better of it. He dropped onto the sofa beside Butterfly, sighing contentedly as she curled up against him. "So come on, tell me about it," he said after they'd both taken a moment to drink in the precious silence.

"The headaches are getting worse," she said. "But it's not just that..." She hesitated as if unsure she wanted to say more.

"What else is it?" Jack gently pressed.

"Today at the nursing home I lost my temper with Charlie."

"It happens."

"No I mean I *really* lost my temper." Butterfly's eyes dropped away from Jack's, heavy with shame. "I almost hit him."

Jack frowned. "But you didn't."

"No," Butterfly replied quickly, shaking her head for emphasis. "I'd never..." She faded off into uncertainty. "Would I?" she murmured as much to herself as Jack.

"Of course you wouldn't."

"You weren't there this afternoon, Jack. It wasn't only Charlie I lost it with. I was ready to swing for anyone who came near me. It was like..." She searched for the right description. "It was like I wasn't myself... Or maybe I *was* myself. Maybe that's who I really am."

Now it was Jack's turn to shake his head. "It's the bullet. Doctor Summers said that if you experienced these kinds of mood swings you should contact him at once. Have you?"

"No."

"Why not?"

"Because I'm sick of it. The scans, the blood tests, the medication. What good does it all do?"

"If the bullet's moved there might be a chance they can operate and take it out."

A strange, troubled light flickered in Butterfly's eyes. "And what if they can take it out, Jack? What then?"

"What do you mean?"

"What if when they take the bullet out it changes me? Changes me back to who I was before. I might become a person you don't know. Someone you can't love."

Jack took Butterfly's hands in his. "I'll always love you."

She looked at him with a questioning hope. "Are you sure of that?"

In answer, he leaned in to kiss her. He kept his lips pressed to hers until he felt the tension leave her. "Promise me you'll call Doctor Summers," he murmured.

"I promise." She pulled him in for another kiss. Then they held each other, listening to the blissful silence.

CHAPTER 3

She was running through a gloomy wood – or rather, she was trying to. Her movements were maddeningly slow, as if she was wading through glue. She was gasping for breath, not simply from exertion, but from terror. Her breathing became even more strained as a voice rang out, "Run, run as fast as you can."

She tried to do so, but her limbs refused to obey. She sobbed with frustration.

The voice came again, "Stop! We want to eat you." Laughter followed, growing louder, until it seemed to be coming from all around her...

Charlie's cries yanked Butterfly out of the dream. Her heart was going like a runaway train. Her eyes goggled, trying to work out where she was. Then she remembered and exhaled in relief.

She slid from beneath the duvet, grabbed the bottle of milk that had been prepared for such an eventuality and hurried to the nursery. Shushing Charlie, she lifted him out of his cot and placed the bottle's teat between his lips. He sucked on it hungrily. After he'd finished feeding, she walked around the room, rocking him until she was sure he was fast asleep. As gently as if she was handling high explosives, she lowered him back into the cot.

She padded back towards her bedroom, halting as a wave of dizziness engulfed her. Reeling into the bathroom, she bent over the toilet. She took deep breaths, fighting an urge to retch. The nausea slowly subsided. As she straightened, she caught sight of herself in the mirror – almond eyes, rosebud lips, a spray of freckles on her slender nose. For an instant, she was hit by the strongest feeling that the face didn't belong to her.

"Run, run as fast as you can," she murmured.

She suddenly found herself wrestling with an impulse to run from the house. She saw herself running and running, not going anywhere in particular, simply putting as much distance as possible between herself and a life that, like the face in the mirror, sometimes felt completely alien to her. She clutched the sink as if to anchor herself in place. Like the dizziness, the impulse subsided.

Instead of returning to bed, Butterfly went downstairs. She ducked into the cupboard underneath the stairs and lifted out a cardboard box. She opened it on the kitchen table. It was full of plastic folders. The top one was labelled 'Tracy Ridley'. Butterfly flipped it open revealing a photo of a young girl. Reddish-brown hair framed a round-cheeked, freckly face. She scrutinised the photo as if searching for something. That same disconnected feeling nibbled at her. She and the girl in the photo were one and the same person. And yet they were also totally different people. They shared the same body, but they were as separate as the two halves of an apple.

Butterfly flipped past the photo to a printout and read 'Tracy Ridley. POB: Prestwich, Manchester; DOB: 14-04-1987; Eye Colour: Brown; Hair Colour: Auburn; Scars, Birth Marks etc: scar on left ankle.' She lifted her leg, running a finger along the almost invisible thin white scar that stretched from the knuckle of her ankle four or five centimetres up her calve.

She turned the page to a document entitled 'Incident Report'. The document was dated '30th July 1998'. The location was recorded as 'Lane Side/Low Lonning'. The incident was identified as 'Multiple Homicides'. The attending officer was 'Constable Eric Ramsden'. Butterfly's eyes skimmed over Constable Ramsden's report.

'At approximately 14:35 on Thursday the 30th of July I responded to a call from Bray Farm. Alistair Bray informed me that a young girl had arrived at his house in a state of distress. Mr Bray said the girl was too upset to talk on the phone. I set off from Whitehaven police station and arrived at Bray Farm at approximately 15:05. The girl told me her name was Tracy Ridley and that she had been walking on Low Lonning bridleway with her parents Marcus and Andrea and her older sister Charlie. She claimed that a masked man armed with a shotgun had approached her family intending to rob them. She had escaped and made her way to Bray Farm. Having reason to believe that the Ridleys were in danger, I decided to investigate further immediately. I left Tracy Ridley with Mr and Mrs Bray and drove to Low Lonning. I walked along the bridleway for approximately 150 metres to the spot Tracy had described. There was no sign of her parents, sister or an armed man. There were signs that something had been dragged into the woods to the north of the bridleway. I conducted a search and approximately 50 metres from the bridleway I discovered the bodies of Marcus Ridley, his wife Andrea and their daughter Charlie lying side by side. All three were deceased. Marcus Ridley's throat appeared to have been cut. Andrea and Charlie Ridley appeared to have been shot in the face at close range. Additionally, there were signs that the females had been sexually assaulted and wounded multiple times with a knife or some other sharp instrument. I returned to my vehicle, radioed my colleagues and waited for backup units.'

Butterfly heaved a sigh. She'd read the report dozens of times before, but that didn't stop each subsequent reading from leaving her feeling as if she'd been punched in the stomach. She took a moment to gather herself before scanning through more photocopies of police reports and newspaper cuttings. In the aftermath of Constable Ramsden's grisly discovery, a massive investigation had been launched. A sweep of the area failed to find the gunman or his accomplice. Nor had anyone in the vicinity seen anything suspicious. Scenes of crime officers had confirmed that Constable Ramsden's initial assessment of the injuries inflicted on the Ridleys was accurate. Marcus had suffered a deep wound to his throat that severed the carotid arteries and perforated his windpipe. Loss of consciousness would have ensued in 15-20 seconds, followed by death in 2-4 minutes. Andrea had suffered multiple slicing wounds to her breasts, lower abdomen, buttocks, pubic area and upper thighs. The massive damage to her skull, along with the clustering of pellets, the presence of metal fragments and wadding from a cartridge shell, powder-burn tattooing and singeing of hairs indicated that a shotgun had been discharged at a distance of 15-30cm. Death would have been instantaneous. Charlie had suffered almost identical injuries to her mother, although her vagina had also been penetrated by a sharp object that lacerated her vaginal wall and cervix.

No semen was recovered from either Andrea or Charlie's bodies. Nor was any of the killers' blood or hair found at the scene. The bags that had been used to blindfold the Ridleys were nowhere to be found. Likewise, the murder weapons were never found. Added to that, the absence of any fingerprints meant there was little or no forensic evidence.

One notable lead was generated by the examination of the bodies – Charlie had been wearing a silver jigsaw piece necklace with 'Big Sis' engraved on it. The necklace was missing. Investigators believed the killers may have taken it as a trophy. It was designed to fit together with a 'Little Sis' necklace worn by Tracy.

Butterfly frowned in thought. She hadn't been wearing the 'Little Sis' necklace when she was taken into hospital after being shot in the head. She'd done what she could to find it – which only amounted to searching her grandma's jewellery box – without success.

"I had a feeling I'd find you going through this stuff."

Butterfly turned at Jack's voice, giving him an apologetic look. "Did I wake you?"

He shook his head and motioned to the pile of folders. "We've been over it all a hundred times. It's a dead end."

"You don't know that for certain. There might be something here that we're missing."

"Like what?"

Butterfly's eyebrows pinched together. "If I knew that, it wouldn't be missing, would it?"

Jack reached for her hand. "Come back to bed."

"You just don't get it, do you Jack?" She pulled her hand away and stabbed a finger at the files. "This is all I've got left of who I used to be."

"No it's not." Jack picked up the photo of Tracy. "I don't believe you and Tracy are all that different. Eric spent a lot of time talking to Tracy. Do you remember what he said about her?"

A crooked smile tugged at Butterfly's mouth. "He said she was a remarkable young girl. And I agree with him. She ran away and left her parents and sister to die. I'd call that remarkable."

Jack sighed. "Are we really going to do this again? Tracy had no choice but to run. It was either that or she would have died too. What would you have had her do?"

Butterfly sat in frowning uncertainty. She knew Jack was right and yet... yet her mind always circled back to the fact that she'd left them to die. "Maybe there was nothing Tracy could have done, but I *can* do something."

She pulled two photographs from a folder. One was of a man with a long face, sharp cheekbones and a broken-veined nose. Dark hair was slicked back from his high forehead. Dark stubble fringed his thin lips. Heavy-lidded eyes completed a sleazy portrait. 'Phil Beech. July 1998' was written on the back of the photo. Tracy and her family had encountered him in the bar of The Rose & Crown on the day of the murders. Beech was a gamekeeper responsible for a large tract of land between Wasdale and the hamlet of Wellington, which included the woods around Low Lonning. Tracy and he had clashed over whether the Ridleys owned a dog. Apparently a dog belonging to some hikers had killed a pheasant the day before. Like the shotgun-wielding masked figure, Beech was tall and wiry. He also had a local accent. Most importantly, he'd known where Tracy and her family would be that afternoon.

The name on the second photo was 'Dale Sutton'. Sutton couldn't have looked more different from Beech – pudgy pink face, piggish upturned nose, cheeks as smooth as a baby's bum. Close-set blue eyes stared out of fatty pouches. A tonsure of fine blonde hair encircled his chrome dome. There was something about him – nothing you could point your finger at – but something not quite right. It always made Butterfly's skin crawl to look at him.

Back in 1998 Phil and Dale had been best mates. Dale hadn't been in The Rose & Crown that lunchtime, but he'd quickly appeared on the police's radar, nonetheless.

"I can go up to The Lakes and track these two down," said Butterfly. "Find out what they have to say for themselves."

"That would be a really bad idea."

"Why?"

"Well for starters, look at you. For weeks you've been suffering from headaches, nausea, mood swings. Charging up to The Lakes is liable to make you ten times worse. You need to rest."

Irritation thumped at Butterfly's skull. "And just how the hell am I supposed to do that with a ten-month-old to look after?"

"Maybe I could take some time off work."

Butterfly closed her eyes. She knew she should have been grateful for Jack's offer, but it only intensified the pounding in her head. "Why can't you understand? This isn't about Charlie. It's about finding out if those fuckers murdered my family."

"Beech and Sutton were questioned multiple times. There was no hard evidence to connect them to the murders."

"The killers used a shotgun. Beech owns a shotgun."

"Yes but your mum and sister were shot at such close range that the cartridges had pretty much disintegrated. And before you say that several intact cartridges were recovered from near the scene, Beech admitted that some of them had probably been fired from his gun. He'd been shooting foxes and rabbits in that area for years."

45

"OK, forget the shotgun. What about the fact that Dale Sutton is a child molester? Don't you call *that* hard evidence?"

"No, I don't. Sutton was sacked from his job as caretaker at Egremont High School for allegedly having inappropriate relationships with several girls, but he was never charged with anything."

"*Allegedly?*" Butterfly echoed, her voice sharpening. "He was inviting teenage girls back to his house and getting them drunk. A fourteen-year-old fell pregnant but refused to identify him as the father. The police said she was terrified of him. All the kids at the school knew Sutton was a deviant. They nicknamed him Pervy Pig. I don't call that *allegedly*. I call it pretty fucking damning."

Jack gestured for her to lower her voice. "You'll wake the kids."

"Beech and Sutton stole my life!" That same white hot rage was in full flow now. Butterfly pummelled a fist into the photos. "I want to look them in the eyes and see how they react when I tell them who I am."

"Why? What good would it do? Even if they are guilty, they're hardly likely to admit it after all these years."

With a sudden sweep of her arms, Butterfly thrust the folders off the kitchen table. "Oh they'll admit it," she spat with a wild light blazing in her eyes. "Because I'll cut pieces off them until they do."

For a second, Jack felt as if he was looking at a stranger, someone who had more in common with the likes of Darren McNeill than the woman he loved. Then the light died and Butterfly clapped a hand to her mouth as if she couldn't believe what she'd said.

"It's OK," soothed Jack, putting his arms around her. "We'll find a way through this."

"Will we?" she murmured doubtfully.

"Yes, we will. First things first, we'll find out what Doctor Summers has to say. And as for this…" Jack nudged the folders with his foot. "We can go over everything again. See if there's anything we missed. I'll even call Eric

Butterfly wondered about her own pregnancy. Had she suffered from morning sickness? Had she had cravings? Had Charlie kept her awake moving around in her womb? Thinking about such questions was like staring into a black hole. "Are you working today?"

"Not until this evening. Why? Do you need me to look after Charlie?"

"I have a hospital appointment, but if you're not up to it I can take him with me."

"I'd love to look after him." Laura added with a touch of dry humour, "I need all the practice I can get."

"No you don't. You'll be a great mum." *A lot better than me,* Butterfly said to herself.

"I hope so."

The line was silent for a moment as if both women were pondering what the future might hold. Then Butterfly said, "I'll drop Charlie off after the school run."

After getting off the phone, she threw herself into the usual daily tasks. She dressed Charlie, made Naomi's packed lunch, negotiated her way through the morning traffic to drop Naomi at school, then went to the supermarket to pick up nappies and formula milk. Once or twice, she glanced in the rear mirror, watching out for the sleek black car. It was nowhere to be seen.

She headed to Laura's house – a smart little two-up, two-down terrace. Laura came to the front door munching on a pickled onion. Her six-months-pregnant belly was developing a pronounced bump. She looked vaguely green around the gills.

"Even though I feel as sick as a dog, I can't stop eating these frigging things," she explained, popping another onion into her mouth.

Butterfly dumped a bag bulging with bottles, baby wipes, rusks and the like in the hallway before returning to the car for Charlie. His big blue-grey eyes widened with delight at the sight of Laura. "Come here you," she said stretching her arms out. "Wow, look at him!" she exclaimed as Butterfly handed over Charlie. "He's getting so big."

"Tell me about it," said Butterfly, massaging an ache in her lower back.

Laura gave Butterfly an appraising look. "Is it just a routine check-up?"

"No. The headaches have been getting worse."

"It's not necessarily a bad thing. If the bullet's dropped lower, they might be able to remove it."

Butterfly smiled at Laura's optimism, but there was little confidence in her voice as she replied, "That's what Jack said." She stooped to kiss Charlie. "See you soon, beautiful. Be good for your Auntie Laura."

"M...m..." babbled Charlie.

"It won't be long before he's talking," said Laura.

Butterfly's smile faded. Not so long ago, she'd wondered whether she would survive to see Charlie take his first steps. Now that milestone had been passed, she found herself waiting on tenterhooks for him to say his first word. She hesitated to move away from him. It had only been in the past couple of months that she'd been able to bring herself to leave him in the care of anyone else. She was still reluctant to spend her first night away from him. Jack had been trying to convince her that they should go away for a weekend and leave Charlie and Naomi with Laura. There would be little chance to do so after Laura had her own baby. But the mere thought of being away from Charlie for two whole days tied Butterfly's insides into knots.

"You don't want to be late for your appointment," prompted Laura. "Don't worry about Charlie. We'll have a great time." Tickling him under his chin, she added, "Won't we?"

As if breaking loose from a tight grip, Butterfly turned abruptly to head for her car. She gave Charlie and Laura a wave as she drove away. The knot in her stomach didn't ease off until she was several miles away from Laura's house. She headed across the city to North Manchester General Hospital. She parked opposite the modern, three-storey brick building and made her way through the familiar, antiseptic-smelling corridors. After a short wait in Neurology's reception area, she was summoned into Doctor Summers's office.

Doctor Summers – a precisely spoken, bespectacled man in his fifties – got straight down to business. He started with the usual battery of neurological tests, using a tuning fork, flashlight, reflex hammer and ophthalmoscope to check Butterfly's motor and sensory functions.

"Everything appears to be normal," he said, "but I'd like to run further tests. I'm sure you know the routine by now. Bloods to make sure there's no sign of infection. An EEG to assess your brain activity. CT scan to monitor the position of the bullet."

Butterfly sighed heavily. In the past ten months, she'd been subjected to more medical tests than most people were in a lifetime. Part of her wanted to walk out of the doctor's office and never come back. If it hadn't been for Charlie, she might have done so. For him she would have endured any number of tests. Even if it only meant she got to hear him say 'Mum' before she died, it would be worth it.

She spent the next few hours having needles poked into her limbs, electrodes stuck to her head and x-rays passed through her skull.

Back in Doctor Summers's office, Butterfly watched him comparing eerily illuminated cross-sections of her head. A snub-nosed cylinder half the length of her little finger was outlined in black near the bottom left side of her walnut-like brain.

"The good news is, there's no sign of blood clots, swelling or infection and your brain's electrical activity is normal." The doctor traced his finger along a slender white line where the bullet had penetrated the frontal bone and burrowed diagonally downwards. "The scarring also appears to be healing as well as can be expected."

"So what's the bad news?" Butterfly asked in an ominously calm voice.

"I'm not sure there is any bad news. It depends on how you look at it." Doctor Summers superimposed two side-on images of Butterfly's brain. "The bullet has dropped about two millimetres. This almost certainly accounts for the symptoms you've been experiencing. We're in something of a catch-22 situation. The bullet is still so deeply embedded that if we attempt to remove it we could cause all sorts of damage. However, if it moves in the wrong direction of its own accord, the prognosis might be even worse. There's also the possibility that gravity will naturally draw the bullet towards the top of your neck, putting it in a position where we can remove it without the same risk of complications. At this moment I would be reluctant to go down the surgery route. I'm afraid it's a case of waiting to see what happens and hoping for the best."

"But expecting the worst," Butterfly said with a dry twist of her lips.

"I wish I could say more, but the outcomes for these types of injuries are difficult to predict at best. I've booked you in for further scans a week from now. I want to keep a close eye on the situation."

Butterfly heaved another sigh. It seemed like she spent half her life in hospital rooms. *You know what, Doctor, thanks but no thanks, I'll take my chances,* she felt like saying, but as always Charlie's cherubic face rose into her mind. "OK, thank you, Doctor." The conversation seemed to be over, but Butterfly remained seated. "There was one more thing," she began, shifting uneasily in her chair. "I've been having that dream again."

"The one where you're running away from the men who killed–"

"Yes that one," Butterfly broke in as if she couldn't bear to hear the dream described out loud. "It feels like an actual memory."

"Maybe it is. Unfortunately we can't know that for sure because the dreams started after you found out about what happened to your family. Are there any new details? Something you haven't read about?"

Butterfly re-ran the dream in her mind. It was always the same – her fleeing in slow-motion through the woods, the voice calling out, *Run, run as fast as you can...* "No. But what if it is a memory, Doctor? What if, as the bullet moves, my memory starts to come back? Will it change me?"

"Change you how?"

Butterfly strove to put what she meant into words. "Will I lose who I am now? What I mean is, will my old memories wipe out my new ones?"

"When the bullet entered your brain, it seemingly destroyed the part of it that contained your autobiographical memories," explained Doctor Summers, choosing his words carefully. "Logic would therefore dictate that those memories can't be retrieved. The same logic also dictates that unless your brain suffers a fresh trauma, you will retain your newly formed memories. That said, there's a possibility that your memory impairment is not simply a result of tissue damage. The trauma your brain suffered may have disrupted its memory retrieval systems. In which case, a portion of your memories might not be lost forever, they might only be temporarily misplaced. And as your recovery progresses, those memories might return. Or they might not. I'm sorry for being so vague, but as I said, the workings of the brain are still very much a mystery to us, especially where amnesia is concerned. In a situation like this, it's always best to focus on the positives. Your semantic and procedural memory appear to be intact. You remember how to drive and know how to find your way around Manchester, even if you don't remember when or where you learnt how to do these things. Your working memory also functions well. You're able to look after your son. You don't forget to attend your appointments. All these things make me optimistic about what the future holds in store for you."

"Focus on the positives," Butterfly said to herself. She gave an unconvincing little nod. "I'll try, Doctor."

After promising that she'd be in touch if there were any further changes to her symptoms, Butterfly headed for the hospital pharmacy to pick up the higher dosage medication Doctor Summers had prescribed. She returned to her car and sat frowning at the tablets. Debilitating headaches or lethargy and constipation. What a choice. She popped a tablet from a blister strip and swallowed it. Her frown intensified as she lifted her gaze. A car had pulled in front of the people carrier, boxing it in. Not just any car. A sporty black car. That was three times in the space of two days. Surely it couldn't be a coincidence. Was the driver following her? If so, what did they want? Was it because she'd almost crashed into their car? Or was there more to it? Whatever the case, she wasn't taking any chances.

She took out her phone and scrolled to Jack's number. Her finger hovered over the screen as a man got out of the black car. The man was about six foot tall with the broad shoulders and narrow waist of a boxer. He was dressed head-to-toe in black – black boots, skinny black jeans, black leather jacket. In contrast his skin was very pale and his crewcut hair was almost equally white. The precise black beard covering his chiselled cheeks suggested his hair was bleached. His dark eyes stared at her with an almost violent intensity. But it wasn't his eyes that made the hairs on the nape of her neck stand on end, it was his tattoo. She took in the concentric circles of white and black, the rusty red expanse beyond them, the ragged line of brown along the wing's edge. The tattoo was identical to hers in every respect except one. It was on the opposite side of the man's face.

She stared at him as if hypnotised. Who was he? She had no idea. The intensity of his gaze told her he wasn't at the same disadvantage. He approached her door. Her hand darted out to lock it, but she still didn't call Jack. How could she when there were so many questions swirling in her mind? She'd been searching for so long for something that would bridge the chasm between Tracy and Butterfly. Something that would help make sense of her past and present. Maybe she was looking at that 'something'.

The man stopped a few paces from her door. He spread his hands as if to show he was no threat. A broad smile lit up his face, balancing out the intensity of his eyes.

Butterfly stared at him for a moment longer before getting out of the car. Keeping the door between her and the man, she waited from him to speak.

"Hello Io," he said, pronouncing the name *eye-o.*

His deep, smooth voice shuddered through Butterfly. "My name's not Io," she replied, struggling to keep her own voice steady.

"Yes it is. You're my Io."

"I don't know you."

The man winced as if she'd dragged her nails down his face. "So it's true what the newspaper's said – you don't remember."

"Who are you?"

"Look at my face, Io. Tell me you don't know the answer to that question."

"I..." Butterfly's voice faltered. Her headache was coming on with a vengeance, drumming at her skull. *Thud...thud...* "I don't know the answer."

"Think, Io," urged the man. "You know me. What's my name?"

Butterfly's knuckles whitened on the door. The drumming was getting faster and louder. *Thud, thud...* She seemed to feel the bullet vibrating against the soft tissue encasing it. Her voice whistled through her teeth. "Look, I don't know your name. So either tell me it or move your fucking car out of my way."

The man's smile returned as if he'd seen something that delighted him. "I'm Karl. With a K."

"Well Karl with a K, let's hear it. Where did you get that tattoo? Why have you suddenly decided to look me up? What do you want from me?"

Karl chuckled softly and the drum's volume turned up another twist. *Thud! thud!* Butterfly bit her tongue against the pain.

"Ooh questions, questions," he said. "Are you sure you're ready for the answers?" Without waiting for a reply, he continued, "I got the tattoo from the same place you did. I didn't suddenly decide to look you up. I just didn't have a chance to until now. And I want only one thing from you – I want you to make me whole again." The intensity flared back into his eyes as he pointed to his tattoo. "I'm only half a person without you, Io."

Butterfly's mouth was so dry she could hardly speak. "Are you saying we're married?"

Karl laughed as if the idea was absurd. "What we've got goes way deeper than marriage." He stretched a hand towards Butterfly. On the back of it was a green tattoo of a Roman numeral clock with no hands. The clock face spiralled downwards, transforming into a red rose. "You promised you'd wait for me no matter how long I was gone."

"I…" Butterfly's voice snagged in her throat again. Suddenly, from some unknown place inside her came an almost overwhelming impulse to take Karl's hand. Her fingers twitched. She lifted her hand as if to obey the impulse, but ducked back into the car instead and jerked the door shut.

No matter what this man knew about who she used to be, right that instant she had to get away from him. It wasn't simply the pain his voice inflicted, it was the fear of what might lurk in that 'unknown place'. What if her past wasn't a destroyed or misplaced memory? What if it was a caged animal desperate to break out and attack her present? Would she have the strength to fight it? She doubted it. Her limbs were shaking. She felt weak right down to her toes.

"Move your car," she mouthed at Karl.

He remained where he was, giving her a look of wide-eyed appeal.

"Move!" exclaimed Butterfly, hammering the horn. A couple of passers-by paused to see what the commotion was about. Karl glanced unconcernedly at them. His gaze returning to Butterfly, he pointed at the tattoo on his hand and mouthed three words. Just three words but it was enough to make her edge the car forwards until it was millimetres from his car. Keeping his gaze fixed on Butterfly, he retreated to get into his car. The engine flared into life. As he sped away, she grabbed a pen and wrote his registration and the make of the car on her hand.

Her phone rang. She wasn't surprised to see 'Jack' flash up on the screen. She'd messaged him that she was heading home from the hospital. She put the receiver to her ear. The drum was still banging away so loudly in her head that she could barely hear his voice as he asked with the usual mixture of eagerness and trepidation, "How did it go?"

"It went fine. Listen, Jack, I need to speak to you about something and I'd rather not do it over the phone."

"Why? What's happened?" Jack was suddenly outright apprehensive. "I thought you said it went fine?"

"It did. This is about something else."

"Where are you?"

"I'm just leaving the hospital."

"Then I'll meet you at HQ's front entrance. See you soon. I love you."

Something like guilt twisted Butterfly's stomach as she thought about how she'd almost taken Karl's hand. "I love you too, Jack."

CHAPTER 5

It was only a five minute drive through streets of redbrick terraced houses, pebbledash council houses, bookies, takeaways, pound shops and off-licences to the soulless light-industrial estate where Greater Manchester Police HQ was located. Butterfly pulled into a small visitors' carpark shadowed by a wall of glass as tall as the building. A Union Jack fluttered atop a flagpole adjacent to broad stone steps leading up to glass doors. Jack waved to Butterfly from the top of the steps. She got out and approached him.

"You look pale," he said, eyeing her intently.

She pushed out a smile. "So what's new?"

Jack took her hand and drew her through the doors into a glass-roofed atrium. Six storeys of open-plan offices overlooked a central area furnished with white tables and matching stools. A trio of potted magnolia trees were lined up like suspects in front of a café counter. Uniformed constables and suited staff were chatting and refuelling on caffeine. A mural of densely packed trees – black trunks with almost luminous strips of green in-between – decorated one wall.

Run, run as fast as you can...

The words seemed to echo in Butterfly's ears at the sight of the mural. Jack directed her to a table and moved off to grab them both a coffee. As usual when she visited the HQ, Butterfly found herself glancing about uneasily. The glass-enclosed offices gave the feeling of being watched from all sides. Without thinking about it, she lifted a hand to cover her tattoo.

"Don't do that," said Jack, placing a cup in front of her as he sat down. "You've got nothing to be ashamed of."

Butterfly eyed him uncertainly. "Are you sure about that? What do you think your colleagues see when they look at me? They see a misfit. A potential criminal."

"I couldn't give a toss what they see. All I care about is what I see. And I love your tattoo. It's part of you. You wouldn't be you without it."

Butterfly's smile relaxed into something less forced. "Yeah well, let's face it Jack, you're not like most of your colleagues."

Jack smiled too. "I'm not sure whether to take that as a compliment." His smile fading, he looked at Butterfly expectantly.

Not wanting to keep him on tenterhooks, she told him, "The bullet has moved. Not much. Just two millimetres."

His brow furrowed. "That doesn't sound good."

"Doctor Summers didn't seem sure if it was a bad or a good thing." Butterfly explained the conundrum about whether or not to perform surgery, adding, "The doctor says I should focus on the positives."

"He's right." Jack rested his hand on hers. She tensed at his touch, thinking once again about the feeling that had reached out from that 'unknown place'. The lines on his brow deepened. "What's the matter, Butterfly? Is something else bothering you?"

She heaved a sigh. "I've put so much on you, Jack. Sometimes I feel as if all I am is a burden to you."

"You haven't put anything on me. You've given me a new life. After Rebecca died, I wasn't sure I'd ever be able to love again. Then I met you." Jack squeezed Butterfly's hand. "Listen, whatever's going on, just tell me and we'll deal with it together."

She lifted his hand and kissed the back of it. "Sometimes I'm almost glad I got shot. Otherwise I wouldn't have met you."

He laughed. "Now that is definitely focusing on the positives."

Butterfly said nothing for a moment. Jack didn't press her further. He knew when to talk and when to let silence do the work. Sometimes a suspect who'd kept their mouth shut through hours of questioning would suddenly open up after being left in silence for a few minutes.

"Yesterday I almost crashed into a car," began Butterfly.

Jack's eyes widened in alarm. "What? Where?"

"Outside the nursing home. A car pulled in front of me. A black Porsche 718 Cayman, to be precise." Butterfly showed Jack the make and registration scribbled on her hand.

He whistled. "That's an expensive car. Whose fault was it?"

"I thought at first that it was my fault. My head was killing me. I could barely see straight." Butterfly put a hand to her forehead, rubbing the red indent. The new painkillers were kicking in, gradually silencing the drumming.

"You thought at first?" Jack gently prompted.

"This morning I saw the same car outside the house. And I saw it again at the hospital just now. Its driver was a man with a tattoo." Her finger moved to trace the outline of the rusty red wing. "The same tattoo as mine only on the opposite side of his face."

Jack gave her a look that was equal parts troubled and intrigued. "Did he say anything?"

Butterfly cleared her throat. It felt like a betrayal of Jack just saying it. "He said he loved me."

His face gave away nothing, but he drew his hand away from hers. "What else did he say?"

"Not much. Some crap about us being two halves of the same person." She added quickly, "That doesn't mean we're married or anything like that. He said his name was Karl and that he'd read about what happened to me in the newspaper. He called me Io."

"Io," repeated Jack. "Not Tracy?"

"No. Maybe I used an alias."

"Hang on, let's not get ahead of ourselves. For all we know this Karl could be some nutter who's become infatuated with you after seeing you in the papers."

"I don't think so. I think he was telling the truth."

"How do you know?"

Butterfly resisted an urge to drop her eyes from Jack's keen gaze. "It's difficult to explain. I just got the feeling that I'd met him before."

"But you don't remember him?"

"No I don't."

Jack was thoughtfully silent, then he took out a pen and notebook. "OK, I want you to tell me everything he said." He jotted down notes as Butterfly recounted her conversation with Karl.

"What do you think?" Butterfly asked when she was finished.

"I think this guy sounds like trouble. I've seen tattoos of clocks without hands on ex-cons who've done a lot of time. If this guy was recently released from prison that would explain why he's only just come looking for you."

"What about the red rose?"

Jack took out his phone and Googled 'Clock and red rose tattoo'. "It says here that a clock combined with a red rose symbolises everlasting love."

Butterfly squeezed her eyes shut. "Oh Jesus, this guy's not going to take no for an answer, is he?"

"Do you want him to?"

Hearing the tightness in Jack's voice, Butterfly looked at him earnestly. "Yes I want him to, but…" Conflicting emotions pulled her face in different directions. "But I also want to ask him about who I used to be. Why did I call myself Io? What happened to Tracy?"

"I think talking to this guy would be a bad idea. He could well be dangerous. I know one thing, he's either a liar or he didn't mean as much to you as he claims. He said you promised to wait for him, but while he was away you fell pregnant with another man's baby."

63

The same thought had already occurred to Butterfly. If she and Karl had been so in love, why had she climbed into bed with Dennis 'Phoenix' Smith? Something about Karl's story didn't add up. And yet... And yet he might be her only chance to rebuild the shattered bridge between her past and present. Maybe he even knew something about what happened to her parents and sister.

Looking into Jack's eyes, Butterfly reached for his hand. "I want you to know that you've got nothing to worry about. Whatever there was between this Karl and me, well it simply doesn't exist anymore. You, Charlie and Naomi are all I want."

"I sense there's a but coming."

A smile fluttered across Butterfly's lips at Jack's intuition. "But if Karl shows up again, I have to talk to him. You understand, don't you?"

Jack nodded. "But I don't like it. And in the meantime, I'm going to find out everything I can about the guy."

Butterfly kissed Jack's hand again. "Perhaps *we* should get matching tattoos," she joked.

He couldn't help but laugh. "Can you imagine what Laura would have to say about that? Bloody hell, I'd never hear the end of it."

The mention of Laura reminded Butterfly about Charlie. She felt a sudden urgency to see him. "I'd better get going," she said, swallowing the dregs of her coffee. "Laura will be wondering where I am."

Jack walked her to the people carrier. She noticed him scanning the street. There was no sign of the Porsche. "Just do me a favour," he said. "If you really must speak to this guy, make sure you do it in a public place. Or even better, do it when I'm around."

"Don't worry. I can look after myself."

An uneasy smile creased Jack's lips. The last man who'd forced Butterfly to prove just how well she could look after herself had ended up in hospital. "I'll see you back at the house. I shouldn't be late."

CHAPTER 6

Jack waved Butterfly off. After she was out of sight, he waited around for a moment, his gaze moving over the street. He went back inside, caught the lift to the Serious Crime Division's floor and made his way past detectives chatting, tapping away at keyboards and making phone calls. At his desk, he logged onto the PNC and ran the Porsche's registration through the DVLA database. He got a hit – the car was owned by a Mick Kelly. Jack's eyes narrowed as they scanned the section of the database that was visible only to the police. Kelly lived in Peckham, North London. He had criminal convictions dating back to the early 1980s – burglary, robbery, assault with intent to rob, forgery, extortion... The list went on and on. He'd done time in HMP Coldingley, Wormwood Scrubs and Belmarsh. More than half his adult life had been spent behind bars. He was currently at liberty, but suspected of involvement in robberies, burglaries and racketeering across London. At the grand old age of 66, Kelly clearly wasn't ready for retirement. The car hadn't been reported as stolen. Perhaps Karl had borrowed it. If he'd just got out of prison, he most likely wouldn't have a car of his own.

"What are you working on?" asked Steve, peering over Jack's shoulder at the screen.

"Nothing much."

Steve smiled crookedly. "Don't bullshit a bullshitter, Jack. Why are you swotting up on north London scumbags?"

Jack eyed him uncertainly. "It would be best if you don't get involved in this, Steve."

Steve raised an intrigued eyebrow. "Now I *really* want to know what this is about. Come on, out with it." He prodded Jack's arm. "You know I'll just keep poking away until you tell me."

His expression balanced between amusement and irritation, Jack swatted Steve's hand away. "You really are a pain in the arse sometimes."

"Only sometimes?" smirked Steve.

Jack rose, motioning for Steve to follow him into an empty office. "This is to go no further than us. And by that I mean–"

"Don't worry," broke in Steve. "I won't breathe a word to Laura. Now come on. Let's hear it."

As Jack recounted Butterfly's encounter with Karl, Steve went from smirking to tugging tensely at his moustache. "This is not good," he said when Jack reached the end of his story. "If this Karl associates with scumbags like Mick Kelly, he's not someone to be taken lightly. You know what we should do? We should track this guy down and tell him to get the fuck out of Dodge."

"What if he ignores us?"

"We'll put it to him in terms he won't be able to ignore." Steve cracked his knuckles meaningfully.

Jack shook his head. "That could make things ten times worse."

"Well we've got to do something. This bloke's not just going to go away. He wants what you've got, Jack, and he'll do whatever it takes to get it. At the very least, let's put his number plate into the ANPR. That way we'll have fair warning if it flags up anywhere near your house."

Jack frowned at the thought of Karl snooping around near his house. "Maybe I should contact Mick Kelly. Find out what he has to say."

Steve wrinkled his nose dubiously. "I doubt he'll tell you much. You know what these old-school scumbags are like when it comes to keeping their trap shut. It's pathological with them."

"Yeah but this is different. And you never know, Kelly might have a beef with Karl. Perhaps the Porsche was a debt repayment."

"Maybe, but just in case I'm right, I'll start looking into associates of Kelly and recent releases from south eastern prisons." Steve clapped Jack on the back as they headed back into the main office. "One way or another, we'll send this arsehole packing with his tail between his legs."

Jack returned to his desk and dialled the contact number on file for Kelly. A voice reduced to a hoarse rasp by a lifetime of smoking answered, "Hello?"

"Is this Mick Kelly?"

"Who wants to know?"

The predictably cagey response told Jack that he was speaking to the very man. "This is Detective Inspector Jack Anderson of Greater Manchester Police, Mr Kelly. I'm calling in regard to a Porsche 718 Cayman. Registration number–"

Jack broke off as wheezy laughter filled the line. "You're him, aren't you?" said Kelly. "You're the copper Karl's woman is shacked up with. I was wondering when I'd hear from you."

"Why's that?" Jack kept his voice neutral. Career criminals like Kelly were like wolves. They would eat you alive if they sniffed out the slightest sign of weakness. The best policy was to treat them as impersonally as possible.

Kelly's laughter grew so loud that he began to cough. "You know why. I'll bet you're shitting your pants, aren't you? You should be."

"Is that a threat?"

"I wouldn't threaten a man like you, Inspector Anderson," Kelly said in a faux-fawning voice. "You killed one of the Mahon brothers and put the other away for life. Oh no, Inspector, I'm much too old for those kinds of games. Mind you, I can't say the same about Karl."

"What's Karl's full name?" Jack asked calmly, not rising to the bait.

"Karl Robinson. He won't mind me telling you that. In fact he wants you to know his name. You should know this too. I've never known anyone love a woman more than he loves her. He'd do anything for her. And I mean absolutely anything, if you get me."

67

"No I don't get you, Mr Kelly. Why don't you explain it to me in more detail?"

Kelly's wheezy laughter clogged the line for another few seconds. "Oh you're a shrewd one. I can see Karl's going to have his work cut out with you. You have a young daughter, don't you? How old is she? Ten? Eleven?"

A rush of heat hit Jack's face. It was all he could do not to spit fire into the phone, but there was only the faintest tremor in his voice as he said, "Can I ask what your relationship is to Mr Robinson?"

"You can ask what you like, copper. Doesn't mean you'll get an answer."

Jack held his anger down. Kelly had been in the system most of his life. Dealing with the police was second nature to him. He knew how to flip questions back on his questioner, push their buttons, divert them from what they were trying to find out. That might have worked with a rookie detective, but Jack had been in the system most of his life too. Dealing with pricks like Mick Kelly was second nature to him. The key was not to play their game. And if you did play, then go all in. Catch the fuckers off guard. "When you call Karl, tell him Jack says hello. And if he ever wants to meet up for a chat or whatever, he knows where to find me."

Jack's voice was relaxed. Anyone overhearing him might have thought he was chatting to a friend, but his dark eyes told a different story.

A small space of silence passed, as if Kelly wasn't sure how to respond. There was no laughter in his voice as he said, "Oh I'll tell him alright. What I wouldn't give to be a fly on the wall when you two meet."

"Thank you Mr Kelly."

"My pleasure, Inspector Anderson." Kelly couldn't resist a parting shot. "By the way, you want to know what they called Karl in the nick? Smooth-talking donkey. And that's not just because the bloke's got the gift of the gab, if you catch my drift."

So you've done time together, thought Jack. He cut off the call with Kelly's laughter echoing in his ears. He sat grinding his teeth for a moment before typing 'Karl Robinson' into the PNC search-term box. A mugshot came up of a square-jawed man with a razor-sharp beard and equally sharp-looking eyes. Jack stared at the butterfly wing tattoo. He'd thought it was unique to Butterfly. More a work of art than a tattoo. Seeing the same tattoo on a stranger's face somehow seemed to cheapen it.

"Bollocks, I thought I'd beaten you to it," said Steve.

Jack's eyes shifted darkly to his colleague.

"You look as if you're ready to knock someone's block off," observed Steve. "I take it you managed to contact Kelly?"

Jack nodded. "Don't ask me what he said because I don't want to talk about it."

"Have you had a chance to read Robinson's rap sheet?" When Jack shook his head, Steve continued, "It's a big one."

Jack gave a humourless little laugh. "So I hear."

"What?" Steve asked bemusedly.

Jack made a dismissive gesture. "Let's hear the good news then."

"This Robinson guy is a major piece of shit. He was released from Wormwood Scrubs two weeks ago. He did two-and-a-half years for credit card fraud. Between January and July 2016, he used stolen chip and pin machines and credit cards to make fraudulent transactions to the tune of £126,750."

"Not bad work if you can get it," Jack commented sardonically. "Is Wormwood scrubs where he met Kelly?"

"No. That was in Belmarsh in 2009. Robinson was doing five years for his part in robbing a house in Kensington. He and an accomplice tied up the couple who lived there and made off with £75,000 in cash, jewellery, antiques, paintings and get this," with an amused shake of his head, Steve added, "a silk duvet cover and two pillow cases. They must have needed a new bed set, eh?"

"Who was the accomplice?"

"We don't know. Robinson never gave her up."

Jack's eyebrow pinched together. "Her?"

Steve glanced around furtively. His voice dropped low. "The burglars were wearing masks. But the house's owners were convinced Robinson's accomplice was a woman of slim build, about 5'5. Sound familiar?"

Jack closed his eyes, pinching the bridge of his nose. "How was Karl caught?"

"The MET picked up the guy the stolen antiques and whatnot were fenced through. He gave up Robinson. Robinson was offered a reduced sentence in return for naming his accomplice. He kept shtum. Seems like he really loves her."

Jack shot Steve a sharp look. "If it was *her*."

"I know you love her too, Jack," said Steve, his craggy features softening. "But don't let that blind you."

Jack wrestled with Steve's words, remembering his own of the previous night to Butterfly – *It's important to see things the way they are, not the way you want them to be.* "Say it was her, what do you expect me to do about it?"

Steve spread his hands. "That's up to you. She's living in your house not mine."

"Are you saying I shouldn't trust her?"

"All I know is I wouldn't sleep very well at night if a woman like that was looking after my kids."

"A woman like *that*?" Jack retorted loud enough to draw curious glances from nearby colleagues. He lowered his voice. "I thought you liked Butterfly."

"I do."

"Then how can you talk about her like that? Whatever she was before, that person died when Ryan Mahon put a bullet in her head."

"I'm sure you're right, Jack. I'm only trying to look out for you." Steve tapped a printout of Karl Robinson's criminal record. "You still haven't heard the worst of this. In 2008 the MET tried to get Robinson on attempted murder. He beat a fellow scumbag called Bryan Hall so badly the guy ended up in a wheelchair. Apparently it was common knowledge on the street that Robinson had done it. He and Hall had some sort of beef going on, but Hall refused to press charges. He was too scared to finger the guy who crippled him. Do you know what that tells me? We shouldn't play around with Robinson. We need to find him and come down on him like the proverbial ton of bricks."

"What was the beef over?"

Steve shrugged. "What are these things always about? Money? A woman?"

"A woman," Jack echoed uneasily, his gaze returning to Karl's mugshot. He looked at it with a pinched brow, then said, "Alright, Steve. We'll do it your way."

Steve nodded approvingly. "I'll circulate Robinson's particulars. I suggest you get yourself home and keep an eye out for him." He handed Jack the printout. "Make sure Butterfly knows exactly what she's dealing with too." As Jack stood to leave, Steve added, "Listen, sorry about what I said before. Thing is, if I let anything happen to you Laura will have my bollocks." His tone was only half-joking.

Jack smiled. But his smile rapidly faded as his thoughts turned to Butterfly's confession that she'd almost hit Charlie. He knew she was capable of extreme violence. He'd watched her do to Ryan Mahon what she'd threatened to do to Phil Beech and Dale Sutton. But Ryan had abducted her child and tried to kill her. She could never turn that part of herself against her family. Could she? He shook his head in an attempt to dislodge the question, but it kept nagging at him as he headed for his car.

CHAPTER 7

Jack scanned the street outside his house. No Porsche. He headed inside to a familiar scene. Naomi and Charlie were playing in the living-room. Butterfly was simultaneously preparing a meal, sterilising baby bottles and sorting through a mound of bibs in the kitchen. As Jack looked at her beautiful, tired face, he felt a stab of guilt. She'd fought tooth-and-nail to get her baby back. Now she was fighting through constant pain to look after her family. How could he have questioned whether she was capable of hurting the ones she loved? He put his arms around her and held her for a moment.

"So what did you find out?" Butterfly asked as they drew apart.

Jack handed her the printout. A cleft formed between her eyes as she flipped through the pages. She put the printout down as if she couldn't bring herself to read any more, lowering her head and closing her eyes. *Thud... thud...* went the drum at the centre of her brain.

"So now we know who I was," she murmured.

"Not for sure."

Butterfly looked at him from under heavy eyelids. "No more kidding ourselves, Jack. I was no better than the lowlifes you lock up."

"Maybe, but you're not that person anymore."

"Aren't I?" A tremor ran through Butterfly's voice. She pressed her fingers to the scar on her forehead. "Sometimes I feel like there's something inside of me. Something that's looking for a way out. It scares me, Jack."

He made to put his arms around her again. "Whatever happens, we'll deal with it together."

Butterfly moved away from his touch. "I'm so tired, Jack. I don't know if I've got the strength to deal with it." She pointed at the printout. "Or with him."

Jack's voice hardened. "You don't have to deal with him. I'll do that."

Butterfly gave him an uncertain look. "What are you going to do?"

"I'm going to talk to him. That's all. Let him know he's not welcome around here." A faintly apprehensive note found its way into Jack's voice. "He's not, is he?"

Irritation flashed in Butterfly's eyes. "What do you want me to say, Jack? Am I going to get back together with him? Of course I'm not. Part of me hopes I never see him again. Another part has a thousand questions it wants to ask him." She clasped the sides of her head. "Sometimes I feel like that's all my life is. Fucking questions!" Seeing the hurt in Jack's eyes, she added quickly, "Sorry, I didn't mean that."

He summoned up a small smile. "I know. And I get it. It's like with my job. The questions never end. Why did this guy murder his wife? Why did that guy rape someone? Sometimes you just want to close your eyes to it all. But you can't. You have to know the answers, even if they make you sick to the pit of your stomach. But I can't let those answers define who I am. If I did, I'd..." He trailed off. He'd been about to say, *I'd chuck myself off the nearest cliff,* but an image of Rebecca rose into his mind. His voice thick with pain, he continued, "Rebecca allowed herself to be overwhelmed by those types of questions."

Now Butterfly moved to put her arms around Jack. "I'm not Rebecca. I know what I've got here and god help anyone who tries to take it away from me."

The fiercely protective edge to Butterfly's voice chased away Jack's pain, but he still held onto her as if afraid she might dissolve through his hands. They drew apart as Naomi entered the kitchen, carrying Charlie on her hip. "Yuck, get a room," she said at the sight of them.

Smiling more broadly, Jack stretched his arms towards her and Charlie. "The hug monster's gonna get you!"

They both squealed with delight as he enveloped them. From the corner of his eye, he watched Butterfly put the printout into a drawer.

73

Karl Robinson and all the rest of it receded from thought as they sat down to eat. Mealtime was the usual fun and games. Jack and Butterfly spent most of it trying to prevent Charlie from decorating the walls with his vegetable gloop. Afterwards, Jack took Charlie upstairs to bath him.

It wasn't until Charlie was in his cot that Karl returned to Jack's mind. As he closed the curtains, his gaze swept the street. Again, no Porsche. *Maybe he's given up and gone back to London,* he said to himself. He seriously doubted it. Assuming Karl's accomplice in the Kensington burglary was Butterfly – or rather, Io – he'd kept his mouth shut for five years. That wasn't the behaviour of a man who gave up easily.

Jack peered into the cot. Charlie was asleep on his back with his arms stretched over his head. "Sleep tight, little man," murmured Jack before tiptoeing from the room.

He found Butterfly at the kitchen table poring over the murder case files. "What if this Karl knows something about the killings?" she said.

"What can he possibly know that we don't? We have access to all sorts of information that he doesn't."

"Except for my memories."

Jack tapped the files. "It's all in there. Tracy told the police everything that happened."

"Did she though?" The old shadow crossed Butterfly's features. "What if there were things she was too scared or ashamed to tell them?"

"That's just your survivor's guilt talking. Believe me, Butterfly, if you'd known anything that would have helped capture the killers, the police would have gotten it out of you."

"Did you speak to Eric?"

Jack nodded. "Briefly. There wasn't much to talk about. Beech still works as a gamekeeper and lives in the same house. Sutton lives in Seascale. He hasn't worked since being sacked from his caretaker job. Apparently he spends most of his time drinking White Lightning on benches around town.

They both live alone. Beech has no family. Sutton has a daughter from the schoolgirl he got pregnant, although for obvious reasons he has no access to her. I'd say they both have pretty shitty lives."

"Is that supposed to be some sort of consolation?" Butterfly asked with a warning glint in her eyes.

"Of course not. I'm just…" Jack sighed. "I suppose I'm just trying to make you feel better about all of this."

"The only thing that would do that is finding the killers."

"I hate to say this, but I'm not sure that's ever going to happen. Not after all this time." Jack gestured to the papers spread over the table. "I mean, what have we got to work with besides a truckload of circumstantial evidence? Yes, Beech knew the Ridleys were going for a walk on Low Lonning. So did the landlord of The Rose and Crown. So did the two men drinking with Beech that lunchtime. Those men worked at Bleng Farm less than a mile from the crime scene. They had access to shotguns. Why not focus on them instead of Beech and Sutton? You passed three farms on the drive out to Low Lonning. Perhaps the killers came from one of those farms. Maybe Alistair Bray, the farmer who phoned the police was involved. Have you considered that?"

"Alistair Bray?" scoffed Butterfly. "He saved my life."

"You saved your own life. All Alistair did was phone the police. He could hardly have done otherwise, that is unless his wife was involved too."

Butterfly gave an incredulous snort. "Pam Bray was a forty-five-year-old housewife with two kids."

"I'm not saying she was directly involved, but she could have been covering for her husband."

Butterfly shook her head. "Pam stated that she, Alistair and their children were stacking hay in their barn shortly before I showed up. A farmer from Holmrook confirmed that he'd made a delivery of hay to Bray Farm that day. The Bray's fourteen-year-old son, Neal, and twelve-year-old daughter,

Hayley, both backed up their mum's statement. Neither Alistair nor Pam has a criminal record. They didn't hesitate to help me. Alistair owned a…" She leafed through several pages and read, 'Cogswell and Harrison shotgun. He'd recently purchased the gun and had not yet shot it, as was confirmed by the absence of carbon residue or wire brush marks."

"I agree, it's extremely unlikely that the Brays had any involvement in the murders."

"Just as it's extremely unlikely that the landlord, Len Simmons, was involved, given that he was at a Cash and Carry in Whitehaven half an hour after the murders. He would have had to drive at a hundred miles an hour the entire way to make it from Low Lonning to Whitehaven in that time. That's just not possible on the roads around there. And those two farm labourers who were drinking with Beech…" Again, Butterfly leafed through the well-thumbed files to the required page. "Kenneth Davies and Jeffery Gardner. They both spent that afternoon helping a local vet worm sheep. The vet and the owner of the farm vouched for their whereabouts. Which brings us back to…"

"Beech and Sutton," Jack admitted with a sigh.

"Phil Beech left The Rose and Crown approximately five minutes after my family. Dale Sutton had no alibi for his whereabouts that afternoon. He claimed he was at home watching a rerun of Minder. In his statement he even talks about what Arthur Daley got up to in that day's episode, as if that somehow proves his innocence. How fucking idiotic can you get?"

"Yeah, it's idiotic," agreed Jack. "That's why it has a ring of truth. You should hear all the bullshit perps come up with. They drag in friends and family, anyone who might cover for them. Sutton didn't do any of that. He gave a story that could have buried him. To me, that doesn't feel like the action of a guilty man. Same with Beech. He claimed he was restocking pheasant feeder barrels in woods along the River Bleng north of Wellington. He had no one to back up his story either."

"So what? So Beech and Sutton are a pair of psychopathic morons. What's so difficult to believe about that?"

"Nothing. If it looks and quacks like a duck, then it probably is a duck. I'm just telling you what my instincts tell me."

Butterfly stared intensely at the case files as if she could will herself to see something that had so far remained hidden. Her finger drew rapid little circles around the entry wound scar. Jack looked on worriedly, resisting an impulse to gather up the files and dump them in the bin. He knew this was something she had to do. He simply had to let her work it out of her system, if that was possible, and try to make sure she came to no harm in doing so.

He rose and moved off to find Naomi. She was on her bed, staring into her iPad. He watched her with a faint frown. She and Butterfly had a lot in common. They were both incredibly strong-willed. When they wanted something, nothing could stop them. If not for sheer willpower, Butterfly might have been dead twice over. But there was a flip side to that coin. Refusing to back down was just as likely to land you in trouble as it was to get you what you wanted.

Jack found himself glancing out of the window in search of the Porsche again. A sardonic smile touched his lips. At least Karl didn't drive a run-of-the-mill car. If all criminals went around in Porsches, it would make his job a lot easier.

"What are you looking at out there?" asked Naomi, eyeing him as if she sensed his tension.

Jack smiled at her. "Nothing." As he stooped to kiss her head, his phone rang. He put it to his ear. "What's up, Steve?"

"We've located Robinson," Steve declared triumphantly. "A traffic camera picked him up on Barlow Moor Road."

Jack's frown returned, more pronounced. Barlow Moor Road ran through Chorlton, passing the street they lived on. "Where is he now?"

"Sat in his car outside McDonald's. A couple of constables are keeping an eye on him. They haven't approached him. How do you want to play this?"

"Tell them I'll be with them in five."

"Will do. Don't do anything without me, Jack." Steve sounded as eager as a boy determined not to miss out on some mischief.

"Would I dare?"

As Jack hung up, Naomi asked, "Work?"

Nodding, he pointed to her iPad. "Don't stay on that thing too long."

He returned downstairs, wondering how much he should say to Butterfly. When he saw her still scrutinising the files, he decided to say as little as possible. "Steve called. I have to go out."

Butterfly looked up from the files. "Is it about Karl?"

"No. I shouldn't be long." He hated to lie, but the tightness around her eyes told him her stress levels were already dangerously high. He didn't want her worrying or, even worse, insisting on coming with him. He bent to kiss her.

She held him to her lips for a moment before murmuring, "Be careful."

CHAPTER 8

Twilight was softening the sky as Jack drove along Barlow Moor Road past restaurants, bars and pubs just starting to fill with evening clientele. The police car was inconspicuously parked on the corner of Beech Road about a hundred metres away from McDonalds. Jack pulled over alongside it and wound his window down.

"He's parked at the right-hand side of McDonalds," the constable behind the steering wheel told him.

"Thanks," said Jack. "You head off. I'll take it from here."

Jack cruised past McDonalds. Next-door to it was an auto repair garage that had shut up for the day. The Porsche was between McDonalds and the garage. Jack turned into a parking space in front of a takeaway joint on the opposite side of the road. He got out of the car and crossed the road. He turned at the sound of feet fast approaching from behind and saw Steve running towards him.

"I thought you were going to wait for me," Steve said, giving him a puppyish aggrieved look.

"This isn't your problem, Steve. I don't want to get you in trouble."

Steve grinned. "The only person I'm worried about getting in trouble with is your sister."

"Alright, have it your own way, but no heavy stuff."

Steve pointed at himself. "Moi, would I?"

The Porsche was facing the street. Steve positioned himself in front of it. Jack approached the driver side door and rapped on its window. It slid down revealing a mid-thirties man with the telltale off-white pallor of a recent parolee. Karl was polishing off the remnants of a burger. He gave Jack a friendly smile that didn't fool the detective for a second. Jack could see the tension coiled behind Karl's dark, calculating eyes. Displaying his police ID, Jack said, "Karl Robinson?"

"Detective Inspector Jack Anderson," Karl read out loud, showing no sign of surprise or nervousness. "What can I do for you?" His tone was almost jaunty. A soft drink cup gurgled as he sucked on its straw.

Jack couldn't help but stare at the tattoo flaring outwards from Karl's left eye. He found himself thinking that if you put Butterfly and Karl's faces together it would make something quite beautiful in a grotesque sort of way. "Get out of the car." His tone was neutral.

Karl got out, still sucking on his drink. He threw Steve a smiling glance. Steve responded with an unsmiling little wave.

"Have I done something wrong, officers?" Karl asked in a tone of disingenuous bemusement.

"Let's cut the shit, shall we Karl?" said Jack. "I know who you are and what you want. I'm here to tell you it's never going to happen."

Karl's smile didn't falter. "Is that right?"

"Yeah that's right, dickhead," put in Steve. "So you might as well sod off back to whatever London shithole you crawled out of."

"Shithole?" Karl let out a reedy laugh. "That's rich coming from a Manc."

"I don't know what there was between you and Butterfly," said Jack. "And frankly I don't give a toss–"

"Who's Butterfly?" Karl broke in with the same provokingly insincere tone.

"You know exactly who she is. Butterfly's with me now."

"Is she?

"I think this prick's got a hearing problem," said Steve. "Maybe we should rinse his ears out."

"Listen, Karl," said Jack. "I'm trying to do this the nice way."

Karl arched an eyebrow. "Really?" He thumbed at Steve. "Is that why you brought that cunt with you? To put me at ease?"

Steve grinned as if that was what he'd been waiting to hear. He stepped forwards, flexing his fists. "What did you call me?"

His smile vanishing, Karl eyeballed Steve without a trace of intimidation. "Perhaps it's you who's got the hearing problem."

Jack stepped between the two men. "Look, Karl, I don't want trouble. Like I said, I'm here to tell you what Butterfly told me. She doesn't remember you. She has no feelings for you. Whatever there was between you is over."

"Why don't we go see her, let her tell me that for herself?"

Jack shook his head. "That's not going to happen."

"Why? What are you afraid of?" The smile crawled back onto Karl's face. "I'll tell you what you're afraid of. You know that deep down in here and here," he pointed at his head and chest, "she remembers the love we had. I'm not talking about any ordinary love. I'm talking about something incandescent."

"Incandescent," chuckled Steve. "Look at who knows big words."

Karl kept his gaze fixed on Jack. "That kind of love never burns out."

"You sound like a cheap Valentine's card," said Steve.

"You know what, Jack? I'm grateful to you. You've looked after my Io, helped nurse her through a bad time. For that I thank you." There was no hint of Karl's earlier insincerity. He appeared to mean what he said. "But I'm here now, so..." He made a little shooing gesture as if giving Jack permission to leave.

Jack felt no anger, just a rising tide of inevitability. "So what you're saying is, you're going to be hanging around here for the foreseeable future."

"For as long as it takes." Karl raised his hand to display the tattoo of the handless clock. "Days, weeks, months, it's all the same to me. All I care about is Io. And one day she'll realise that you're just a tiny little flame, a match that blows out in the wind, and I'm the sun–"

"Oh Jesus, here we go again," Steve broke in with a roll of his eyes. "This moron could give Barbara Cartland a run for her money."

81

Karl threw him a lewd grin. "I've got a lot more to offer than big words. My nickname in Belmarsh–"

"I've already heard it from your mate Mick," interrupted Jack.

"Yeah, he told us how popular you were in the showers," said Steve.

Karl laughed. "Don't project your fantasies on me, little boy blue." He pointedly lifted his soft drink and resumed sucking on its straw. *Gurgle, gurgle...*

With a sighing shake of his head, Jack took out his phone and dialled. He gave the switchboard operator his name, rank and warrant number, before adding, "I need a tow truck to remove an illegally parked car outside McDonalds on Barlow Moor Road, Chorlton."

"What the fuck are you talking about?" demanded Karl. "I'm not illegally parked."

Jack pointed to the Porsche's rear wheel, which was just barely touching a double yellow line. Karl laughed again, but there was no amusement in his eyes as Jack continued into the phone, "It's a black Porsche 718 Cayman."

"With a scratch on its bonnet," put in Steve, taking out a key and scouring a white line along the pristine paintwork.

A gleam of gold showed as Karl's lips peeled away from his gums in a clench-toothed grimace. For an instant, he glared at Steve as if contemplating punching a hole through his face. Then, his lips relaxing back into a smile, he shook his head as if to say, *Uh-uh, you're not going to get me like that.*

Jack gestured towards his own car parked across the street. "If you'd please come with us, Mr Robinson."

"What about my car?"

"There will be a parking fine to pay, plus a recovery fee. A letter will be sent out with all the relevant details."

"And where are you going to take me?"

"Piccadilly Train Station. I'm putting you on a train to London."

Karl snorted. "You think that'll stop me?"

"No. But when you return to Manchester, I'll find you again and put you back on a train. And I'll keep on doing it until you get the message."

One of them on either side of him, Jack and Steve shepherded Karl across the road. "Watch your head," said Steve, none too gently pushing Karl towards the backseat. He ducked into the car alongside Karl. Jack got behind the steering wheel.

They headed into the city centre. Massed ranks of terraced houses gave way to lo-rise blocks of flats, which in turn gave way to towers of glittering glass and steel. Huge cranes punctuated the skyline. "Looks like this place is on the up and up," commented Karl. "Maybe it's not such a shithole. You know, I could even see myself living here."

"Keep your mouth shut," growled Steve.

Karl found his reedy laugh again. "Why do you guys always have to be so predictable?"

"What if I was to shove my hand in your gob and tear your tongue out? Would that be predictable?"

"Steve," Jack said in a cautioning voice.

The ring road ferried them into the city centre where bland modern buildings competed for space with elaborate Georgian and Victorian architecture. A grimy, exhaust-fume filled tunnel brought them to the contrasting blend of old and new that was Piccadilly Station. A curving building of metal and glass squatted atop a Victorian facade of brick and stone.

They found a parking spot. Steve and Jack each kept a hand on Karl's arms as they joined a steady stream of people passing between the station's sliding doors. To their left train platforms with echoing vaulted-roofs were visible through walls of glass. To their right escalators led up to shops, cafes and fast-food restaurants. Steve stayed with Karl whilst Jack followed a sign for 'Tickets and Travel Centre'.

When they were alone, Steve leaned in close to Karl. "Jack's a nice guy." His voice was a menacing murmur. "I'm not. I see you back around here, I'm not just going to put you on a train."

Karl gave him a thin-lipped smile. "I guess we'll see about that."

"I've got a tattoo too, you know." Steve took off his jacket and pulled up his polo-shirt's sleeve, exposing a grinning skull wearing a maroon beret at a jaunty angle. "That's ten years in the Paras. We shit on wannabe tough guys like you. So if you feel like making a move..." He trailed off meaningfully.

Karl spread his hands. "You've got me all wrong, Inspector. I'm not looking for trouble."

Steve and Karl competed in a staring contest. Neither broke eye contact until Jack returned with the ticket. He pointed them in the direction of a platform where people were boarding a bullet-headed Intercity train. "Looks like we're just in time," said Steve, prodding Karl towards the platform.

"Shame," said Karl as they passed between two rows of steel pillars that supported the soaring roof. "I was hoping to spend more time with you. Get to know you better."

Steve broke into a deep belly laugh. "Oh this one is priceless."

They stopped by a carriage's open door. Jack pressed the ticket into Karl's hand, looking him in the eyes without animosity. His voice was almost apologetic as he said, "I understand how it feels to lose someone you love. There's nothing worse. I hope you can move on and find happiness. I really do."

Karl stared back, frowning faintly as if unsure how to take his words.

"Tell your pal Mick Kelly he's got twenty eight days to come up here and get his car back," said Steve. "After that it'll be sold at auction." With a mischievous twinkle in his eyes, he added, "That is if we don't have it crushed."

Karl's cocky grin returned as if he was back on familiar territory. He turned to board the train. The detectives watched him take a seat and waited for the train to pull out of the station. Steve waved Karl off with a taunting waggle of his fingers. Karl blew him a kiss.

Steve swiped his hands together as if wiping off dirt. "Well that's that."

Pursing his lips doubtfully, Jack headed for the street.

"I take it you don't think that's the last we've seen of our new friend," said Steve, following him.

"He loves her," Jack stated as if that was the only answer necessary.

"Yeah, but she doesn't love him." Steve patted Jack's shoulder. "Stop looking so worried. If he shows his face again, we'll come down on him even harder. Maybe we'll even magic up a parole violation, get him sent back to Wormwood Scrubs."

Jack heaved a sigh. "Why can't life ever be simple?"

Steve laughed again. "Where would the fun be in that? Come on, let's go for a drink. I know a great little boozer just around the corner from here."

"I don't drink, remember?"

"So I'll buy you a lemonade."

Jack shook his head. "I need to get home. This whole thing has left Butterfly in a right old state." He gave Steve a grateful glance. "Thanks."

"It was nothing, mate. I enjoyed it. I haven't had a buzz like that in ages." As Jack got into the car, Steve added with a lewd grin, "You and Butterfly should get out of the city for a few days. A dirty weekend in Blackpool. Best stress relief in the world. Laura and I can look after the kids."

"Sounds like a good idea, except for the Blackpool part."

"There's nowt wrong with Blackpool. You know what you are, Jack? You're a southern snob."

Jack laughed despite the lump of tension in his stomach. "I've been called a lot of things, but never that. Besides, it would make no difference whether it was Blackpool or Barcelona. Butterfly won't leave Charlie."

Steve gave him a nod of sympathy. "See you tomorrow then."

Jack's smile faded as he drove away. The future held so much uncertainty, but he felt sure of one thing – Karl Robinson would be on the next train back to Manchester.

CHAPTER 9

When Jack got home, the house was eerily silent. He found Butterfly asleep on the sofa with the case notes spread over her chest and the carpet. Even in sleep, there was a crease between her eyebrows. He watched her for a moment before padding upstairs. Naomi and Charlie were asleep too. He fetched a blanket and returned to Butterfly. As he draped it over her, she opened her eyes. "Hello there," she said, smiling. "How did whatever it was go?"

He smiled back, feeling a ripple of guilt. "Fine."

Butterfly cheeks were flushed with sleep. Her lips slightly parted, she drew him to her and kissed him. She lifted the blanket for him to get underneath. A tingle of arousal coursed through him as she hooked a leg around his waist. "How's your headache?" he asked.

"Fuck my headache," she said breathily, moving in to kiss him again. "You smell sweaty."

Jack thought about how striving to keep calm and impersonal with Karl had made sweat seep from his armpits. "I'll get a shower."

Butterfly pulled him even closer. "No, I like it."

Then they were kissing again and peeling off each other's clothes. The knot of tension in Jack's stomach untied itself as he thrust between her thighs. Butterfly moaned, pulling him deeper into her. He kissed her face and neck, took her lower lip between his and sucked it. This was usually when Charlie woke up as if he had some sort of ESP and started bawling. But not tonight. Tonight they moved in unison until they climaxed together. Then they lay in each other's arms, warm and heavy, not thinking about the murders or Karl Robinson or anything except being there with each other.

"Let's go to bed," Butterfly suggested after a while.

Jack gathered up their clothes while Butterfly returned the box of case notes to the cupboard under the stairs. "I never want to be anywhere else but here," Butterfly murmured as they curled up against each other beneath the duvet.

"Me neither," he replied, proprietarily wrapping an arm around her. He drifted off to sleep with his nose buried in her soft auburn hair.

It seemed as if he'd only been asleep for seconds when his eyes sprang open. Charlie was crying, but that wasn't what had woken him. He couldn't breathe. There were hands on his throat, fingers constricting his windpipe, nails digging into his flesh.

His first thought was – *Karl!*

By the faint light seeping into the room from the landing, he saw something that horrified him far more than that thought. It wasn't Karl's hands on his throat, it was Butterfly's. She was straddling him. He couldn't make out her features, but he recognised the shape of her body and the curl of her hair.

"What are you doing?" His voice scraped out. With one hand, he tried to prise her off his throat. With the other, he groped for his bedside lamp.

"Who are you?" she demanded.

It wasn't only the question that sent a chill through him, it was the flat, unrecognisable tone of Butterfly's voice. His hand found the lamp and switched it on. For an instant he saw an ice-cold light in her eyes, then she blinked and it was extinguished. Her eyes swelled, moving from confusion and surprise to horror. She snatched her hands away from his throat, looked at them as if they didn't belong to her, then buried her face in them. Deep sobs racked her body. Her distraught voice shuddered through her fingers, "Oh my God, what's happening to me?"

Jack sat up and tried to put his arms around her, but she recoiled from him.

Naomi poked her head into the room. "Charlie's awake–" she started to say, but broke off at the sight of Butterfly.

"It's OK, she just had a bad dream," Jack told her.

"I'll go see Charlie."

Thanks, mouthed Jack. Butterfly was facedown on the bed with her knees folded beneath her. "That's all it was," he said to her, "just a bad dream."

She shook her head hard, sobbing, "It wasn't a dream." She stabbed a finger at her head. "Io's in there. She wants to destroy everything I've got. Oh god, Jack, what am I going to do? What am I going to do?" Her voice was ragged with desperation.

Jack didn't have an answer. He rested his hand on her back, his forehead folded into helpless creases. This time she didn't move away from his touch. Charlie's crying stopped. Once again, the house was eerily silent.

CHAPTER 10

A bell rang out and a voice shouted, "Time!"

Steve raised a hand to catch the barman's attention. He ordered another pint of lager and swilled half of it down in one. He glanced around blearily. Drinkers were chatting and laughing at little round tables. Some numpty was chucking his money away on a fruit machine. A TV was showing highlights of the footy. He drew in a deep breath, savouring the smells and sounds of the pub. God, he loved these places. But when the bun cooking in Laura's oven found its way into the world all this would come to a stop. He'd made a promise to himself. It wouldn't be like with his other kids. This time he would be there to change the little blighter's nappies, feed it and do anything else that needed doing. He would be there for Laura too. He knew a good thing when he saw one and he was determined not to throw it away.

He smiled at his pint somewhat mournfully as if saying a last goodbye to an old friend, before swallowing its remnants and turning to leave. On his way out of the pub, he texted Laura 'On my way home. See you soon. Can't wait to get my hands on that gorgeous arse of yours.'

She messaged him back 'Are you drunk? I told you I'm working the graveyard shift tonight.'

Steve chuckled to himself. Laura was always quick to put him in his place, but he didn't mind. He needed someone to tell him how it was, keep him on the straight and narrow. And she *did* have a gorgeous soft round arse, an arse you could get a real handful of. He swayed along the deserted street daydreaming about doing just that. A black cab passed by. He raised a hand to flag it down, but it didn't stop. No matter. There would be plenty of taxis outside the railway station.

He passed beneath an arched steel-and-stone railway bridge. On its far side was a lonely patch of rubbish-strewn wasteland and a shop with graffiti-scarred roller-shutters. A figure stepped from behind one of the scrubby trees that dotted the wasteland.

Steve stopped abruptly. The figure was dressed all in black and wearing a balaclava. Steve found himself wishing he hadn't had that final pint as the masked figure blocked his path. He noted with some relief that the figure wasn't holding a weapon in their gloved hands. He took out his warrant card. "I'm a policeman, dickhead."

He expected the figure to either take to their heels or demand his wallet and phone, but they simply stood there as if waiting for him to do something.

"You stay right where you bloody are," Steve warned needlessly, taking out his phone to dial for assistance. The figure's hand flashed out like a whip to slap the phone to the pavement.

"I dunno what your fucking game is, but you're in deep shit," scowled Steve, putting up his hands, fists clenched.

The figure put up their hands too, crouching into a boxer's stance.

A glimmer of realisation twinkled in Steve's eyes as he surveyed broad shoulders that tapered down to a narrow waist. "Robinson, is that you?"

No reply.

Steve's teeth flashed in a wolfish grin under his salt n' pepper moustache. "Yeah, it's you. Take that mask off so I can see the look on your face when I put my fist in it."

The figure silently held their position, poised to strike.

"One last chance, Robinson," offered Steve. "Fuck off back to London and I'll forget this ever—"

Before Steve could finish, the figure darted in. Steve just barely evaded a right hook. Instead of retreating, he stepped in closer, thrusting out an elbow. The figure grunted as the elbow connected with their face. They tried to dodge out of reach, but Steve wrapped one hand around the back of their neck and pressed the thumb of his other hand into their eye. It was

BEN CHEETHAM

something that had been drummed into him as a Para – always go for the weak points – the eyes, neck and groin. At the same time, he pulled his attacker in even closer, not giving them any room to land a hard strike. The masked figure gave out a yelp as Steve twisted them around and put them in a headlock. He grinned as his hand slid under the figure's chin. A quick squeeze against the carotid arteries and it would be nighty-nighty for this prick.

The figure struck backwards at Steve. A white light seemed to explode in front of Steve's eyes. He reeled away in pain and confusion. The blow should have glanced harmlessly off his skull, but hot blood was streaming down his face. His vision cleared just in time to see a flurry of punches coming his way. He flung up his guard. The punches bounced off his forearms. Fresh pain lanced through him. He caught a glimpse of its cause – the figure was wearing a black ring on their right hand adorned with a spike two or three centimetres long.

"You dirty fucker," gasped Steve, squinting as blood half-blinded him. The figure jabbed at him again. He grabbed their arm and tried to wrench the spiked ring off their finger. The figure took the opportunity to land a thunderous blow against his unguarded head. Steve dropped to his knees, holding on grimly to the ring. His vision swam in an out of focus as more punches crashed into his face. He yanked at the ring again and felt it slide off his attacker's finger. Now it was his turn to strike back. He thrust the ring at his attacker's groin. There wasn't much force behind the blow, but it was enough to make the figure cry out and spring backwards.

Steve clambered to his feet, panting. His legs felt like melted rubber, a light breeze could have knocked him over, but he wasn't about to let his attacker see that. Grinning, he spat blood at the bastard's feet. "Come on then, Robinson," he said, raising his hands with the spike protruding between his fingers. "Let's see how tough you are now."

92

Dark eyes stared at Steve through the balaclava slit. The combatants faced each other for a few rapid heartbeats, then the figure pivoted and sprinted away.

Steve took several staggering steps after his attacker, yelling, "Fucking coward!"

He stumbled to his knees again, blood streaming from his forehead onto the pavement. More blood was seeping through the arms of his jacket. He felt at a gouge that ran from above his right eye past his temple. A centimetre lower and he would have lost an eye. Fighting a surge of dizziness, he crawled on his hands and knees to his phone. Keeping an eye out lest his attacker returned, he dialled 999 and in a slurring voice told the operator to send police and an ambulance. Then he phoned Jack, but got no answer. "Robinson's back," he said after the voicemail beep. He rested his back against a tree, turning the spiked ring over in his hand. It was smooth and beautifully crafted. He chuckled as a thought popped into his head – *Maybe you should get down on one knee and offer it to Laura?*

CHAPTER 11

Jack was sitting up in bed with Butterfly's head on his lap. She'd eventually fallen into a fitful sleep. He'd lain awake all night, watching her. He kept thinking about the feel of her hands on his throat. What if he hadn't woken up? Would she have strangled him to death? He pushed the questions away, telling himself their answers were irrelevant. They had to find a way through this. There was no other option. The thought of life without her or, indeed, without Charlie was more than he could bear.

The sound of Charlie mewling came through the open door. Jack glanced at the alarm clock – 6:45 AM. Charlie would be hungry. Slowly, so as not to wake her, Jack moved Butterfly onto a pillow and slid from beneath the duvet. He picked Charlie out of his cot, kissing his milky-sweet hair and murmuring, "Morning beautiful."

A sting of tears welled up in Jack's eyes as Charlie smiled at him. What if he found himself bringing up two children who'd lost their mums? He shook his head. *No more questions. Focus on the positives. Butterfly is alive and she loves you.* Nothing would change that last part. "Nothing," he said in a voice of soft determination, cradling Charlie against his shoulder.

He went downstairs, mixed up a bottle of milk and fed Charlie on the sofa. Gurgling contentedly, Charlie gulped down his breakfast. Jack's mobile phone rang. It was Laura. He frowned faintly. Why was she phoning at this early hour? "Morning, sis," he said.

"Have you heard?" she replied in a way that made the wrinkles on in forehead deepen.

"Heard what?"

"Steve's in hospital."

"What? Why?"

"They brought him into the Royal Infirmary last night. I only found out a short while ago. A nurse I know over there called me. He was found unconscious in the city centre. Someone had beaten him up."

Jack grimaced. "How is he now?"

"He's concussed, but he'll be OK."

"Had he been robbed?"

"I don't know. I haven't spoken to him. I'm on my way over there." Laura told him which ward Steve was on, before asking, "Has this got something to do with you? The last time I saw him he was heading out to meet you."

"It might have," admitted Jack. "I'll see you at the hospital. I'll tell you all about it then."

Jack got off the phone, his brows knitted in thought. Had Steve got drunk and fallen prey to a mugger? No, it had to be Karl. It was too coincidental. He headed back upstairs with Charlie burbling in his ear. He gently shook Butterfly awake. Looking up at him with puffy, painfully apologetic eyes, she squeezed his hand and mouthed, *I'm sorry.*

He stooped to kiss her knuckles. "You've got nothing to be sorry for."

"I could… I could have killed you," Butterfly said haltingly.

"No you couldn't. You were disorientated and scared." Jack cupped his hand over her cheek, feathering the tattoo with a fingertip. "I trust you, Butterfly, with my life and the life of my child."

She pressed her face against his palm, her eyes glazing with tears.

"Listen, I have to go out. Something's happened to Steve. I'm not sure if he's been mugged or if he just fell over drunk and hit his head, but he's in hospital." Seeing Butterfly's eyes widen with concern, Jack added, "He's fine. Just a concussion. As soon as I've seen him, I'm coming straight back here. Are you up to doing the school run? I can take Naomi with–"

"I'll be fine," broke in Butterfly. "I just want things to be as normal as possible. You know?"

Jack nodded understanding. He handed over Charlie. Wrenching his eyes from Butterfly, he dressed in jeans and a polo-shirt and hurried from the room. He looked in on Naomi. She was still fast asleep. He crouched at her side, whispering her name. As she opened her eyes, he put a finger to his lips. "I have to go out," he said. "I need you to keep an eye on Butterfly. If she falls ill or... I don't know, acts odd in any way, I want you to call me at once. OK?"

Naomi nodded. Jack kissed her on the cheek. "Good girl. Have a good day at school."

He felt a twinge of guilt for having effectively asked Naomi to spy on Butterfly. He told himself it wasn't because he didn't trust Butterfly, it was because he was worried about her health. But his eyes glimmered with uncertainty as he headed for his car.

His thoughts turned to Steve as he drove through the beginnings of rush-hour to the angular mirrored-glass building that housed Manchester Royal Infirmary. When he got to the ward, he found Laura at the end of Steve's bed, perusing his charts. She hadn't changed out of her nursing uniform. Jack noted that her bump had become considerably more prominent in the week since he'd last seen her.

Steve was propped up on pillows, tucking into tea and toast. His head was swathed in a bandage. His right eye was blackened and swollen shut. Strips of butterfly stitches crisscrossed his forearms. "Bloody hell, mate," said Jack. "You look as if you've been hit by a truck."

Steve made a dismissive gesture as if to say, *It's nothing.* "Did you get my message?"

"No."

Steve glanced at Laura as if uncertain whether to speak his mind in front of her. Jack motioned for him to go ahead. Even if he'd wanted to, there would have been little point trying to hide anything from Laura. Once she caught a scent, she was like a bloodhound. Right then, she was treating both men to a narrow look through her black-rimmed spectacles.

"I'm sure it was Robinson who put me here," said Steve.

"Who's Robinson?" asked Laura.

"Karl Robinson's an ex-con who claims he was in a relationship with Butterfly before… Well, before she *was* Butterfly," said Jack. "Now he wants her back."

"And how long's this been going on?"

"A couple of days. Butterfly wants nothing to do with him. Steve and I tried to warn him off but–"

"But it obviously didn't have the desired effect," Laura interrupted with a glance at Steve's battered face.

"I would have wiped the floor with the bastard if he'd played fair," said Steve.

"You were punched in the face with a metal spike," chided Laura. "You were lucky you weren't killed."

Grinning, Steve rapped his head with his knuckles. "Nah, I've got a head like a bag of cement. It'll take a lot more than that to do me in."

Laura's hand went to her swollen belly. "This isn't a joke, Steve. You do want to be around to see your baby, don't you?"

Steve's grin faltered. "Of course I do," he said with a gentleness that belied his rugged appearance.

"Then stop playing these stupid sodding games!"

Jack was surprised to hear a wobble of tears in Laura's voice. She'd never been the type to cry. She turned her head away as if she didn't want them to see the tears welling into her eyes.

"I'm sorry, Laura. I…" Steve trailed off as if he didn't know what else to say. He looked at Jack as if appealing for backup.

"This isn't Steve's fault, Laura," said Jack. "I got him involved him in this. I'm the one you should be angry at."

"I'm not angry at you. I'm..." Laura heaved a sigh. "I don't know what I am. Christ, why do I constantly feel like crying these days?" She cupped a hand over her belly in a manner that suggested she knew the answer to her question.

"Just wait until the little bugger's born, then you really will feel like having a breakdown," said Steve, rediscovering his grin.

She arched an eyebrow that warned him not to push his luck. "I'm going to get a coffee and leave you two to plan your next disaster."

Steve watched her step out of the curtained cubicle with awed eyes. He puffed his cheeks at Jack. "I'd rather take on a thousand Karl Robinsons than one pregnant Laura."

"So what happened?" asked Jack.

Steve described the fight with the masked figure. He chuckled when he came to the part where he jabbed the spike into the figure's groin. "Whatever he's got down his pants, he won't be sticking it in anything anytime soon."

"Where's the ring?"

"Forensics have got it. If they come up with Robinson's fingerprints, he'll be back in Wormwood Scrubs faster than you can say smooth-talking donkey."

"Sorry about all this, Steve."

"Ah forget it. I shouldn't have been out on the lash." An unusually thoughtful look crossed Steve's face. "Sometimes I wonder if I invite this crap on myself. The ex-wife used to say that all I'm good for is trouble."

"She sounds like a perceptive woman," Jack commented dryly.

Steve laughed, then winced and put a hand to his bandaged head. *Fuck you*, he mouthed.

As Laura returned with her coffee, Jack bent in to kiss her cheek. "I have to go. Keep an eye on him. Make sure he doesn't sneak out to the pub."

"Oh believe me, he won't be seeing the inside of a pub for quite some time." Laura gave Steve an ominous look. "Will you?"

Steve's grimace intensified. He stared at Laura for a moment before caving in with a mournful shake of his head. As Jack turned to leave, Steve said, "Be careful. Robinson's a tricky bugger."

Jack gave him a nod. He took out his phone and dialled Butterfly. The call went through to voicemail. Why wasn't she picking up? He looked at his watch – 8:27. She was probably dropping Naomi off at school. He wondered whether to leave a message warning her about Karl, but decided against it. He didn't want to risk triggering another of her episodes. His rapid footsteps echoed along the corridors.

CHAPTER 12

After swallowing her painkillers, Butterfly changed Charlie's nappy and took him downstairs. Naomi was munching cereal in the kitchen. She cast a lingering look at Butterfly. A smile spread over Naomi's face as she turned her attention to Charlie. "Morning Charlie."

He waved his pudgy hands, burbling at her.

Butterfly put Charlie in his highchair and mashed up a banana for him. She felt gritty-eyed with tiredness, but she was glad to be busy. Anything was better than lying around worrying about what was going on inside her damaged brain.

Half-an-hour later the three of them were in the people carrier, negotiating the congested streets around Naomi's school. Butterfly kept glancing in the rearview mirror. Despite there being no sign of Karl's Porsche, she insisted on walking Naomi to the school gates. Naomi gave her an even more enthusiastic cuddle and kiss than usual and treated her to another searching look before heading into school. Jack had obviously said something to her. Butterfly didn't blame him, but she felt a pang of sadness. Why did it have to be this way? Why couldn't things just be normal? *Normal.* She heaved a sigh. It seemed as if she would never learn the true meaning of that word.

They were running low on baby wipes, but she drove straight home, too weary to face the shops. By the time they got there, Charlie was hungry for his next feed. She returned him to his highchair and set about sterilising a day's worth of bottles for his milk.

There was a knock at the front door. Leaving Charlie in his chair, Butterfly went to see who it was. As she opened the door, she stiffened at the sight that confronted her. Karl's left eye was weepy and shot through with red veins. He was smiling, but there was zero amusement in his expression.

"Hello Io."

Butterfly made to slam the door in his face. He jammed a foot against it.

"Move your foot!" she demanded.

"Please, Io, I just want to talk."

"Move your foot or I'll scream."

Karl removed his foot from the door, taking a step backwards, hands spread. "Like I said, I just want to talk. We've got so much to say to each other, Io."

"Stop calling me that. My name's Butterfly."

"OK, Butterfly. I'm happy to call you whatever you want."

Butterfly eyed Karl uncertainly, poised to slam the door. "And what if I say I want you to go away and never come back? Will you?"

"If that's truly what you want, then I'll accept it. But first let me say what I came to say. I think I deserve that after all the years we spent together."

"I don't remember those years."

"That doesn't mean they didn't happen. Thirteen years. We were together for thirteen, almost fourteen years. We had something…" Karl sought for the words to describe what they'd had. "Nothing and no one else mattered. It was just us against the world."

"If what we had was so great why did I have another man's baby?"

Karl winced as if Butterfly had poked a finger into his good eye. "The last time I saw you before this week we had a big old row."

"About what?"

"You came to see me in prison. You wanted something from me, but I wouldn't give it to you." Karl reached inside his t-shirt and pulled out a silver necklace with a jigsaw piece pendant dangling from it. 'Little Sis' was engraved on the pendant.

Butterfly's mouth dropped open. The drum started up in her head. *Thud… Thud…* "Tracy's necklace."

"So you do remember some things."

Butterfly shook her head. "I've read about the murders."

"Then you know that whoever has the other piece of this jigsaw killed your parents and sister." Karl took off the necklace and proffered it to Butterfly. Warily, as if fearing he might grab her, she made to accept it. He closed his hand around it. "Let me come inside and speak to you. Five minutes. That's all I'm asking for."

Butterfly's gaze flicked from the necklace to Karl and back. She stepped aside. "Five minutes," she echoed as he entered the house.

"M...m...m..." Charlie was calling from the kitchen.

Butterfly lifted him out of his highchair. "Hi there, little one," said Karl, reaching to tickle Charlie's cheek. "Aren't you beautiful? Just like your mummy."

Butterfly moved out of Karl's reach, holding Charlie protectively against her chest.

"What's his name?" asked Karl.

"Charlie."

Karl nodded as if he wasn't surprised. "You always said if you had a kid you'd name it after your sister. Seems to me there's a lot left of who you used to be in that head of yours."

"You're wrong." Butterfly tried to say it with conviction, but the doubt in her voice was unmistakable.

Karl gave a smiling shake of his head. "I never thought you'd actually have a baby though. I just couldn't see you changing nappies and cleaning up sick. You hated getting your hands dirty."

Butterfly cocked an eyebrow at him. "So what was I doing with a scumbag like you?"

Karl laughed. "There it is. There's that bitchy streak. God, I've missed that."

Butterfly gritted her teeth. The drum was thundering in her ears loudly enough to make her sway on her feet. Karl darted out a hand to steady her.

She pushed him away, saying, "I'm fine." She drew a deep breath through her nostrils – in for seven, out for eleven. The thundering receded to a slow thudding. "It's the bullet," she explained a touch hoarsely. "I get these headaches."

"If I ever get my hands on the fucker who shot you, I'll tear his heart out and feed it to him," Karl said with such vehemence that Butterfly gave him a reassessing, almost sympathetic look.

"You really did love me, didn't you?" she said.

"I *do* love you," corrected Karl.

"No you don't," she stated. "The woman you loved is dead."

"No, you're wrong. Io's still in there. I can see her in your–"

"Stop," cut in Butterfly, pressing a hand to her head. Charlie let out a distressed mewl at the sharpness of her voice. She stroked his back, shushing him into silence. "You have to stop this," she said to Karl in a tone that was part demanding, part pleading. "If you do still love me, you'll accept that whatever there was between us died with my memories."

Karl was silent for a moment, his lips compressed into a tight line. Very slowly, as if unsure he was doing the right thing, he placed the necklace on the table. "I wouldn't give this to you when I was in prison because I didn't want you to go up to The Lakes alone and get yourself hurt. But it didn't make any difference. You went up there anyway. You always did exactly what you wanted to do."

Butterfly picked up the necklace. As if it was a sacred artefact, she reverently traced a finger around the jigsaw piece's outline.

"Your parents gave you that necklace," said Karl, dabbing his bloodshot eye with a tissue. "Your sister Charlie had one too. You and she were very different, but your mum and dad wanted you to know that you were pieces of the same puzzle. You fitted together. The same as you and me. We fit together. We–"

Karl fell silent at a warning glance from Butterfly. "How were Charlie and I different?"

"She was a normal teenage girl. She was into boys, pop stars all that bollocks. You were into…" Karl chuckled, "other things."

"What other things?"

Butterfly's forehead furrowed as he replied, "You used to read to me from the papers every day. Stabbings, shootings, serial killers, jihadis. You couldn't get enough of that shit."

An uneasy smile crept up Butterfly's face. "I got off on that stuff, did I?"

"Nah, you were just keeping yourself on your toes. Staring the world straight in the face." Karl dabbed his eye again, wincing. "This fucking eye."

"What's wrong with it?"

"I think it's infected."

"You should see a doctor."

Karl gave a dismissive flick of his hand. "I've got a sore eye, you're walking around with a bullet in your head." He shook his head in awe. "You always were the toughest bitch in the entire universe."

"Yeah well it doesn't matter how tough I am. This bullet moves one millimetre in the wrong direction and that'll be the end of me."

"Nah, there's no way you're going out like that. You'll be kicking the shit out of the world long after I'm dead and buried." Karl motioned to Charlie. "Especially now you've got this little man to keep you on your toes."

As if on cue, Charlie threw back his head and let out a little wail. "Are you hungry?" asked Butterfly, reaching for a packet of rusks. He eagerly accepted the biscuit and jammed it into his mouth.

Karl chuckled. "I can see he's gonna be a handful."

Butterfly's gaze returned to the 'Little Sis' pendant. "Thank you for giving me this." She smiled at Karl for the first time.

He pressed a hand to his chest as if her smile had hit him there. "I just hope it helps you find the fuckers that killed them."

"I hope so too." Butterfly glanced pointedly at a clock on the wall. "Listen, I've got things to do. So…" Her gaze moved to the front door.

Karl continued to look at Butterfly as if he couldn't take his eyes off her. "When can I see you again?"

She shifted uneasily under his intense gaze. "I don't think we should do this again."

"But there's still so much I haven't told you. About you. About us. About who killed your parents and sister."

"What else do you know about their deaths?" Butterfly asked with piqued interest.

"You collected boxes of stuff about the murders. Newspaper clippings, files you put together on everyone the police spoke to."

"Have you still got it all?"

"Yeah. It's with Mick."

"Mick?"

"Mick Kelly. He's a good mate of ours. But we don't need all that stuff." Karl prodded a finger at his temple. "It's all in there. Names, addresses, the lot. I've got one of them what d'you call it, photographic memories." His eyes lit up as if he'd had an idea. "Hey, I know, why don't we take a trip up to The Lakes? You, me and Charlie boy. We'll pay some of those names a surprise visit."

Just for a second, as if she was considering the proposal, Butterfly hesitated to reply. Then she shook her head. "No."

"Why not? We always used to talk about doing it."

"Because I'm not well enough to go up there. And because… Well, because if I do go up there, it won't be with you. Do you understand?" There was a softness in Butterfly's voice that hadn't been there earlier, but also a finality that dampened down the light in Karl's eyes.

His gaze dropped away from hers. He pressed the tissue to a fresh welling of moisture from his injured eye. His shoulders slumped like a defeated boxer's, he turned and took several slow steps towards the front door. With a quiet breath of relief, Butterfly returned Charlie to his highchair and followed Karl. He stopped suddenly, his face knotted as if wrestling with an internal debate. The knot smoothed out as he shook his head.

"You know what?" he said as much to himself as Butterfly. "I can't accept it." His hand slid into his jacket pocket. It emerged gripping a pistol with the distinctive square barrel of a Glock.

"What are you doing?" gasped Butterfly, her eyes like saucers.

"I didn't want to do this, but you've given me no choice." Karl's voice swayed between anger and apology. He flicked his wrist. "Backup."

Butterfly retreated into the kitchen, darting a panicky glance at Charlie who was obliviously sucking on his rusk. She backed up against the work surface. She didn't want the gun pointing anywhere near Charlie. "Please don't hurt him."

"What the fuck do you think I am?" retorted Karl as if insulted by the suggestion that he would do such a thing.

Butterfly's hand groped across the drainer behind her back. Her fingers closed around the handle of a knife. She let go of it as Karl sidestepped towards the highchair and scooped up Charlie.

"Don't," exclaimed Butterfly, holding her hands out pleadingly.

"Don't what? I told you, I'm not going to hurt him." Karl playfully nuzzled Charlie with his black beard. Charlie laughed as the bristles tickled his cheek. "See, he likes me. We're gonna be great mates. Aren't we Charlie?"

"I'm begging you. Put him down and I'll do anything you want. We can go to The Lakes."

"Oh we're going to The Lakes. All three of us." Karl motioned to the baby paraphernalia cluttering the table and work surfaces. "Pack what you need."

As suddenly as a switch being flipped, the fear left Butterfly's eyes. "No." Her tone was flat and hard. She took a step towards Karl. "You won't hurt me. Now put Charlie down and get out of my house."

A smile crawled over Karl's lips. "Is that you Io?"

"Do as I say. Walk out of here now and I'll forget this ever happened. You can get on with your life and I'll get on with mine."

Pain twisted Karl's smile out of shape. "*You* are my life. If I can't have you then–"

"Then what?" cut in Butterfly, taking another step towards him. "You won't hurt me," she repeated. "Not if you love me."

"That's why I will hurt you." Karl took aim at Butterfly's head. "I'll put another bullet in your brain, then I'll put one in my own. I don't want to do it, but I swear to fucking god I will if you make me."

The desperate, agonised sincerity in Karl's voice stopped Butterfly in her tracks. He motioned towards the baby paraphernalia again. This time, she reluctantly set about packing bottles, formula milk, rusks, bibs, nappies, teethers and all the rest of it into a cloth bag.

When she was done, Karl backed into the hallway with Charlie in the crook of his arm. Slinging the bag over her shoulder, Butterfly followed him. She pointed to the under-stairs cupboard. "I need Charlie's pushchair."

Karl gestured for her to go ahead. She dragged the box of case files from the cupboard before lifting out the pushchair. She closed the cupboard, leaving the box in the middle of the hallway. Karl jerked his chin at a bunch of keys dangling from a hook. "Are those your car keys?" When Butterfly nodded, he added, "Bring them and leave your mobile phone."

Butterfly placed her phone on the hallway sideboard.

Karl stepped outside, glancing around as if to make sure no one was about. He slid the gun into his pocket, but kept hold of it. "Put the buggy in the boot." As Butterfly opened the people carrier's boot, Karl lowered Charlie into the baby seat. "Strap him in."

Butterfly slung the rest of Charlie's clobber onto the backseat and secured the straps across him. Her hands lingered on him, her forehead puckering with indecision.

"Don't try anything stupid," warned Karl.

Butterfly straightened, giving him a *What now?* look.

"Keys," he said, holding out his hand.

Tension quivered through Butterfly as she made to place the keys in his palm. This was her chance. If she stabbed a key into Karl's good eye, she might be able to overpower him. As if reading her mind, he said, "Think about Charlie."

She exhaled resignedly, knowing he was right. She couldn't risk a stray bullet hitting Charlie. She released the keys. "Get in the front passenger seat," said Karl.

"Can I sit in the back with Charlie?"

Karl smiled thinly. "What and then the pair of you make a run for it at the first set of traffic lights? I don't think so, sweetheart."

Thud, thud! The drum reverberated through Butterfly's brain. "I'm not your fucking sweetheart," she scowled, a savage light flaring in her eyes. For an instant, it was all she could do not to swing for Karl regardless of the consequences.

He retreated a step, his smile broadening. "Oh I can see this is going to be a fun trip."

Keep it together! Think about Charlie, Butterfly commanded herself, turning down the drum's volume with a seven-eleven breath. She headed around to the front passenger door and ducked into the car. Karl got behind the steering wheel. He took out the Glock, wedged it under his right thigh and started the engine. "OK," he said with an excited look at Butterfly. "Here we go! Our first family holiday."

CHAPTER 13

On the way home, Jack phoned the office. Detective Chief Inspector Paul Gunn picked up the phone. "What's this I'm hearing about you and DI Platts using police resources to locate an ex-boyfriend of Butterfly's?" he asked in a disapproving tone.

"Karl Robinson isn't just any old ex."

"I know. I've read his rap sheet. Butterfly used to keep dubious company to say the least."

Jack held in a sigh. He didn't want to get into a discussion about Butterfly's past. He already knew the DCI's views on such things. The private lives of Paul's detectives were their own business, unless they had the potential to reflect badly on the Serious Crime Division. The division had a spotless reputation under Paul's watch. He intended to keep it that way. If anyone but Jack had been caught using the PNC for personal reasons, Paul would have had them up on a misconduct charge. But Jack and Paul went way back. Jack knew Paul was far from the white knight he projected himself to be. The two men had enough dirt on each other to derail their respective careers. The result was an uneasy understanding – you stay out of my business and I'll stay out of yours. "I'm sorry, Paul, I should have come to you about Robinson."

"You're damn right you should of. We could have done this the right way – taken out a restraining order against him. But it's too late for that now. I've got an officer in the hospital and a suspect at large. What the hell did you do to this man that made him retaliate like that?"

"We put him on a train to London and told him not to show his face around here again."

"For Christ's sake, Jack." Paul sounded annoyed but not surprised. "What if Robinson goes to the press? This isn't the Wild West. We don't run criminals out of town."

"He's not going to the press. And even if he did, it would be the word of a career criminal against two DIs. Who do you think they would believe?"

"That's not the point. I shouldn't be put in a position where I might have to lie to cover for my detectives." Paul's voice grew heavy with regret. "Look, Jack, I realise what I did can never be made right, but things can't keep going on like this. At some point, I have to say enough is enough."

"You're dead-on, Paul, what you did can never be made right." The old resentment found its way into Jack's tone as he thought about how Paul and Rebecca – his onetime closest friend and the woman he'd worshipped – had been meeting up for sex. The feeling faded as fast as it had arisen. He barely ever thought about Paul and Rebecca's betrayal these days. Not since getting together with Butterfly. The more he fell in love with Butterfly, the less it hurt to see the photo of Rebecca that Naomi kept on her bedside table.

A momentary silence filled the phone line. His voice impersonal once again, Jack said, "I'm not asking you to lie for me, Paul. If it comes to it, I'm willing to take full responsibility for my actions." *More than willing,* he added to himself. In some ways it would be a relief. There had been a time when he'd allowed the job to define him. He'd lost sight of what truly mattered and it had almost cost him everything. He would never make that mistake again. "I called to let you know I won't be coming in today. I'd also appreciate it if you could let me know if we pick up Robinson or if Forensics come up with any prints."

"Of course I will. I know you don't trust me, Jack, but I'm your DCI. As far as I'm concerned, if someone's threatening you, they're threatening me. So if there's anything else I can do to help…" Paul left the offer hanging.

Jack hesitated before saying, "Thanks." It was only the space of a breath, but it was enough to let Paul know his offer wouldn't be taken up unless there was no other choice. A rueful smile crossed Jack's face. If love was a healer, then pride was a motherfucker.

He got off the phone and dialled Butterfly. Once again, his call went through to voicemail. He put his foot down. His expression grew more troubled when he arrived at the semi-detached house. He'd been hoping to see Butterfly's car, but the driveway was empty. He parked up and hurried into the house, calling out, "Butterfly."

No response.

His gaze came to land on the box of case files. What was it doing in the middle of the hallway? Butterfly knew better than to leave it out. The box contained crime scene photos of corpses with their faces shredded by shotgun pellets. He would have been devastated if Naomi saw them. He dodged around the box into the kitchen. The breakfast pots were still on the table. Charlie's highchair was splotched with mushed banana and biscuit crumbs. That wasn't unusual. There generally wasn't time to clean up before taking Naomi to school. And on the way back from the school run, Butterfly would often stop off at the supermarket. Doubtless that's where she was now. They'd been running low on baby wipes.

Jack cleared the table, washed and dried the pots and began to put them away. He paused, his eyes narrowing pensively. The shelf where they stored the baby bottles and formula milk was empty. Butterfly always took one or more pre-prepared bottles with her when she went out with Charlie, depending on how long they would be gone for. But why would she need *all* the bottles? Jack looked in the drawer where they kept Charlie's bibs, dummies, teething powders, nappy rash cream and Calpol. Empty.

He gave a baffled shake of his head. Butterfly had packed as if she would be gone for days. His gaze returned to the box of case files as a worrying thought occurred to him – might Butterfly have gone up to The Lakes? She'd assured him she wouldn't, but she hadn't exactly been in her right mind. Perhaps she was scared that if she didn't go to The Lakes now, she would become too ill to do so. He moved to open the box and leaf through the folders. None appeared to be missing, including those that contained Phil Beech and Dale Sutton's home addresses. He went up to their bedroom and looked in the wardrobe and drawers. Butterfly didn't appear to have taken any of her clothes. The bag she used whenever they went away overnight was still under the bed. Somewhat reassured that he was wrong about The Lakes, he returned downstairs.

He caught sight of something on the sideboard that momentarily stopped him in his tracks. He hastened to pick up the object. Butterfly's phone. Why would she have left her phone behind? Even if she had gone to The Lakes, surely she would have taken it with her. Had she simply forgotten it? Another more disturbing possibility occurred to him. What if she'd been forced to leave it behind by someone who wanted to prevent her whereabouts from being tracked? Had Karl been here?

Carefully, as if afraid of contaminating potential evidence, he made his way around the house. There was no sign of forced entrance on any of the windows or doors. Nor were there any signs of struggle. The only things out of place were the box and the missing baby gear. Neither thing was necessarily sinister, yet his instincts yelled that something was amiss.

He phoned Naomi's school and told the receptionist he needed to speak to his daughter. After a wait of several minutes, Naomi came on the phone. "Hi Dad. What is it?" She sounded worried.

"How did Butterfly seem to you this morning?"

"She seemed OK. A bit tired. Why?"

"Did she take any bags with her when you left the house?"

"Just Charlie's things."

"How much of Charlie's stuff did she have?"

"Two bottles, some nappies and spare clothes."

"Only two bottles. Are you certain about that?"

"Pretty much, yeah. What's going on, Dad?"

"Nothing for you to worry about. I've got to go. I'll see you later, sweetheart."

Jack hung up and stared uncertainly at Butterfly's iPhone. After a moment, he tapped in the unlock code and looked through the phone's contents. He wasn't comfortable with snooping on her – he'd told himself he would never allow Rebecca's unfaithfulness to poison his and Butterfly's relationship with suspicion and jealousy – but surely it was justified in this instance. His stomach felt as tight as a fist. What if he found that Butterfly had been in contact with Karl?

She'd made no calls and sent no texts that day. The only calls she'd received were from him. Jack wasn't sure how to feel. On the one hand, it eased his tension to know she hadn't spoken to Karl behind his back. On the other, it left him no closer to solving the mystery of her whereabouts.

He briefly lowered his head in thought before striding out of the house. Perhaps one of his neighbours could shed some light on the matter. He didn't bother with his immediate neighbours. Both those houses were inhabited by young families too busy to notice comings and goings on the street. Instead, he headed for a house on the opposite side of the street. Mrs Turner, an eighty-seven-year-old widow lived there. She sat in an armchair by her living-room window all day long. Nothing much got by her.

Jack knocked on her door and called through her letterbox. "Mrs Turner, it's Jack Anderson from number twenty four."

A five-foot-nothing barrel of a woman with a grey perm tottered into the hallway, surfing between the furniture to keep herself upright like Charlie did. With frustrating slowness, she made her way to the front door and struggled to slot the key into the lock. Eventually she managed to get the door open. "What can I do for you love?" she asked, turning an ear toward Jack in anticipation of his reply.

"I'm looking for Butterfly."

"Who?"

"The lady who lives with me."

"Oh, the young lady with *that* great big tattoo on her face." The way she said it made it clear what she thought of the tattoo.

Jack was too worried to be irritated by her disapproving tone. "Have you seen her?"

Mrs Turner thought for a moment. "Now then, I did see her earlier. I was watering the plants in the front window and I happened to see her driving away in her car."

"What time was this?"

"How should I know? I don't keep tabs on her," bristled Mrs Turner.

"I know that, Mrs Turner," said Jack, smiling patiently. The old lady was obviously keen not to be labelled as a curtain-twitcher. He subtly shifted tack. "So you were watering your plants..." He trailed off so that the old lady could fill in the blanks.

"Yes, I water them every morning after breakfast."

"What time do you have breakfast?"

"Well I wake up at seven, but I only have a cup of tea. My appetite isn't what it used to be. At nine o'clock I have a slice of toast."

"Nine o'clock," echoed Jack, frowning. Butterfly took Naomi to school at around half-past eight. If she didn't stop at the shops and depending on traffic, she usually got back home at around a quarter-past nine. "Was anyone with her? I mean other than the baby? Possibly a man with a dark beard and short white-blond hair?"

"I've no idea. Now that I think about it, I didn't see her. I only saw the back of her car as she drove away." Mrs Turner peered at Jack through thick-lensed spectacles. "Is this man a friend of hers?"

The knowing question told Jack it was time to bring the conversation to a swift conclusion. "Which way was the car going?"

Mrs Turner pointed south towards Edge Lane.

"Thanks for your help, Mrs Turner. Have a good day."

Jack hastened back to his house. He knew now why Naomi hadn't seen Butterfly with the missing baby clobber. Butterfly had taken Naomi to school, returned home, packed Charlie's bottles and other things, then headed out again. But why? And where had she gone? If she'd been heading into the city centre to do some shopping, she would have gone towards Manchester Road, not Edge Lane. Edge Lane snaked northwest through Stretford towards the M60, which joined with the M61 north of the city. The M61 in turn curved north towards Preston and the M6. From there it was a straight run up to The Lakes.

Jack paced around the living-room, darting glances out of the window every time a car passed. Ten minutes crawled by. Twenty...

Why would she go out without her phone? He kept asking himself. *Especially considering everything that's happened?* His gaze was continually drawn to the box of case files and the more he looked at it the more it seemed like some sort of sign. He glanced at the clock. It was edging towards eleven. With a sudden decisive movement, he took out his phone and called Laura. "I'm sorry about this, sis, but I need a favour?" he said. "Can you pick up Naomi from school and look after her for a few hours?"

"What about Butterfly?"

"That's the thing. She's not at the house, her car's gone and I can't get hold of her."

"Do you think it's got something to do with this ex-boyfriend?"

"Possibly," Jack admitted. "There's another possibility. I have a horrible feeling she might be on her way up to The Lakes to confront the men she thinks murdered her parents and sister."

"Bloody hell, Jack. Are you going to head up there yourself?"

"What else can I do?"

"Speak to Paul. Get him to put out an APB or whatever you call it for Butterfly's car."

"I don't think we're at that point yet. She's not even been gone two hours. She might just be at the shops."

"Or maybe she's visiting her grandma."

A little lift of hope came into Jack's voice. "You could be onto something there. I'll give the nursing home a call."

"OK. Let me know if you still need me to pick up Naomi."

"Will do. Speak soon."

Jack hung up and scrolled through Butterfly's contacts list to 'Gran'. He pressed dial, and a woman answered, "Golden Year's nursing home. How can I help?"

"I'm calling about Shirley Ridley. Has her granddaughter visited her today?"

"Shirley's not had any visitors this morning."

"Thank you."

Jack cut off the call, scrolled through his own contacts to 'Eric Ramsden' and dialled. A man with a soft Cumbrian accent came on the line, "Hello Jack. I didn't expect to be hearing from you again so soon."

"I'm afraid we may have something of a situation on our hands, Eric."

"Sounds ominous." There was an apprehensive note in Eric's voice. Last time Jack had called him about a 'situation' in his neck of the woods, twenty one people had ended up dead at the hands of a psychotic cult leader. Jack explained what was going on. "This Robinson character sounds like a real piece of work," commented Eric. "I'll tell my constables to keep an eye out. There's something else you should bear in mind, Jack. There's still a lot of anger around here about what happened at Hawkshead Manor. If Butterfly bumps into the wrong people, she could find herself in all sorts of trouble."

Jack grimaced as his mind flashed back to that horrific night – the flames consuming the manor house, the women and children racked with agony after being fed a deadly brew of death cap mushrooms by their would-be saviour. "I'm about to set off. I'll call you when I get to Gosforth."

Jack found a pen and paper and wrote, 'Butterfly. You weren't here when I got home. I was worried so I've gone out looking for you. If you read this, give me a call. I love you. Jack.' He weighted the note down with Butterfly's phone, then hurried to his car.

CHAPTER 14

"Shh," soothed Butterfly, reaching back to gently rock Charlie's chair. They were cruising in the fast lane along a stretch of motorway sunken between banks of bushes and trees. Charlie quietened down. His eyes drifted shut. His breathing softened as sleep descended over him.

Butterfly's gaze returned to Karl. "You realise you're going to prison for a long time."

He smiled, revealing a gold canine tooth. "I don't think so. I think this trip will bring out the best of you."

Butterfly thought about what she'd learnt about who she used to be – a bitch, a criminal. "You mean the worst."

"That depends on your perspective."

"The robbery you went to prison for back in 2009, the victims said you had an accomplice. That was me, wasn't it?"

Karl shot her a sidelong glance. "I think you know the answer to that. You and me were a good team. The best."

Butterfly released a contemptuous breath at the pride in his voice. "If we were that good, how come you got caught?"

Karl scowled. "Bryan-fucking-Hall."

"Who's he?"

"A whiny small-time cunt I had a falling out with."

"Over what?"

Karl gave Butterfly a meaningful look.

She touched a hand to her chest. "Over me?"

"Hall thought he was god's gift. Thought all he had to do was reach out and take whatever he wanted. Turned out that what he wanted was you. I put him right on that score." Karl ran his tongue over his teeth as if savouring a pleasant taste. "He won't ever try to stick his cock in anyone else's woman again."

"You killed him."

"Next best thing – I put him in a wheelchair. I should have finished the job. The bloke I fenced the Kensington stuff through turned out to be a mate of Bryan's. When the coppers picked him up, it took him about ten seconds to start flapping his tongue. That mistake cost me five years of my life. I could have done half that time If I'd given you up."

"So why didn't you?"

Karl turned to her with soulfully big eyes. "You know the answer to that as well."

Butterfly dropped her gaze. Part of her was drawn to those eyes. The realisation was more frightening than the gun wedged under Karl's thigh.

"I'd have done a life sentence for you," he continued in an almost imploringly soft voice.

Butterfly fought the urge to lift her eyes to Karl's. The drum was playing a rapid beat in her head. *Slow breaths,* she told herself. *Seven in, eleven out...*

The motorway flared out into a tangle of crisscrossing lanes, slip roads and flyovers. "This is near where you were shot, isn't it?" said Karl.

Butterfly lifted her head. To the left of the motorway were grassy fields grazed by cows. To the right was an expanse of woodland. She'd returned to those woods with Jack once after the shooting to see if they sparked her memory. Nothing of *that* night – the night Dennis 'Phoenix' Smith stole Charlie from her womb and Ryan Mahon put a bullet in her brain – had come back to her. The woods were just woods. They held no fear for her. Was that a curse or a mercy?

"I still can't get over the thought of you with a copper," said Karl. "The woman I knew wouldn't have pissed on him if he was on fire."

"Then I'm glad she's gone."

"Oh she's not gone. She's just..." Karl sought the right word, "sleeping." He grinned. "My sleeping lioness."

The drum rolled a warning through Butterfly's head. She swiftly changed the subject. "So what's the plan?"

Karl shrugged. "I thought we could stop somewhere for a bite to eat."

Butterfly narrowed her eyes as if struggling to work him out. "Are you joking?"

"I've heard there's a pub in Gosforth that does a decent steak. The Rose and Crown. Or we could take a picnic out to Low Lonning. It's supposed to be beautiful around there. Maybe after that we could pay a visit to Bray Farm. Then we could mosey on down to Phil Beech's cottage by the River Bleng or Dale Sutton's bungalow in Seascale." Karl chuckled at Butterfly's astonished expression. "I told you, I know everything the coppers know about the murders. And a shit load they don't."

"Such as?"

"Ah, that would be telling, wouldn't it now? Let's just say that necklace isn't the only thing I could give you that'll help us get those murdering fucks. The real question is, what are you going to do when we find them?"

"What do you mean?"

Karl let out a thin laugh that shivered down Butterfly's spine. "You just love asking questions you already know the answer to. You know exactly what I mean. Are you going to unload a shotgun in their faces, like they did to your mum and sister? That's what you always said you'd do."

Butterfly shook her head vehemently enough to send a shaft of pain through it. "They're going to prison for the rest of their lives for what they did."

Karl threw her a searching glance. "Are you sure about that? Sounds to me like that copper put those words in your mouth. I want to hear what you have to say. What do you think they deserve?"

Thud...thud... went the drum. Butterfly pressed a hand to her forehead. The daylight suddenly seemed wincingly bright. She closed her eyes, but the darkness behind them was illuminated by lurid images of Beech and Sutton's faces reduced to bloody pulps. She counted her breaths, but the images didn't fade. If anything they became even more vivid. Oh Christ, was that what she truly wanted to do to them?

A shrill sound drew her attention to the backseat. For once, she was relieved to hear Charlie crying. She reached for him. "He's hungry," she said when he grabbed one of her fingers and pulled it towards his mouth. "We need to pull over so I can feed him."

They were passing grassy fields speckled with woodland. A sign alerted them to an upcoming slip road for Wigan and Bolton. Karl turned off the motorway and pulled over at an isolated layby. "Stay there," he said to Butterfly. Taking the keys out of the ignition and pocketing the Glock, he got out of the car. He opened the backdoors, flicked on the child locks, then motioned for Butterfly to climb between the seats into the back.

Dabbing his weepy eye, Karl watched her slide the teat of a bottle into Charlie's mouth. As was her habit, she hummed to him as he guzzled his milk. Afterwards, she laid him out on a changing mat, removed his dirty nappy, wiped him clean and strapped on a fresh nappy.

Karl shook his head as if he couldn't quite believe what he'd just seen. "You're a natural."

"No I'm not," said Butterfly. "Most days I feel like I'm having a nervous breakdown."

"*You* have a nervous breakdown?" Karl scoffed at the idea. "I used to say you had ice for blood. Nothing fazed you."

"Yeah well, if you think robbing houses is nerve-racking, you should try listening to a baby with colic cry for four hours straight." Butterfly nuzzled Charlie's nose with hers.

"M...m...m..." he babbled.

"Yes I'm talking about you," she cooed. "My beautiful little bundle of trouble."

She returned him to his seat and clambered into the front. Karl turned the car around and headed back to the motorway. Charlie was soon fast asleep again. Karl was prattling on about their past, regaling Butterfly with stories of how unflappable she'd been. Instead of listening to him, she concentrated on Charlie's soft, steady breathing, letting it soothe away the drumming in her head.

"We were the best thieves in London," boasted Karl. "We might still be if I'd put that wanker Bryan in a coffin instead of just a wheelchair."

Butterfly pinched the bridge of her nose. "Christ, how could I have loved a man who'd do something like that?"

"Do you know what you did after you found out what I'd done? You jumped all over me. Gave me the fuck of my life. You said it was the most romantic thing anyone had ever done for you."

Butterfly pushed at the coin-shaped divot in her skull, using the pain to distract her from other feelings. "Please can we not talk for a while?"

"No problem. I'm used to your silence. You always were a quiet one. You just kick back and enjoy the scenery. We'll be there soon. It won't take long to get this murder shit sorted out. You know why? Because when we're together we're unstoppable."

Butterfly rested against the headrest, running her thumb over the 'Little Sis' pendant she'd hung around her neck. North of Preston was mile after mile of flat fields peppered with hay bales drying under the August sun. The further north they got the bigger the sky seemed to become. The landscape took on a rolling quality. Low green hills sprouted on the horizon. They left the motorway behind for a dual carriageway that took them north west towards higher, heather-clad hills before narrowing to two lanes and looping south west through seemingly endless sheep-grazed fields.

"Fucking hell, look at it," muttered Karl. "Nothing but grass and sheep. How could you stand living out here?"

Butterfly had no reply to give. She'd apparently spent a year-and-a-half of her life living at Hawkshead Manor, but that time was a blank. The road curved north towards the bottom end of Lake Windermere. She stared at the ribbon of glistening water, and the white cottages nestled in the wooded hills, wondering, *Did I ever pass by here with my parents and sister? Did we stop to enjoy the view or take a walk along the shoreline?* Those were the things she wanted to hear about. Not the shit that Karl spouted. But there was no one left who knew about that part of her life. She heaved a sigh.

After passing the immense mud-flats of Morecambe Bay, the road dipped in and out of wooded valleys. To the north, rugged hills took shape beneath a broad blue sky. The road climbed between slopes of bracken and purple heather, narrowing to a single lane that snaked its way across a vast, empty heathland. To the west, Butterfly caught glimmering blue glimpses of the Irish Sea. Charlie woke up and started bawling again. They stopped for him to be fed.

"I see what you mean," said Karl. "I think I'd have a nervous breakdown if I had to put up with that. Does it ever stop?"

"No, never," Butterfly replied with an edge of weariness.

Karl held out his hands. "Give him to me. I'll feed him."

Butterfly tightened her grip on Charlie, eyeing Karl warily.

"Don't worry," he said. "Lie down. Take a nap. I'll sort Charlie boy out." He made to lift Charlie from Butterfly's arms. She held on to him for a second before reluctantly letting go. She didn't lie down, though. She watched Karl like a hawk as he awkwardly cradled Charlie in his arms. Charlie let out a mewl of annoyance, then fell silent as the bottle's rubber teat touched his lips.

"There you go, little man," said Karl. "Wow, you are hungry, aren't you?" A smile spread over his face as he watched Charlie gulp down his milk. It was a different sort of smile. Less self-conscious. Warmer. When the bottle was empty, Charlie gave a contented gurgle. Karl looked at Butterfly with a boyish twinkle in his eyes. "I think he likes me."

Butterfly reached to take Charlie back. She checked his nappy before strapping him into his seat. "You should smile like that more often," she commented as they got going again.

Karl treated her to another of his soulful looks. "Would I stand a chance with you if I did?"

"No, but some other woman might want you. A woman who could give you a family of your own."

"There's only one woman I'm interested in."

"Fucking hell, Karl." The words hissed through Butterfly's teeth. "How can I get this through to you? We don't have a future together."

His knowing smile returned. "That's the first time you've called me by my name. I call that progress."

Resisting an urge to scream in frustration, Butterfly took a slow breath. The road descended into a softer landscape of lush grassy fields sprinkled with picture-postcard villages of stone cottages. The brooding hills lurked on the eastern skyline now.

When they passed a sign with 'Gosforth ¼' on it, Karl gave Butterfly a grin of anticipation. "I can't wait to see the look on Beech and Sutton's ugly mugs when we rock up."

Butterfly frowned uneasily. "You're not going to do anything crazy, are you?"

Karl chuckled. "You mean crazier than kidnapping you and Charlie? Relax. We'll play it cool, unless they force us to do otherwise."

CHAPTER 15

The road passed a terraced row of white cottages on its way to the centre of Gosforth. Three pubs clustered around a mini-roundabout. To the right was The Lion & Lamb, to the left The Wheatsheaf Inn, straight ahead The Rose & Crown. Between the road and The Wheatsheaf Inn stood a magnolia tree in full pink bloom. The base of the magnolia's trunk was hidden beneath dozens of bunches of flowers. Many of the bouquets were withered and brown. Others looked fresh. In amongst them were teddy bears, dolls and cards sealed in plastic. The village basked sleepily in the midday sun.

Karl blew out his cheeks. "What a fucking graveyard." He nodded at the flowers. "What's that all about?"

"I don't know," murmured Butterfly, but she was thinking about Hawkshead Manor, the thirteen children and seven women who'd drunk Dennis 'Phoenix' Smith's spiritual and literal poison. She recalled seeing news items about people coming from miles around to place offerings at an impromptu memorial outside the grounds of Hawkshead Manor. Another such memorial had seemingly sprung up here.

"The Rose and Crown looks closed."

Butterfly glanced at the dashboard clock – 11:58. "It's not quite twelve."

"Oh yeah, I forgot they're still living in the Stone Age around here."

A man with heavy rounded shoulders and a sagging belly opened the pub's front door. Butterfly recognised Len Simmons from the case file photos, although the intervening twenty years had robbed him of all but a tonsure of grey hair and left his face looking like a wrinkled red apple.

"That the same bloke who was running the place back when you stayed there?" wondered Karl.

"Yes."

Len wedged the door open and disappeared back inside the pub. Butterfly reached to open her door. Karl put a hand on her arm. "What are you doing?"

"I want to see inside the pub."

"What for?" Karl's eyebrows lifted in realisation. "Oh I get it. You want to see if you remember anything." He thought for a moment, then said, "OK, but we'll just have a gander through the windows. And Charlie stays in the car."

Butterfly nodded assent. Karl pulled across the mini-roundabout. With a meaningful glance at her, he slid the pistol into his pocket.

They got out of the car. Karl quickly moved around the bonnet to take hold of Butterfly's elbow. His other hand remained in his pocket. They approached a sash window to the right-hand side of the pub's entrance. A chalked sign advertised 'Home Cooked Food' and 'Cask Ales'. Cupping her hands against the glass, Butterfly peered into the pub. The landlord was nowhere to be seen. She took in the flagstone floor, the sooty fireplace, the dark wood bar counter, stools and tables, the black and white photos of the village adorning the walls. Nothing much had changed since the Ridleys stopped there. The barroom was exactly as she'd expected it to be from scrutinising photos of the pub from the time of the murders. But that was all it was – an image brought to life, not a memory.

"Well?" asked Karl, looking at her as if searching for something he recognised.

She shook her head. "Maybe if I saw the bedroom where I stayed."

"No chance. That would be way too risky. And besides, what about Charlie boy?"

Butterfly allowed herself to be drawn away from the window towards the car. Three men rounded the corner of the pub, striding purposefully towards their first pint of the day. She came to an abrupt halt, half-expecting to see Phil Beech's long, thin face amongst them, but they ranged from perhaps late twenties to early forties. Beech would be in his late fifties by now. Karl gave her arm a sharp squeeze of warning.

The men stopped too, staring at Butterfly and Karl as if they'd just emerged from a spaceship. The oldest of the three – well-built, close-cropped salt n' pepper hair and matching stubble – stepped forwards with a frown on his nut-brown face. "I didn't realise the circus was in town," he said, prompting uneasy laughter from his companions.

Karl smiled humourlessly. "Now that's not very friendly, is it?"

It flashed through Butterfly's mind that she might furtively signal for help, but the way the man was staring at her squashed the idea. His eyes were hard with hate. "I know you." He spat the words in her face. "You were one of *them*."

"We don't want any trouble," said Karl.

"I went up to the manor house that night to help. I saw..." The man choked up for a second before continuing in a trembling growl, "I saw the dead children."

"She's the one who ran away," one of the other men exclaimed.

"Yeah," said the nut-brown man. "She knew what was going on up there and she did nothing." He stabbed an accusing finger at Butterfly. "You let those kids die."

Butterfly winced as if she'd been punched in the chest. "I'm sorry. I'm so, so sorry."

Karl stepped between Butterfly and the man, making a wafting motion towards the pub. "I suggest you gentlemen go inside and enjoy your lunchtime." His words were polite, but there was an unmistakable warning in his tone.

"We'll go inside when we're good and bloody ready," retorted the man, squaring up to him. "This is our village and you're not welcome here."

Karl's lips curled into a slow smile. For a tense moment, the two men eyeballed each other, neither backing down. Butterfly put a hand on Karl's arm. "Come on," she urged. "Let's go."

Not breaking eye contact with the man, Karl retreated towards the car.

"Yeah, that's right. Go on. Piss off," said the man. "Show your ugly faces around here again and you'll be leaving in an ambulance."

Butterfly got into the car. As Karl moved around to the driver side, he made a gun signal at the man and popped off an imaginary shot.

The man lifted his hands, pretending to tremble. Laughing at the taunt, Karl ducked into the car. "That was fun. Where to now?"

Butterfly wordlessly pointed to the road ahead. The tremor in her hand wasn't pretend. She stared at her lap as they accelerated away, her eyes haunted by the accusation – *You let those kids die.* "Why didn't I warn anyone about what was going on at the manor house?" she murmured. It was a question she'd asked Jack dozens of times over the past ten months. His answer was always the same – *You were fleeing for your life. You didn't have chance to warn anyone.* The insinuation was that maybe she would have warned someone if Ryan and Gary Mahon hadn't caught up with her. But the more she found out about who she'd used to be, the more she doubted that was the case.

"Don't let those rednecks bother you," said Karl. "They don't know what the fuck they're talking about." He took out the Glock. "Do you know what they'd do if I pointed this at them? They'd shit themselves. Literally. What did you do? The only thing you thought about was protecting Charlie. That's because you're a lioness and lionesses protect their cubs. Fuck everything else. The law of the wild. That's all it is."

"The law of the wild," Butterfly echoed, giving Karl a curious sidelong glance. Perhaps he was right. Maybe, despite all the civilised words of men like Jack, that's what it always came down to in the end. Animal instinct.

Survival of the fittest. And maybe, just maybe Karl knew her better than Jack would ever do.

"How about we head up to Low Lonning?" suggested Karl. "We'll reconstruct your movements on the day of the murders. You know, like they used to do on Crimewatch."

Butterfly frowned at his jokey tone. "You're enjoying this, aren't you?"

"I'm with my lioness," he said as if that was all the explanation necessary.

As they headed out of Gosforth along a lane lined by cottages and fields of sheep, Karl whistled the incongruously upbeat Crimewatch theme tune. After three-quarters of a mile or so, they came to a fork in the road. The right-hand fork led over a stone bridge that spanned a narrow river. Karl pointed to the left-hand fork, which passed between several small bungalows and a short terrace of stone cottages. "Beech lives down there. We'll pay him a visit later."

They crossed the bridge and ascended a steep slope. Butterfly's eyes passed over the hedgerows and fields of grass, gorse and bracken. How many times had she travelled this route before? Why had she chosen to live at Hawkshead Manor, less than a mile from where the murders occurred? Had she somehow felt closer to her parents and sister there? She'd come up here to find the killer, but somewhere along the way she'd lost sight of that purpose. Or maybe she'd already been lost. Perhaps that was why she'd been taken in by Dennis 'Phoenix' Smith's pseudo-spiritual bullshit. She still felt lost in so many ways. Glancing in the wing mirror, the familiar feeling swept over her that the face staring back belonged to a stranger.

Who are you? her mind demanded to know.

Karl's words echoed back to her, *You're a lioness.*

She repeated them defiantly in her mind and the sense of dislocation subsided. In its place, she felt a welling of strength and determination. She wouldn't lose sight of her purpose this time. The police had failed to find the killers, but she wasn't the police. There were no rules or regulations restricting her.

The road dipped through a tunnel of trees. At the tunnel's end a view of the craggy, shale-strewn fells of Wasdale opened up. About fifty metres off to the right of the road was a white farmhouse. Butterfly knew Bray Farm was hidden somewhere amongst the trees on their left. She stared into the woods she'd fled through as a child. They held no more fear for her than the woods where she'd been shot as an adult.

They pulled over at a bridleway that crossed the lane on its way to another farm nestled amidst the rolling fields. Charlie burst into tears the instant the car came to a stop. Butterfly got out and ducked in at the backdoor to comfort him. Karl watched closely as she lifted Charlie out of his seat and placated him with a rusk.

"Don't worry. I'm not going to run." As Butterfly said it, she was surprised to realise that she meant it. The only thing on her mind at that moment, apart from looking after Charlie, was tracking down the killers.

"I wish I could believe that," Karl said with a note of longing. He lifted Charlie from Butterfly's arms and motioned for her to lead the way. They walked along the pot-holed gravel bridleway, Karl and Charlie on one side of the band of grass at its centre, Butterfly on the other. On their right was an overgrown hedge, then fields sloping down towards woodland that hid the blackened husk of Hawkshead Manor. Beyond that the vast amphitheatre of Wasdale basked in sunshine. Trees overhung the left-hand side of the bridleway, dappling it with shadows. Leaves rustled in the pleasantly cool breeze blowing from the north. Birds sang and twittered. Sheep munched grass. A deep sense of stillness hung over the scene. It was difficult to believe such terrible events could have occurred amidst such beauty.

After what she judged to be a hundred and fifty metres, Butterfly came to a stop. Her gaze moved intently over the bridleway's surface, almost as if she expected to see some clue. "This is where it happened," she murmured hollowly, turning to stare into the woods. She took a steadying breath, then spoke with a forensic dryness, as if reading from the police reports, "The masked gunman came out of the trees. After making us tie each other up, he put bags over our heads. Then the second man came out. The first man sounded nervous. The second man was more confident. He egged on the first man to sexually assault Charlie. The first man began to remove Charlie's t-shirt and bra. He likely intended to rape her, but it seems he ejaculated prematurely. This led to speculation that the first man was more sexually inexperienced than the second man. Dad struggled and shouted for the men to leave Charlie alone. They dragged him about fifty metres into the trees and cut his throat."

Butterfly walked into the woods. At a little clearing carpeted with twigs and leaves, she squatted to inspect the ground. The bodies of her mum, dad and Charlie had been found at this spot, stabbed, slashed, riddled with shotgun pellets. The ground must have been sodden with their blood. "The killers inflicted many more injuries on Mum and Charlie than was necessary to kill them," she continued. "It was speculated that they held some sort of grudge against women."

"Or perhaps they were just pissed off that you escaped and they couldn't take their merry time doing whatever they wanted to do," said Karl.

Moving like someone in a trance, Butterfly returned to the bridleway. She stared at what she reckoned to be the spot where she'd been tied up, picturing herself wriggling free from her bonds. She'd tried to free her mum and sister, but it had come down to a simple choice – stay and die or flee and live. Survival of the fittest. The law of the wild. "I ran back towards the road. My mum shouted, 'Watch out.' There was a gun shot. I wasn't hit, but I fell over. I got up and ran into the woods." They walked back along the lane a short distance before heading into the trees again. A soft gloom enfolded them as they made their way deeper into the wood.

"Run, run as fast as you can," Butterfly said more to herself than Karl.

"Stop! We want to eat you," he added with a shake if his head. "It's some messed up shit. You must have had twenty or thirty copies of The Gingerbread Man."

"Why so many?"

"I guess you were looking for clues. There are loads of different versions of the story. The version that particularly interested you was the one where the old man and woman live in a cottage by a river. Just like you-know-who does."

Butterfly's eyes narrowed as Phil Beech's weasel face rose into her mind. They walked on in silence, crunching dry leaves underfoot. There was no way of knowing the exact route Tracy had taken. At first, she'd run in a blind panic. After regaining her composure, she'd had the presence of mind to keep the sun on her left-hand side. Butterfly looked skyward. It was roughly two hours earlier in the day and a month later in the year than when the murders had been committed. The sun was ahead and slightly to the left.

"Hey look at this," said Karl, dropping to his haunches. A faint animal trail wound its way through the trees. A sturdy branch had been driven into the ground at one side of the trail. At the other side of the trail stood a Y-shaped stick. A noose of twine tied into a slipknot dangled between the sticks. "I think it's a snare." He ran a finger over the thick, furry green twine. "Remind you of anything?"

Butterfly stooped to inspect the twine. Was this the same type of twine that had been used to bind her wrists and ankles?

"There's another one." Karl pointed to an identical snare a few metres further along the trail. "I bet Beech sets them to catch rabbits or foxes or whatever."

"Tracy said the bag that was put over her head had an animal smell," said Butterfly.

"What more proof do you need? The fucker did it. I say we have a gander inside his house."

"How do we get inside?"

Karl grinned. "I'm one of the best house-breakers in London, remember?"

CHAPTER 16

Jack barely took his foot off the accelerator all the way up to The Lakes. The stunning landscape swept by in a blur. With each passing mile that Butterfly didn't call to let him know where she was, he became more convinced his hunch was correct. The question that bothered him most now was – was she alone or with Karl? Other possibilities prodded at him like sharp sticks. Surely she wouldn't have gone with Karl of her own free will. Would she? Not if she was Butterfly. But what if Io had come back again? What if… What if…

He raced north across lonely heaths and hills. When he was a few miles out from Gosforth, he got on the phone to Eric Ramsden. "No reported sightings of them so far," Eric informed him. "I'll meet you outside The Rose and Crown."

Jack pulled in behind a blue and fluorescent yellow chequered Landrover outside the pub. A man in a police-issue short-sleeved white shirt, black tie and black trousers got out of it. Sergeant Eric Ramsden was a stocky forty-something with neat brown hair, a matching beard and a broad, earnest face, the sort of face you could trust. He extended his hand to shake Jack's. "Good to see you, Jack, although I'd hoped next time we met it would be under better circumstances."

Jack offered a grim smile. "Me too."

Eric motioned to the pub. "I thought it would be best to begin at the beginning, so to speak."

Jack nodded agreement and they headed into the pub. The lunchtime trade – a motley collection of old men, tradesmen and farm labourers – were propping up the bar. There was a distinct absence of the hikers and other tourists that usually flooded the area at that time of year. The hum of chatter died and all eyes turned towards the newcomers.

"Hello Len," Eric said to the ruddy-faced landlord.

"Eric," said Len, glancing up from pulling a pint. "What can I do for you?"

Jack held up his phone to display a photo of Butterfly. He swiped to a mugshot of Karl. "Have you seen either of these people today?"

"No."

Jack showed the photos to the drinkers lined up at the bar. "Yeah, I had words with them out front," said a sour-faced man with a greying crewcut. From the way he said 'words' it was evident the conversation hadn't been pleasant.

"Are you sure it was them?"

"Yeah, they're not exactly hard to recognise."

So Butterfly *was* with Karl. A shock of adrenaline flushed through Jack at the knowledge. He struggled to keep his voice steady. "Can I ask your name?"

"Rob Baker."

"At what time did you speak to them, Mr Baker?"

"Opening time." His lips twisting, Rob jabbed a finger at Butterfly's photo. "I recognised her straight away. She's one of them psychos from the manor house."

Jack winced internally at hearing Butterfly described as, *one of them psychos*. "How did she seem?"

Rob shrugged. "What do I give a shit how she seemed? I told her she's not welcome around here. Those nutjobs have ruined this area. Just ask Len. Trade's practically non-existent, isn't it?"

Len nodded morosely.

"My wife worked at a B&B out towards Wasdale," Rob continued to rant. "They had to let her go. There were no guests, apart from a few weirdos who come here because of what happened. What do you call 'em?"

"Murder tourists," put in one of Rob's companions.

"Murder tourists," echoed Rob, scowling. "That's all we're good for now. Do you know what they call this place? The village of the damned."

Jack's gaze travelled along the faces at the bar. The same simmering resentment glowered in all their eyes. It was clear that things could turn nasty if Butterfly showed her face in the village again.

"Why has she come back here?" asked Len.

"I don't give a toss why she's back," spat Rob, eyeballing Jack and Eric. "What I want to know is why haven't you lot locked her up and thrown away the key?"

"As far as we're aware, the woman in question has committed no crime," said Jack.

"Committed no crime?" Rob laughed bitterly. "Is that some sort of sick joke? Well I'll tell you this, I won't let that crazy bitch do anything else to hurt this village. I see her hanging around here again and I'm–"

"That's enough," Eric cut in firmly. "I don't want to hear any more of that talk. Is that understood?" His steady brown eyes moved around the barroom and met with silence. "Now can any of you tell us anything about how the lady in the photo seemed? Did she seem distressed?"

"No," said Rob. "I wouldn't have given her and her husband a second glance if it wasn't for their tattoos."

Jack's eyebrows pinched together. "What makes you think he's her husband?"

"What do you think? They look like a pair of circus freaks."

Biting down on a jolt of anger, Jack asked, "Did they have a baby with them?"

"They drove off in one of those shitty people carriers. Now you mention it, there was a baby seat in the back." Rob shook his head. "Poor little thing. Imagine having parents like them. Wonder how long it is before that bitch shoves poison down its throat?"

Jack's fist clenched involuntarily. Fighting the urge to smash it into Rob's ignorant face, he said, "Which way did they go?"

Rob pointed towards Wasdale Road.

"Thanks for your help." Jack pushed the words through his teeth.

"If you see either of these people again, please contact Whitehaven police station," Eric said to the assembled drinkers.

As they turned to leave, Jack noticed a solitary figure nursing a pint by a window. The man was wearing a battered old wax jacket and flat cap. He had narrow, sloping shoulders and a thin face. Bushy brows shadowed his beady eyes. Wisps of lank grey hair curled from beneath his cap. A ratty moustache fringed his upper lip. He looked to be in his mid-to-late fifties. He stared into his glass, avoiding eye contact with the policemen as they passed by.

Once they were outside, Eric said, "Butterfly could have tried to tell those men she was in trouble, but she didn't. Is that a good thing?"

"She may have thought she'd be worse off with them than Karl." Jack sounded as if he was trying to convince himself of his words.

"So we're proceeding on the assumption that she's with him under duress?"

"Why the fuck else would she be with him?" snapped Jack. He reigned in his anger with a deep breath. "Sorry, Eric."

Eric put up a hand as if to say, *No need to apologise.* "How worried should I be about Karl Robinson?"

"He has a history of violence, but I don't think he'll hurt Butterfly or Charlie."

"I was thinking more about you and me. Should I be calling in backup?"

The *what ifs* returned to torment Jack. What if Butterfly was suffering another of her episodes? Depending on her state of mind, she might indeed be with Karl of her own free will. If that was the case and she was intent on exacting revenge on the killers, then the fewer people involved the better.

"No. I'm heading out to Low Lonning. That's where they'll go next. Maybe it would be best if you don't come with me."

Eric's beard split into a smile. "Do you know how boring it is around here most days, Jack? I could do with some excitement. Not too much, mind."

Jack summoned up a grateful smile in return.

"I'll follow you," said Eric, getting into his Landrover. "Oh by the way, that weasel-faced bloke drinking on his own, did you recognise him?"

Jack nodded. "Phil Beech."

"Do you think we should warn him to stay put until we've found Butterfly and Karl?"

Jack shook his head. "This place is already ready to explode. Best not stir up any more bad memories."

CHAPTER 17

Karl drove back down Leagate Brow while Butterfly fed Charlie. The milk lolled Charlie off to sleep. After crossing the little bridge, they turned right. After a hundred metres or so, the road curved leftwards up a low hill. A narrow lane branched off to the right, running between hedges alongside the River Bleng. There was a 'Private Road' sign at the end of the lane.

Butterfly pointed past the sign. "It's down there."

"Yeah, I know." Karl turned off the road. "Let's hope we don't meet Beech coming the other way."

The car juddered over potholes, passing a farm with a large collection of corrugated barns. Karl screwed up his face at the stench of manure. "And they say London smells like shit."

On their right, trees snaked along the riverbank. The lane headed into a long tunnel of oaks and alders. After maybe a quarter of a mile, it re-crossed the river on a wooden plank bridge and emerged at a grassy clearing with a stone cottage at its centre. The cottage was set a short distance back from the lane behind an overgrown privet hedge. Its dandelion-flecked lawn gently sloped down to the pebbly riverbed. The cottage's slate roof was blanketed with moss. Lichenous streaks stretched down the walls from its leaky gutter. But otherwise it looked well-kept – pale blue front door, matching window frames, little leaded windows, blood-red roses climbing the walls. To the right of the cottage a short gravel driveway led to a wooden garage. There were no vehicles in the driveway. Although it was turning into a warm afternoon, all the windows were shut.

Once upon a time a little old woman and a little old man lived in a cottage by a river... The opening line from The Gingerbread Man played in Butterfly's mind as her gaze moved between the secluded cottage and the sun-splashed river.

"Doesn't look like anyone's home," observed Karl, continuing past the cottage and climbing away from the river up a steady incline. He pulled off the lane into the trees so that the cottage was hidden from view. He looked askance at Butterfly. "So how do you want to play this?"

She glanced uncertainly at Charlie. He hadn't woken despite the car stopping. He usually took a long nap in the early afternoon.

"Bring him with us if you like," said Karl. "But breaking-and-entering is best not done with a baby in tow. Remember, Beech has got a shotgun." He gestured to the woods. "What harm will come to Charlie here? I've been robbing houses since I was nine. I know where people hide the shit they don't want to be found. We'll be in there ten minutes tops."

"Ten minutes," Butterfly echoed, nervously running her tongue over her lips.

"The longer we sit here, the more likely it is that Beech will show up and we'll miss our chance."

"OK, let's do it."

Grinning like a kid on a daytrip, Karl got out of the car. Taking care not to wake Charlie, Butterfly put him in his seat. She placed a rusk and a couple of his favourite toys within his reach. If he woke, hopefully they would keep him from crying. She wound down a window a few centimetres, allowing the cool air of the woods into the car. Then she got out, closing the door as quietly as possible behind her.

They slunk through the trees to the cottage. Karl watched its windows for a moment before stepping into the lane. As if he owned the place, he strode through the gate and along the path. His grin returned when he saw the front door. "Yale lock," he said. "You used to able to pick one of these things in ten seconds flat. Fancy a go? See if you've still got the touch?"

Butterfly gave a frowning shake of her head, motioning for Karl to get on with it.

He opened a leather wallet containing a series of picks of varying lengths and slender metal rods with right-angled flat ends. "This is the torque rod," he said as if he was teaching a protégé. He inserted a rod into the lock. "The rod goes in at the bottom of the lock. The pick goes in at the top like so." He slid a pick with a curved tip into the lock above the rod. "Now you just tickle it over the pins whilst twisting the rod." He withdrew the pick, subtly working it up and down. There was a click and the lock turned. "Et voila!" He looked at Butterfly. "Bring back anything?"

"Let's just get this done as fast as possible," she whispered sharply, doing her best to ignore the faint drumming that had started up behind her forehead.

Holding up a cautioning hand, Karl poked his head through the door and whistled. "Here boy, here boy." Silence greeted his call. "No dog." He opened the door fully and stepped inside.

Butterfly followed him into a gloomy hallway with a low beamed ceiling, a flagstone floor and yellowed Anaglypta wallpaper. To their right were stairs carpeted in threadbare brown. On their left were pegs draped with jackets, fleeces and flat caps. The floor under the pegs was cluttered with mud-encrusted wellies, waders and boots. Beyond the pegs was a panelled, unpainted door. There was an identical door at the opposite end of the hallway. A heavy scent of fried food hung in the air.

Karl headed for the second door. It led to a cramped kitchen with a red quarry-tiled floor. There was an overflowing bin by the backdoor. The walls were lined with rough wooden cupboards and shelves. Blackened pans dangled from hooks. Crockery and utensils stained with grease, egg-yolk and baked bean juice cluttered the work-surface. More crockery was piled in a deep, chipped ceramic sink. A frying pan and whistling kettle occupied what looked to be an old camping stove. Karl touched the kettle.

"Still warm," he said. "Looks like Beech had his lunch and headed out to slaughter a few bunnies." He pointed to the shelves, which were crammed with mismatched crockery, tins, condiments, jars of instant coffee and boxes of teabags and cereal. "Have a look in those tins." As Butterfly did so, he searched the cupboards, checking there were no loose panels that things might be hidden behind.

The tins contained sugar, granulated gravy and the like. Karl motioned to move on. The other door led to a living-room with a tatty sofa and armchair arranged around an incongruously modern flat-screen television. Logs were piled haphazardly to either side of a log burner set in a tall stone fireplace. Ranks of empty beer cans marched across a coffee-table. There was a dining-table with a single chair by the dusty window. The walls were devoid of pictures. There were no ornaments or any other signs of a woman's touch. Butterfly found herself thinking of Jack's living-room when she'd first moved in. *Jack.* He must have returned home and found that she was gone by now. Had he picked up on the significance of her leaving the case files in the hallway? Of course he had. Jack didn't miss signs like that.

The muscles of her jaw pulsed. Part of her wished she hadn't left a clue for him to follow. She was fairly certain Karl wouldn't use his gun on her, but Jack was another matter. There was another consideration too – if Jack caught up with them, she may well lose her best chance to find the killers.

Flipping up the sofa cushions, Karl said with a chuckle, "Way back when I was a kid, I once found over three thousand quid under an old dear's sofa."

The amusement in his voice rankled Butterfly. She wondered once again how she could have been attracted to a man like Karl. The answer was as obvious as it was uncomfortable – because she'd been no better than him. "We're not looking for money."

"Sorry, force of habit." He gave the contents of some shelves the once over, flipping through dog-eared angling and shooting magazines, peering into a collection of pewter tankards.

After a swift search of the fireplace, they left the room and headed upstairs to a little landing with three doors. A bathroom with a stained toilet, an equally grubby basin and bath was visible through one door. Karl wrinkled his nose at the mould-flecked tiles, pube-encrusted soap, grey towels and sour whiff of urine. "This fucker has got serious hygiene issues."

He had a glance in a bathroom cabinet and prodded the side of the bath to see if it was loose, before moving on to the neighbouring door. Beyond it was a box-room with a desk and a computer. Grinning, Karl pointed out a toilet roll next to the monitor. "Wouldn't you like to know what Beech has been looking at?"

Now it was Butterfly's turn to wrinkle her nose. "Not really."

Karl ran his fingers along the edges of the dark-patterned carpet. "Just checking for loose corners," he explained. "You'd be amazed how many people hide their life savings under the floorboards."

He straightened with a shake of his head and made for the final door. Beech's bedroom was as spartan as the rest of the house – an iron-framed double-bed with a jumble of blankets and two pillows, a wardrobe, a chest of drawers, a bedside table with a tea-stained mug on it. But what caught their attention was a tall, grey-metal strong box in one corner. Karl set to work on the lock with a torque rod and pick, applying light twisting pressure on the rod, pushing the pick into the lock and raking it back out. The lock turned a fraction. He repeated the process and it rotated further. The strong-box door swung open, revealing a shotgun, a rifle with a telescopic sight, several boxes of cartridges and bullets and a leather ammo bag. The guns' wooden stocks and black metal barrels gleamed spotlessly.

"Looks like these are the best cared for things in the house," observed Karl.

"No necklace," said Butterfly, pursing her lips in disappointment.

Karl shut the strong-box, inserted the pick again and rammed it upwards with the heel of his hand. "He'll have a hard time opening this now."

"But won't he know that someone's been tampering with the lock?"

"Perhaps, but better that than him coming at us with his shotgun if we need to have words with him."

Butterfly frowned. Karl's tone hinted at much more than simply having words.

"I know you don't like the thought of it," continued Karl, reading her expression, "but if you're serious about getting to the truth, we might have no other choice. Come on, let's search the rest of the room. We've been in here too long."

Butterfly checked out the drawers. "Just socks and underpants."

"Take each drawer all the way out. Make sure there's nothing behind them." Karl drew aside the assortment of shirts, trousers, jeans and jumpers hanging in the wardrobe to check it didn't have a false back. Then he peered under the bed and lifted its mattress. "Nothing but dust and pubes." He puffed his cheeks. "If your sister's necklace is here we're not going to find it without taking this place apart brick by brick."

Butterfly slotted the drawers back into place and headed for the stairs. As much as she wanted to keep looking, she'd already been away from Charlie too long. She opened the front door a crack and peered through it before stepping outside. Karl pointed to the garage. Butterfly nodded and they headed around the side of the house. Karl made short work of the padlock that secured the double-doors. He squinted into the garage's gloomy interior. Bags of 'Mixed Corn' poultry feed were stacked beside the plastic barrel bins used for dispensing it. An array of animal traps – wooden boxes and cages with sliding doors, spring-loaded vermin traps, wire and twine snares – were neatly laid out on a workbench.

There were several bulging hessian sacks under the bench. Butterfly stooped to look inside one. A sickly sweet smell tickled her nostrils. The sack was full to the brim with dead moles. She looked in another sack and found a fox staring blankly back at her, its curved yellow-brown teeth exposed in a rictus of death.

"The gunman wore a hessian bag with eyeholes cut out," Karl quoted from Tracy's police statement.

A search of the garage revealed nothing else of interest. They hastened back to the car. Butterfly was relieved to see that Charlie was still sleeping soundly. "Where to next?" asked Karl.

Butterfly gave the only possible answer. "Dale Sutton."

As they drove back the way they'd come, Karl said, "And what if we don't find the necklace at Sutton's place? How far are you willing to go?"

Butterfly made no reply. But as the car bounced over potholes, the question kept rattling around in her head. Just how far *was* she willing to go?

CHAPTER 18

Eric squatted down to examine the indents of tyre prints in the soft turf at the roadside. "Someone was parked here recently."

He rose to follow Jack along the arrow-straight bridleway. The ground was too dry for footprints. Jack saw no further signs of anyone having been there. After forty or fifty metres, Eric pointed to a patch of flattened nettles at the edge of the woods. "Could be someone went into the trees here."

"If they're retracing Tracy's steps, they would have gone through the woods to Bray Farm."

"But what could they hope to find by doing that?"

Jack thought about Butterfly's hands on his throat. The coldness in her eyes. "Butterfly's been having these episodes recently. I don't know if it's memories trying to come back or... or something else. Maybe she hopes that being here might somehow spark her memory."

"They're a good hour ahead of us. That would give them enough time to walk to the farm, talk to the Brays and come back here."

"No way would Karl risk letting Butterfly talk to the Brays."

"There's only one way to find out if that's the case."

Eric didn't need to say any more. They hurried to their vehicles. With Eric leading the way, they drove towards Leagate Brow. Eric turned right onto a rutted farm track that followed the western fringe of the woods. Beyond a hedge on their left, a field of grazing sheep sloped down towards the trees that flanked the river. Somewhere amongst those trees, Jack knew, was Phil Beech's cottage. The track curved into the woods, terminating at a closed wooden farm gate. A few hens were pecking around a farmyard carpeted with dry mud and straw. At the centre of the yard stood a dusty white farmhouse and stone barn. A Landrover and a tractor were parked between the buildings.

Jack and Eric got out of their vehicles, opened the gate and made their way across the yard. The air was heavy with the musky smell of sheep. From inside the barn came a symphony of bleating. A black and white collie sprinted out of the farmhouse's open front-door. "Hello boy," said Eric, holding out a hand for the dog to sniff.

The collie was followed by a sturdy woman with a broad weather-beaten face and bobbed black hair shot through with grey. The woman looked at them with dark, cheerless eyes. Her flour-stained hands and apron suggested she'd been disturbed in the midst of baking. "Hello, Mr Ramsden. What can I do for you?" Her tone was polite, but with a hint of wariness. No wonder, reflected Jack. Eric had been the first responder on the day of the Ridley murders. That had been twenty years ago, but those kinds of things stayed with you no matter how much time passed.

"Who is it, Mother?" inquired a deep voice from within the barn.

"It's no one, Neal," she replied in a rolling Cumbrian accent. "You just get on with tending to those ewes."

"Sorry for bothering you, Mrs Bray," said Eric. He motioned to Jack. "This is Detective Inspector Jack Anderson from Manchester. We were just wondering if you've had any other visitors today."

Jack's stomach squeezed in anticipation of Pam Bray's response. If she'd spoken to Butterfly, it would surely confirm that Butterfly was with Karl of her own free will. He held in a breath of relief as she said, "Not that I'm aware of." Creases spread from the corners of her eyes. "Why?"

"It's nothing for you to be concerned about," Jack assured her. "We're looking for these two people." He brought up the photo of Butterfly. No hint of recognition showed in Pam's eyes. Butterfly obviously hadn't visited Bray Farm when she was living at Hawkshead Manor. It was also obvious that Pam paid little attention to what was going on in the world beyond her farm. He swiped to the photo of Karl.

147

"Never seen either of them before. They look like strange birds. Who are they?"

"Like I said, Mrs Bray, you've no need to be concerned. Would it be possible for me to speak to your husband and anyone else who's here?"

"My husband's bedridden."

"Oh, I'm sorry to hear that."

"Me too," put in Eric. "Nothing too serious I hope."

"Forty-odd year of farming these hills is what's wrong with him." There was a note of dour resentment in Pam's voice. "They romanticise this life, but I wouldn't wish it on my worst enemy."

Eric glanced towards the barn. "But your son Neal still works here."

"He's forced to. What with his dad being in such a state. Besides, what else would he do around here?"

"We need to talk to him." As Pam pursed her lips reluctantly, Eric added, "I promise you we'll only keep him for a few minutes."

Heaving an annoyed breath, Pam called, "Neal!"

A tall, broad-shouldered man in wellies and blue overalls emerged from the barn. Neal Bray's granite-featured face was weathered beyond its years from working outside come rain or shine. A floppy mop of black hair hung down almost into his eyes. His shirtsleeves were rolled up, exposing forearms corded with veins and muscle. "What's up, Mum?"

"These policemen want to talk to you."

Neal eyed Jack and Eric with eyes as dark and deep-set as his mum's. Jack showed him the photos. "Have you seen either of these people?"

Neal shook his head. "I've not seen anyone today besides Mum and Dad."

Pam treated Jack and Eric to a *there-I-told-you-so* look. With a swipe of her hand, she ushered Neal back to the barn.

"Thanks for talking to us, Mrs Bray," said Eric. "If you do happen to see the people in the photos, could you please contact Whitehaven police station."

Pam nodded. She stood watching with folded arms as Jack and Eric returned to their vehicles. "Not the most talkative bunch, are they?" Jack commented when they were out of earshot.

"They keep themselves to themselves. Frankly I don't blame them after what happened in '98. Sometimes I feel like doing the same myself."

"Believe me, Eric, it doesn't work." Jack's voice was weighed down by experience. "One way or another, the world always finds its way to your door."

"Seems you were right about Karl not letting Butterfly talk to–" Eric broke off as his mobile phone rang. He put it to his ear. His bushy eyebrows lifted. "When was this? OK. I'm on my way. Thanks Tim." He hung up and turned to Jack. "Well, well, the plot thickens. That was the station. A call just came in from Phil Beech. Someone broke into his house."

Without another word, Jack and Eric jumped into their vehicles. They sped back along the farm track. Minutes later they were pulling up outside Beech's stone cottage. The gamekeeper was pacing about the front lawn like a nervous greyhound. His eyes, still glassy from a liquid lunch, narrowed at Jack before shifting to Eric. "Someone's been in my place."

"Have any doors or windows been forced?" asked Eric.

"No."

"Has anything been taken?"

"No."

"Then how do you know someone's been in there?"

Phil jutted his sharp, stubble-flecked chin out in annoyance. "Because I can tell. Things have been moved. And my gun box won't open."

Jack's eyes scoured their surroundings. There was nothing to be seen other than trees and the river. He gave the gamekeeper a narrow look of his own. "Show us the gun box."

"Why are you here?" Phil's eyes twinkled with suspicion. "What's this got to do with Manchester police?"

"Inspector Anderson was in the area working on a separate investigation," said Eric. "He offered to help."

Phil made a phlegmy noise in his throat and turned to head into the house. He pointed to a pile of magazines on a table in the living-room. "Someone's been through my magazines. This week's Angling Times was under last week's. I always keep them in order." He led Jack and Eric to his bedroom. "And then there's this." He reached a key towards the lock of a rectangular strongbox.

"Don't touch that," said Jack. "There might be fingerprints."

"I cleaned my guns only this morning," said Phil as Eric and Jack examined the lock. "So I know the lock wasn't broken before I went to the pub."

Eric pointed out some scratches on the lip of the lock. "Those could have been caused by someone tampering with it. Can I have the key?" Phil handed it over and Eric inserted it into the lock and tried in vain to turn it.

"I'll tell you what happened," said Phil. "Someone damaged the lock while trying to get my guns."

"How many guns do you own?" asked Jack.

"A shotgun and a hunting rifle." Phil added defensively, "You can see the licences if you want."

"Please."

Muttering something under his breath, the gamekeeper left the room.

"What do you think?" asked Eric.

"I think they were here." Jack pointed to the lock. "But I think Beech is wrong about that. Karl Robinson makes a living out of breaking into far

SHE IS GONE

more secure places than this. He wouldn't have had any trouble picking a lock like that."

A frown found its way onto Eric's face. "So you're saying he deliberately damaged the lock after opening the box. Which means the guns might no longer be in there and we could be dealing with an armed man."

Jack nodded.

"I'm sorry, Jack, but I'm going to have to call this in. I can't risk one of my officers stumbling into a confrontation with Karl."

Jack heaved a sigh and gave another nod. Phil returned with the licences. Struggling to hide his distaste at the gamekeeper's hatchet face and mean little eyes, Jack looked at the licences. Everything was in order. "Thank you, Mr Beech." He handed back the papers.

"This has got something to do with what you were talking to the lads in the pub about, hasn't it?"

"I'm afraid I can't discuss an ongoing investigation."

Phil scowled. "Don't give me that. If there's some sort of criminal gang operating in this area, I've got a right to know."

Jack stepped around him and headed for the front door, leaving Eric to do the talking. He suddenly felt that if he opened his mouth all the questions he'd been dying to ask the gamekeeper for months would come rushing out. *Did Tracy make you angry talking to you like that in front of the lads in the pub? Did she make you feel small? You wanted to teach her a lesson. That's why you and your rapist pal went up to Low Lonning and did what you did, isn't it? Come on, admit it. That fat coward hid in the trees while you made the Ridleys tie themselves up. Then the pair of you had your sweet way with them. Isn't that right?*

A flicker of uncertainty passed over at Jack's face. But *was* that right? The way the attackers made the Ridleys tie themselves up had always bothered him. Surely it would have made more sense for one man to hold a gun on the family while the other tied them up. Then there would have been little or no chance of anyone escaping. And as for having their sweet way with them...

One of the attackers – most likely Beech – had seemingly masturbated over Charlie. Her vagina had been penetrated by a sharp object, most likely post-mortem considering the lack of abrasions on her inner thighs. But no semen was recovered from her or Andrea's bodies. Why hadn't Sutton – someone with a history of sexual offences – attempted to rape either of them? There would have been plenty of time to do so, even after Tracy fled the scene. Had he been too panicked to get an erection? Was that why he'd mutilated Charlie's vagina?

Eric interrupted Jack's train of thought. "I've put the word out. Two of my guys are on their way over here. The nearest armed police are in Carlisle. It'll take them a while to get down here."

"What have you told Beech?"

"Nothing yet, but he has the right to know if he's in danger. So does Dale Sutton. You know that's where they're headed next."

"Just do me a favour. Don't tell them who Butterfly really is or you'll be putting her in danger."

"Don't worry, Jack. I won't tell those pair one word more than they need to know." The curl of Eric's lips revealed his dislike for Beech and Sutton. "Although they'll soon cotton-on to what's going on if they speak to each other."

"Then we'd better get to Sutton ASAP. How far is it to Seascale?"

"Four or five miles. We're the closest officers."

"So let's get going."

Eric hesitated. "The guns have changed things. If we find Karl, I need to know you won't go charging in and get yourself or anyone else killed."

"You needn't worry about that, Eric. I'm not going to do anything stupid. I have a daughter to think about."

Reassured, Eric nodded and headed for his Landrover. Jack ducked into his car and rammed it into gear. Things were moving fast. He had to move even faster. Once the armed police arrived, the situation would be out of his hands. Sweat prickled his palms as he thought about how Dennis 'Phoenix' Smith had reacted when he realised the police were closing in. Karl was a different kettle of fish, but who knew what he would be capable of if he was backed into a corner.

Jack's wheels spat stones as he accelerated away from the cottage.

CHAPTER 19

The road descended gently between thick hedges that enclosed flat grassy fields. The craggy fells of Wasdale were receding into the distance behind the car. A few miles to the north, the nuclear chimneys of Sellafield sprouted like a towering forest of concrete and steel. Karl was humming along to the radio and drumming his fingers on the steering-wheel.

"What have you got to be so chirpy about?" Butterfly asked with an edge of irritation.

"Didn't you feel it back there at Beech's house?"

"Feel what?"

"That old buzz."

"I felt scared, if that's what you mean."

"Nah, you didn't. You were as steady as ever."

Butterfly's fingers circled the depression on her forehead. Sometimes she felt as if she wanted to push her fingers through the scar, push them deep into the spongy brain and pull the bullet out. "Are you trying to kill me? Because that's what'll happen if you keep on doing this."

"I'm trying to bring you back to life."

"So you admit it. The woman you loved is dead."

Karl shook his head. "Oh she's still in there alright. Lost in a maze. I'm going to show her the way out."

Butterfly pressed her fingers harder against the scar. Karl's words were hitting their target. Her brain was drumming its painful rhythm once more. "It's not a maze, it's a prison," she muttered. "And I'll do whatever it takes to keep her locked up."

"So *you* admit it," countered Karl. "That bullet didn't kill Io."

Heaving a sigh, Butterfly stared at the drab pebbledash houses on the outskirts of Seascale. The brooding blue line of the Irish Sea came into view as the road curved down into the village. Closer to Seascale's centre, white cottages were dotted in amongst the almost uniformly grey houses. Unlike Gosforth, Seascale had the feel of a place for locals rather than tourists.

Karl thumbed over his shoulder towards Charlie. "He's a good sleeper, isn't he?"

"So I'm told," said Butterfly, glad for the change of subject. "He usually sleeps for two or three hours in the afternoon. When he wakes up, he'll be hungry. I'll need to boil some water for his formula milk."

"Maybe Dale will let us use his kettle."

Butterfly cast Karl an unamused glance. The Sat Nav directed them onto an estate of characterless council houses. Karl pointed to a little bungalow with a postage-stamp of grass in front of it. Net curtains hung in the windows. A rusty Ford Fiesta squatted on its axles in the cracked concrete driveway. There was nothing that marked the bungalow out as the home of a child molester and possible multiple murderer.

Karl continued a short distance past the bungalow and parked alongside a scrap of grass with a swing and seesaw at its centre. There was no one using the play park. The end of the school day was still two hours away. Next to the park was a cluster of garages. Butterfly glanced uneasily at them and the nearby houses. "I don't like the thought of leaving Charlie alone here."

"Why? There's no one around and we'll be quick." Karl clicked his fingers. "In and out like that."

"What if Sutton's in? He doesn't work. He hasn't been able to find a job since getting sacked from the school where he was the caretaker."

"If he's in, we'll come back to the car and have a rethink."

Butterfly considered Karl's proposal for a moment, then took a baby blanket out of her bag. She draped the blanket over Charlie's seat so he wouldn't be seen by anyone passing by, taking care that the material didn't rest on his face. "OK," she said, reaching for the door handle.

Karl rested a hand on her arm. He pointed to an old man walking a dog across the street. They waited for the man to turn a corner before getting out of the car. This time, Karl didn't loiter at the front of the bungalow. He led Butterfly along the side of it, past the car, a wheelie bin and a recycling box full of empty White Lightening bottles. He glanced into a window before moving swiftly on. Butterfly took a quick peek too and found herself looking into a pigsty of a bedroom. A duvet was screwed up on the bed. Clothes were strewn over the carpet. Socks lolled like thirsty tongues from a chest of drawers.

The bungalow's back garden was a square of overgrown grass. Beyond a thin hedge was a field grazed by ponies. A deep-looking pond occupied the nearside of the field. Only the neighbouring bungalow overlooked the garden.

There were two windows and a uPVC door at the rear of the house. The nearest window looked into a kitchen as bland as the bungalow's exterior – white cupboards and tiles, freestanding oven and hob, Formica table with the remnants of fish and chips in greasy paper and a bottle of cider on it. Karl exchanged a glance with Butterfly upon seeing the food. He edged his eyes around the other window. It looked into a living-room that ran the length of the house. The room appeared to have been decorated by an old woman rather than a middle-aged man – chintzy three-piece-suite and curtains, pink carpet and matching fluffy rug, a herd of ceramic pigs on the mantelpiece. Crisp packets and chocolate bar wrappers were scattered over the carpet by the armchair nearest the television. The television wasn't on.

"Looks like Pervy Pig isn't home," whispered Karl. He returned his attention to the door. "Barrel lock. I used to bust these things open in five seconds." He set to work with his lock picking tools. True to his word, seconds later the door swung inwards. Placing a finger to his lips, Karl stood listening for a moment.

Silence.

Bathroom, he mouthed at Butterfly. She nodded understanding – he wanted to make sure Dale wasn't in the bathroom – and they padded through the kitchen. Karl eased the door open. He took a step into the hallway and stopped dead. A figure was blotting out the light from the front door window. Dale Sutton was almost as wide as he was tall. His stomach sagged like a sack of grain over his tracksuit bottoms. His face was as pink and smooth as a baby's with drooping jowls and a triple-chin. His fish-eyes protruded from fleshy pouches. A faint sheen of sweat glistened above his upper lip and on the bald dome of his head.

At first, Butterfly saw none of this. Her gaze was transfixed on the rifle in Dale's hands. It had a wooden stock and a single slender barrel. The rifle butt was pressed into Dale's rounded shoulder. The barrel swayed back and forth between her and Karl.

"Put your hands up," Dale said in a gruff, tremulous voice.

Karl raised his hands. "Is this number fifty five?" His unflustered tone suggested this wasn't the first time he'd had a gun aimed at him.

"Sixty two."

"Oh well we're in the wrong house. A mate of mine lives at–"

"Save it," broke in Dale. He made a jerky motion with the gun towards the living-room. "In there. Go on. Move. And keep your hands up or I'll shoot. Do you hear?"

"We hear," said Karl. "Relax. We won't cause any trouble. This is just a simple misunderstanding."

Karl and Butterfly went into the living-room.

"Sit on the sofa," Dale instructed them. As they did so, he positioned himself in front of them. His tongue flickered nervously over his lips.

"What now?" asked Karl.

"That depends on what you're doing in my house."

Karl motioned to the rifle. "What type of gun is that?"

"Keep your hands where they are," warned Dale.

"Looks like an air rifle I had when I was a kid. I used to shoot rats with it. Proper piece of crap."

"Well this piece of crap could put your eye out no problem."

Karl pushed his lips out. "Maybe."

"What are you going to do to us?" asked Butterfly. Right that second, finding the killers almost seemed like an irrelevance. All she was thinking about was what would happen to Charlie if Dale pulled the trigger.

"I told you, I'll decide that when I know why…" Dale's voice faltered. A glimmer of puzzled curiosity came into his eyes. "I know you."

The words made Butterfly's heart beat even faster. How could Dale know who she was? Did he somehow recognise her from twenty years ago? His next words proved otherwise. "You're the one that got away from Hawkshead Manor. I saw your picture in the paper. What do you want with me?"

Not knowing what to say, Butterfly glanced at Karl. She saw that his right hand was edging towards the pocket containing the Glock.

Don't, her eyes pleaded.

"I asked you a question," Dale persisted.

Karl gave him an amused look. "Is that gun a bit heavy for you, Pervy Pig? Your bingo wings are trembling."

"Don't call me that," retorted Dale.

"What should I call you then? Rapist? Paedo?"

Angry red splotches stained Dale's pudgy cheeks. "I'm not a paedo."

"That's not what I hear. I know all about you. You've got a thing for schoolgirls. Melissa Jones. That was the name of that fourteen-year-old you got pregnant."

Dale took a threatening step towards Karl. "I could shoot you. I'd be within my rights."

"I'll bet you messed Melissa's life up good and proper. Fourteen-years-old and lumbered with the baby of a sad-sack piece of shit. Have you ever even fucked a real woman?" Karl waggled his little finger. "Nah, I don't reckon you could get your dick up for a real woman."

"I'll shoot you." Spittle flecked Dale's lips. "I swear to god I will."

Karl thrust his face towards the gun as if daring Dale to do so.

"Karl," Butterfly hissed. "What are you doing?"

"I'm just having a chat with our friend the fat paedo," he replied, keeping his eyes on Dale.

"I'm not a paedophile!" exploded Dale, his face quivering like a plate of jelly. "I'd never hurt a child. Unlike her." He darted an accusing look at Butterfly. "How many children are dead because of–"

As fast as a striking snake, Karl's hand shot out and swiped the gun aside. There was a hiss of air as Dale reflexively squeezed the trigger. The pellet thunked into the wall to the right of Karl. In the next second, Karl was on his feet, driving a fist into Dale's abdomen. His eyes on stalks, Dale doubled over as the breath whooshed from his lungs. Karl drove his elbow down against the back of Dale's neck. The whole bungalow seemed to shake as Dale crashed to the rug. Karl wrenched the rifle from Dale's hands and tossed it across the room. At the same instant, he whipped out the Glock and aimed it at Dale's head. Within the blink of an eye, the entire situation had been reversed.

"Please," wheezed Dale, tears streaming down his cheeks. "Please don't shoot me."

Karl glanced at Butterfly. "You OK?" When she nodded, he asked Dale, "Who lives next door?"

"W... what? Why?" stammered Dale.

"Just tell me."

"Eileen. She lives on her own."

"Does she go out to work?"

"Yes. She works at the power station."

A slow smile spread over Karl's face. "Well then we can make as much noise as we want."

"No. Oh god no," sobbed Dale.

"We should search the place," said Butterfly. "If we find the necklace, that's all the evidence we need to put him away for life."

"Why bother with searching when Pervy Pig here's going to tell us everything we need to know?" Karl nudged Dale with his foot. "Aren't you?"

Flinching, Dale whimpered, "Just tell me what you want."

"Show him," Karl said to Butterfly.

Watching Dale as if trying to read every crease and fold of his face, Butterfly took out the 'Little Sis' necklace. He stared at it with incomprehension for a few seconds, then his eyes swelled in horrified realisation and darted to Butterfly's face.

"You recognise it, don't you?" said Karl.

Dale's jowls flapped as he shook his head.

"Oh yes you do," continued Karl. "And you know exactly who she is. She's not just the one that got away from Hawkshead Manor, she's the one that got away from you and your pal Phil Beech."

Dale shook his head even more rapidly. "No, no, no," he gasped. "It wasn't us."

Karl looked at Butterfly. "Ask him."

"Where's my sister's necklace?" asked Butterfly.

"Oh god, you've got to believe me," sobbed Dale. "I had nothing to do with–" The air whistled from Dale's lungs as Karl kicked him hard in the gut.

"Don't," exclaimed Butterfly as Karl drew back his foot to kick Dale again.

"Why shouldn't I?" Karl's voice was calm, but his eyes were menacingly bright. "Do you know what we'd do to a fucker like him in prison?" Dale's sobbing became almost hysterical as Karl said, "We'd cut off his dick and feed it to him."

"You're not in prison now," said Butterfly. "And this isn't what I want."

"Isn't it? Look at that fat blubbering bastard. Go on. Look at him."

Butterfly looked down at Dale. His face was a quivering mess of tears and sweat. His eyeballs looked ready to pop out of their sockets. His t-shirt had ruckled up, revealing a lardy, stretch-mark riddled belly with a livid red mark where he'd been kicked. Doubt welled up in her at the sight. Could this pathetic thing really have murdered her parents and sister?

As if in answer, Karl said, "He cut your dad's throat, then blasted Charlie and your mum in the face. But even that wasn't enough. He carried on stabbing them long after they were dead. Do you know why? Because it made him feel like a big man for once in his life. Isn't that right, fat boy?"

Dale shook his head frantically. "No, no, no…"

"Ah bullshit!" scowled Karl. "You did it." He slammed his foot into Dale's midriff again. This time, not only breath hissed between the downed man's lips. He retched up a steaming puddle of cider and partly digested fish and chips.

"Whoo!" laughed Karl. "That's got a tang to it." His probing gaze returned to Butterfly. "Ask him again."

She blinked away from him as if she had something to hide. The drum was beating in her brain. *Thud… thud…* She could feel sweat popping out all over her as she asked Dale, "Where's the necklace you took from my sister?" Her voice was a strange mix of anger and pleading.

"I don't know, honest to–" Dale broke off, retching up more of his lunch.

Butterfly swallowed as queasiness pushed its way up her throat.

"He's lying," Karl stated as if it was a fact. He moved closer to Butterfly, his voice dropping low. "Are you going to let him get away with what he did to you?"

Thud, thud... The drumming was getting louder and faster. A choking fist of rage replaced the queasiness. Butterfly swallowed again, but the feeling kept rising, forcing its way out of her mouth, "Where's the fucking necklace?" she demanded to know. "Either you tell me or... or..." She trailed off as if uncertain of what came next.

Dale squirmed and wept at her feet. Her lips twisted in disgust as, like a prostrated beggar, he wormed a pleading hand towards her. Karl stamped on the hand. A scream burst from Dale. Keeping his heel on Dale's hand, Karl leaned in so close to Butterfly that she could feel his breath hot on her cheek. "Ask him again," he murmured like a lover whispering sweet nothings.

Thud, thud, thud went the drum. Butterfly squinted. Lights were dancing in front of her eyes as if she'd stared into the sun. Her throat was so full of anger that she could barely breathe.

"Go on," Karl urged, his lips almost touching her.

She flinched at the feel of something hard and heavy being pressed into her palm. The drumming leapt up in volume as she saw that she was holding the Glock.

"Ask him," went on Karl, keeping his hand on hers, manoeuvring the pistol towards Dale's head.

Her mouth opened and closed but no words came out. Images were flashing through her mind – the masked man stepping from the trees, her sister and parents' terrified faces. Was she remembering or was her mind painting pictures from things she'd read? She seemed to hear a voice – Dale's voice – call out from some inner place. *Run, run as fast as you can!*

Her finger twitched against the trigger. "It *was* you."

Dale shook his head, gasping, "No."

"Yes!" The word hissed from Butterfly like the pellet had from the air rifle.

Karl's voice tickled her ear. "Pull the trigger, Io."

Butterfly swayed on her feet. The splotches of light were spreading over her vision, blotting out Dale's terrified face.

"Do it. Do it," Karl chanted like a schoolyard taunt.

Thud! THUD! Suddenly all Butterfly could hear was the drumming and all she could see was the blinding light. Then her legs could no longer support her and she was collapsing to the floor. Her face slapped against the warm vomit. Before losing consciousness, she just had time to wonder whether Dale's bloated face would be the last thing she ever saw.

CHAPTER 20

Jack's phone rang. He put it on loudspeaker and Eric's ever-steady voice came over the line, "I've tried Dale's home and mobile numbers. No one's answering."

In response, Jack pressed the accelerator closer to the floor. Fields rushed by. He swore as a tractor blocked his progress. He overtook it, hammering his horn to warn any oncoming vehicles. The glittering line of the sea greeted him as he hit the outskirts of Seascale. He raced through the sleepy streets as if Butterfly's life hung on the next few minutes. He eased up on the accelerator as the Sat Nav informed him that he was approaching his destination. His gaze darted along a row of nondescript grey houses, homing in on Dale Sutton's small semi-detached bungalow.

Nothing appeared to be out of the ordinary. Butterfly's people carrier was nowhere to be seen. He pulled over by a rectangle of communal grass with a swing and seesaw on it. He got out of the car, just barely resisting the impulse to rush headlong to the bungalow. Eric's Landrover drew in behind him. The sergeant got out and approached him, cautiously keeping the vehicles between himself and the bungalow.

"What do you think?" asked Eric, squinting at the bungalow.

"The windows are closed. Sutton might simply have gone out. Maybe Butterfly and Karl haven't been here." Although Jack's tone was hopeful, he didn't believe his words. Dale's bungalow would certainly be Butterfly and Karl's next port of call. He estimated them to be at least forty-five minutes ahead of himself and Eric, which would have given them plenty of time to do their thing. He prayed that 'thing' amounted to no more than breaking in and searching the bungalow. "How far away are the AFOs?"

"I'd say about an hour."

"I can't wait that long. I think Butterfly and Karl have been and gone. That means every second we stand here, they're getting further away from us."

Eric ran his fingers through his beard, eyeballing the row of garages to the left of the bungalow and the houses to its right. The street was silent, except for the murmur of a lawnmower. "OK, we'll take a look. But you follow my lead."

Jack motioned for Eric to lead the way.

They crossed the play park and the strip of tarmac that led to the garages' forecourt. Eric pointed to the bungalow's front window. Nodding understanding, Jack followed him past the rusty old car in the driveway. They peered around the edge of the window. A three-piece-suite and a television were visible through the net-curtains. There was no sign of life or of any disturbance having taken place. Jack listened at the letterbox. Not a sound.

They headed around back, peeping into the side window. Dale's bedroom looked as if it had been ransacked – duvet scrunched on the bed, drawers half-open with clothes hanging out. Then again, maybe Dale was just messy. The kitchen was similarly devoid of life. Eric pointed to a half-eaten portion of fish and chips on a little table against the inner wall, whispering, "Looks like he's in after all. So why isn't he answering his phone?"

Ducking down below the kitchen windowsill, they crept to the backdoor. Eric pointed to the lawn. The grass looked as if it hadn't been mowed in months. A strip of the long blades had been flattened as if something approximately Dale Sutton-sized had crawled or been dragged towards the hedge that divided the garden from the field beyond. Eric took out his steel baton and extended it. Motioning for Jack to stay where he was, he followed the flattened grass to a gap in the hedge. He hurried back to Jack and told him, "It continues towards the pond. No sign of whatever made it."

Looking askance at Eric, Jack reached for the door handle. Eric nodded and Jack depressed the handle. The door swung inwards. The scent of vinegar and something more acrid tickled their nostrils as they padded into the kitchen. With his baton poised to strike, Eric peered into the hallway and bathroom. Empty. He edged into the lounge and stopped dead, pointing to a puddle of vomit on the carpet.

"Looks like Dale's lunch didn't agree with him," observed Eric. "That might explain his absence. Maybe he had to rush out for something to settle his stomach."

"Or maybe he vomited after someone punched him in the stomach. Then that same someone killed him and wrapped him in the rug that was here." Jack squatted down to trace his fingers along a line that marked out a faint rectangle on the carpet. Beyond the line the carpet was several shades darker as if it had been shielded from the sun's bleaching effects.

"And then they dragged him outside and dumped him in the pond," finished Eric.

"Sounds about right."

"It sounds like what it is – speculation."

"There's only one way to find out if it's speculation – dredge the pond."

"Let me make a few calls first, just in case Dale *has* popped down the chemists."

With another glance of revulsion at the vomit, Eric took out his phone and stepped into the hallway. Jack scrutinised the room. His gaze came to rest on a small circular hole in the wall above the sofa. He ran his fingers over it. There was something embedded in the plaster. He dug at the hole with his car key. A flat-nosed pellet popped out of it into his palm.

"I've been on to the chemists and the doctors. Dale hasn't been seen at either place."

Jack showed Eric the pellet.

"It's an airgun pellet," said Eric. "That didn't come from one of Phil's guns."

"I don't see an airgun around here." Jack glanced towards the pond.

Catching his meaning, Eric said, "OK, Jack, we'll do it your way. But if this is a crime scene, we'd better not touch anything else."

Eric got on the phone again as they returned to the back garden. Jack sidled through a gap in the hedge and followed the flattened grass to the pond. The water was impenetrably brown and flecked with algae. Jack stared at it, feeling as if he'd swallowed a lump of concrete.

Oh Jesus, Butterfly, he thought. *What have you done?*

Eric came up behind him. "SOCO and a dredging team are on their way."

"If Sutton's in there, you know what that means."

"That Butterfly and Karl are looking for Phil."

"We should head back to his house."

"I say we wait and see what comes out of the pond. Two of my men are with Phil, and the AFOs will be here soon. For all we know, Dale might be drunk on a bench somewhere around town. We could be putting him at risk if we go back to Gosforth now."

"It's not him I'm worried about."

"I know and I'd feel the same way if I were you," Eric said sympathetically. "But we need to get a proper handle on what's going on here. And we can't do that if we keep charging blindly back and forth."

With a heavy sigh, Jack reluctantly accepted that Eric was right.

"Let's go speak to the neighbours," suggested Eric.

They worked their way along the street, knocking on doors. There was no one in the neighbouring bungalow. A woman was hurrying out of a house a few doors along to pick her kids up from school. She hadn't seen anything. The old man next door to her had been dozing in his chair with the television turned up to full volume. No one answered their knocks at the next couple of houses. A woman in the last house in the row had seen Dale leaving his bungalow at about half-past twelve to buy fish and chips – as he did every day. The houses facing the bungalow were a good hundred metres away and partially screened by trees. The chances of their inhabitants having seen anyone coming and going from the bungalow were low.

By the time they were knocking on the final door, a 'SCIENTIFIC SUPPORT' police van was pulling up. A solidly built middle-aged woman with shoulder-length chestnut hair got out of it. Eric waved, heading over to her. Beaming at him, she said, "Hello Sergeant."

"Hello love."

"Hey, less of the 'love', we're on duty," the woman gently admonished.

Smiling back at her, Eric said, "Jack meet Crime Scene Examiner Susan Ramsden. My wife."

Jack shook Susan's hand. "Good to meet you, Susan."

"You too, Jack." Susan's smile turned serious. "Eric told me what's going on. You must be half out of your mind with worry."

Jack confirmed her words with another heavy sigh.

Susan surveyed his unshaven face. "I'll bet you haven't had a chance to eat lunch, have you?" She pointed to a Tupperware container and a flask on the van's passenger seat. "There are ham sandwiches and tea there. Even if you're not hungry, you should try to eat or you'll be no good to anyone."

"My wife loves to feed people," commented Eric as Susan opened the back of the van and began sorting through a plethora of Forensic gear – fingerprint and DNA kits, photographic equipment, latex gloves, crime scene tape.

"I heard that," she shot back. "A sandwich and a cuppa can solve a lot of problems."

With a glimmer of amusement in his eyes, Eric glanced at Jack. "You'd better do as she says."

Jack opened the Tupperware box. His stomach grumbled at the smell of ham. As he took a bite of a sandwich, he thought about Butterfly. Had she had anything to eat? And what about Charlie? If he hadn't been fed, he would be screaming blue murder by now.

He poured himself a cup of tea and sipped it, eyeing the group of residents gathering in dribs and drabs by the play park. An old woman with crossed arms called to Eric, "What's he done now?"

"Please go back to your houses," replied Eric. "There's nothing for you to be concerned about."

"Nothing for us to be concerned about?" snorted a thirty-something woman. "I've got two young daughters. That pervert shouldn't be allowed to live around here."

"Then where *should* he live?" Eric said as an aside to Jack. "At least in a small community like this people can keep an eye on him."

"They weren't keeping an eye on him in '98," said Jack. "He was able to make his way to Low Lonning and back without being seen."

"So you really believe he killed that family?" put in Susan.

"Do you know of anyone else with a history of sexual offences who was aware the Ridleys would be there that afternoon?"

"No, but do *you* know there have been dozens of different theories over the years as to who killed the Ridleys?"

"People love to play armchair detective," said Eric.

Susan passed a box of evidence markers to him. "Help me carry this stuff around back."

Jack picked up a box of kit too. As the three of them headed for the backdoor, Eric told Susan what they'd touched and where they'd been in the house. She set to work, photographing the flattened grass. "So tell me about these other theories," said Jack.

"Gypsies did it. Several people said they saw gypsies in the area that day. That was one theory that did the rounds. Total nonsense. There were a fair few other theories about killers from outside the area. I suppose it's easier to believe that no one from around here would be capable of such a thing. That being said, some rumours did circulate about the Brays. And then, of course, there was that theory about the killers being strange little orange people, about ten centimetres tall with currants for eyes."

Jack's brow briefly wrinkled in confusion. Then his lips curved into a wry smile.

"Sorry," said Susan. "Bad taste, I know, but I can't think about the case without hearing those words – *Run, run as fast as you can.*"

"I think we can be sure the Ridleys weren't killed by gingerbread men," said Eric

"No, but Susan has a point," said Jack. "That's the one thing that sticks with me too."

Eric turned at the sound of another police vehicle pulling up outside the house. The group of onlookers had swelled to a dozen or so. "I'd better set up a perimeter."

"You mentioned the Brays before," Jack said to Susan as Eric headed for the street.

"Yes, there were some nasty little whispers about them, mainly put about by Phil Beech and his mates."

"What sort of whispers?"

"Just the usual rubbish – they're oddballs, inbreeds with webbed feet. They were easy targets you see. They keep themselves to themselves. Always have done. Except for Hayley. That's Alistair and Pam's daughter. She lives in Gosforth. From what I hear she doesn't have any contact with her parents. Apparently they had some sort of falling out. Don't ask me what about."

Jack's eyebrows drew together thoughtfully. "I wonder if it's got anything to do with Alistair Bray's illness."

"Alistair's ill? I didn't know that. What wrong with him?"

"I don't know, but according to Pam he was too ill to speak to us this morning. She blamed his illness on the farm."

"Well it's a hard way of life. I've been called out to more than one farm where the farmer's put both barrels of a shotgun in his mouth. Depression's rife in the farming community and people are often reluctant to seek help for mental health problems, especially the older generation."

"Do you know where Hayley lives?"

"She's got a little house on Whitecroft Road opposite the Methodist church. Why?"

"I'd like to have a chat with her."

Susan frowned. "I thought you were convinced Beech and Sutton are the killers."

"I am apart from one or two doubts, but I'd rather keep busy than hang around here worrying about Butterfly and Charlie."

Susan gave Jack a smile of understanding.

"Thanks for the sandwiches," he said.

She made an *it's nothing* gesture. "When this is over, you and Butterfly will have to come over to the house for a proper meal."

Jack found a small smile of his own. "I'd like that."

He returned to the front garden. Eric and a constable were stringing blue and white striped tape across the driveway. A van with 'SPECIALIST SEARCH AND RECOVERY TEAM' emblazoned on it had joined the police vehicles. Officers were sorting through dredging equipment – full-body waders, rakes, shovels and pumps.

"I'm told the pond isn't all that deep," said Eric. "It shouldn't take long to find out if Dale's in there."

Jack told Eric about Hayley. Eric scratched his beard doubtfully. "Doesn't sound like anything to me."

"Me neither but…" Jack tailed off into a sigh. He didn't have the energy to repeat the conversation he'd had with Susan.

"I'll call you as soon as there's anything to tell."

With a nod of thanks, Jack got into his car. As he pulled away from the bungalow, the eyes of those gathered by the play park followed him suspiciously.

CHAPTER 21

Butterfly regained consciousness with a gasp as if surfacing from the depths of a lake. For an instant, she didn't know where she was, then it came flooding back. She opened her eyes, expecting to see Dale Sutton's living-room. Instead, she saw that she was slumped in the front-passenger seat of her car. *Karl must have carried me here,* she thought, straightening up. She winced as a needle of pain pierced her skull. She felt as if she was coming around from an all-night bender. But at least she *had* come around. Her unconsciousness had been as dreamless as death, and yet here she was alive. How much longer would she remain that way though? Days? Hours? Would she live to hear Charlie say his first word?

Charlie! Where was Charlie?

Heedless of the pain, she jerked her head around. She was alone in the car. Outside was a winding gravel lane hemmed in by trees and bushes. Karl was leaning against the bonnet, cradling Charlie in his arms and feeding him a bottle of milk. Karl was smiling in that unguarded way that made his face boyishly handsome. The lines of anxiety receded from Butterfly's forehead, but reappeared as she reached for the door handle. There were rusty red smears on her fingers. Was it Sutton's blood? Who else's could it be?

Oh Shit, oh shit! What had happened? Had she pulled the trigger? No, she'd wanted to, but she hadn't actually done it... Had She? Her eyes were racked with doubt as she got out of the car. The ground felt like the deck of a boat in choppy waters. She clutched the door to steady herself.

"Welcome back." Karl's voice was as soft as a purr. "How are you feeling?"

Butterfly held out her hands. "Give him to me." Her tone was both pleading and sharp.

"Relax. He likes me." Karl stroked under Charlie's chin. "Don't you, Charlie boy? Yes, you like your Uncle Karl."

"Give him to me," repeated Butterfly. The sharpness was gone. Only the pleading was left.

Karl frowned as if troubled by what he heard. He held out Charlie. She took Charlie into her arms and removed the teat from his mouth. He let out a mewl of disapproval, pawing at the bottle.

"Don't worry." Karl pointed to an electric kettle on the backseat. "I made the milk with boiled water as per the instructions."

Butterfly seemed to remember seeing just such a kettle in the bungalow's kitchen. "What did you do to Sutton?" she asked hesitatingly as if afraid of the answer.

Karl pointed at his chest, his face a picture of faux-innocence. "Me? Nothing."

"So he's still alive?"

Karl's lips curled away from his teeth in a way that made Butterfly shudder. "I'd say Pervy Pig's about as far from alive as you can get."

"Are you saying I—" Butterfly broke off, strangled by the realisation of what he was insinuating. The colour leached from her lips as if she might faint. Karl moved as if to catch her.

"No," she spat at him, retreating unsteadily, clutching Charlie to her chest. Charlie's mewling ratcheted up to a cry of distress.

Karl countered with an almost gleeful, "Yes! You gave that fat fuck what he deserved – a bullet right there." He pointed at his forehead.

"You're lying."

"You came back to me, Io. You came back and did what needed to be done. Don't you remember?"

"I...I..." stammered Butterfly, searching her mind for the truth of what had happened. It was like trying to see the bottom of a muddy river.

"I knew you were still in there, Io. You just needed something to bring you out."

"I'm not Io!" Butterfly's voice was a tremulous shriek. Whirling away from Karl, she broke into a staggering run.

He caught her up in seconds, wrapping his arms around her in something between an embrace and a restraint. "Yes you are," he murmured in her ear. "And soon you'll come back to me for good. All you need to do is finish what you've started. Only one more to go."

Tears tracking her cheeks, Butterfly tried to twist free. "Please stop this."

"It's too late for that. We're in this together. All the way."

Butterfly gave up resisting. Her head hung down against Charlie as Karl guided her back to the car. Charlie's eyes were swimming with tears. His warbling cries were like knives twisting in her brain.

"Shh," she soothed, her voice heavy with resignation.

She dropped onto the backseat. The milk bottle felt as heavy as a brick as she lifted it to Charlie's lips. He fell mercifully silent as he resumed sucking on it. Karl closed the backdoor, got behind the steering-wheel and reversed along the lane. "We're only a mile or two from Beech's place. With any luck, we'll deal with him and be on our way within the hour."

"Be on our way where?"

"Wherever you want. The world's our oyster. I know a bloke who knows a bloke who's the Picasso of fake passports."

"You're delusional."

Karl gave Butterfly one of his *we'll see* smiles.

They pulled onto a tarmac road that crossed a humped stone bridge. A foam-flecked river babbled between pebbly banks. Anyone passing by would have thought they were just a family enjoying a day out, the same as the Ridleys all those years ago. Butterfly was suddenly overcome by the strongest feeling that maybe she hadn't escaped the killers after all. Maybe she was still on Low Lonning with a bag over her head, unconscious, trapped in a nightmare from which the only escape was death.

"What if Sutton and Beech are innocent?" she asked.

"But they're not. They killed your parents and sister. Sutton admitted it just before you put a bullet in him."

Butterfly gave Karl a searching, doubtful look. "What did he say exactly?"

"He said Beech was the one who did the killing. He claimed he tried to stop him."

"Do you think he was telling the truth?"

"What does it matter? The fucker was there that day. Him and Beech took something from you. Now they're going to give you something back."

Frowning thoughtfully, Butterfly touched her 'Little Sis' necklace. "You didn't find my sister's necklace."

"Sutton said Beech has it."

"How convenient."

Karl chuckled at Butterfly's sardonic tone. "You know I just love it when you do your cold-hearted bitch thing."

She made a conscious effort to soften her voice. "I keep asking myself how I could have loved someone like you. The same question goes for you. How can you love someone like Io?"

Karl shrugged. "Maybe I'm a glutton for punishment." He looked at Butterfly in the mirror with almost pitifully pained eyes. "I always said you were my cocaine. I couldn't give you up even though I knew you were bad for me. Pretty fucked up, eh?"

"Pretty fucked up," agreed Butterfly.

They passed a 'Welcome to GOSFORTH' sign at the outskirts of the village. Butterfly felt an urge to duck down – not in fear but in shame – lest they were recognised.

"Not far now," Karl said excitedly as they turned onto Wasdale Road.

"I won't do it." Butterfly tried to say it with conviction, but there was a telltale tremor in her voice.

"Yeah you will," grinned Karl. "You'll finish this and we'll get our life back. Only this time it'll be so much better. Do you know why? Because now we know what it's like to lose each other. Every night in that prison, alone in bed I felt…" he sought for the right word, "empty. Like someone had ripped my insides out. I never want to feel like that again. I'd rather be dead."

"You don't mean that," said Butterfly, but when she looked in Karl's eyes she saw that he did.

"No one will ever love you like I do."

She thought of Jack, of everything he'd risked for her. "You're wrong." Now there was real conviction in her voice.

Karl's eyes flared like a blowtorch. "You'd better hope I'm not, because if your copper tries to get between us I'll cut his fucking heart out."

Charlie scrunched his face and let out at wail at the anger in Karl's voice. Butterfly stroked his fluffy hair, shushing him. She stared out of the windows, her eyes riddled with anxious uncertainty. Was Jack somewhere nearby or was he with Naomi back in Manchester? She was no longer sure what to hope for.

When they passed the 'Private Road' sign, Karl slowed almost to a jogging pace. The potholed lane snaked its way through the trees to the wooden plank bridge. He edged onto it, craning his neck to see the little cottage. He braked abruptly and shoved the car into reverse.

"What is it?" asked Butterfly.

Karl didn't reply. After reversing a couple of hundred metres, he pulled off the lane into a gap between the trees. The car juddered over a stony track that crossed the river on another wooden bridge, beyond which was an open farm gate and grassy field.

"Shit," hissed Karl, braking.

"What did you see?"

"A police car."

A mixture of emotions swept through Butterfly. There was relief, but there was also disappointment. Now she would almost certainly never find out if Beech *did* have her sister's necklace. Were the police at the cottage because of Jack? Or had Beech realised that someone had broken in? Either way, the end result was the same. "It's over."

"Depends how many of them there are. I only saw one car, but coppers are like rats – where there's one there's always another."

"Give it up, Karl."

"No!" The retort was loud enough to set Charlie off crying again. "I've waited too long to get you back." Karl's eyes searched Butterfly's. "Besides, you don't want me to stop. Not really. I can see it in your eyes."

Her arms protectively encircled Charlie as Karl pulled out a pocket knife. He grabbed the bag of baby paraphernalia, emptied it out and began sawing it into strips. "Sorry, but I'm going to have to tie you up," he explained. "I wish I could trust you, but…" he faded off with a rueful shake of his head. "Turn around and put your hands behind your back."

Before doing so, Butterfly strapped Charlie into his seat. As Karl expertly tied her wrists, she said, "You're going to get yourself killed."

"So what if I do? If I don't get my Io back, I'm dead anyway."

"That not true. You said it yourself, Io was bad for you. It wasn't love you felt for her. It was addiction."

"Maybe so." Karl stroked his knuckles down Butterfly's face. "But I did five years in Belmarsh for you. And do you know what?" His voice thickened as if he was fighting tears. "You never came to visit me. Not once. But that didn't change the way I feel about you. Just like–" The words snagged in his throat. Grimacing as if they were fishhooks, he forced them out. "Just like when I found out you'd been fucking Bryan Hall, that didn't change anything either. So what difference does it make whether it's addiction or love? Either way, I can't live without you."

Butterfly blinked away from Karl's gaze. "I'm sorry for everything I've done to you." Her tone was leaden with regret.

Karl rediscovered his grin. "No you're not. Io never apologised to anyone."

He tied Butterfly's ankles, manoeuvred her onto her belly and tied her feet to her hands. "Not bad," he said, surveying his handiwork. "Not as good as you could have done. You used to tie people up so tight that Houdini wouldn't have been able to escape." He gagged Butterfly, then leaned in to brush his lips over her ear and whisper, "I won't be long."

He smiled at Charlie who was burbling, "M...m..." and playing with the straps of his seat.

"See you soon little buddy."

Karl got out of the car and closed the door softly behind himself. Butterfly strained at her bonds, but they were tied securely enough to give her pins and needles. There was no way she would be able to wriggle free. Not this time.

CHAPTER 22

Hayley Bray lived in a little mid-terrace cottage whose front door opened directly onto the main road through Gosforth. The place had a faint air of neglect about it – peeling white paint on the windows and door, cracks in the pebbledash. A window-box overflowing with purple and pink flowers hinted at how close to nature Hayley's upbringing had been.

Jack knocked on the door. A woman almost as tall and well-built as him opened it. Hayley was dressed in jeans and a t-shirt. She had her mum's thick brown hair – minus the grey streaks – and her dad's keen blue eyes. Her windswept complexion and the crow's feet at the corners of her eyes were the product of a lifetime spent outdoors. A girl of two or three peered up at Jack from between Hayley's legs. The girl too was unmistakably a Bray – rosy-cheeked, dark-haired, strong-featured.

Jack smiled down at her and she hid shyly behind her mum's legs. "Hayley Bray?" he asked.

Hayley nodded, eyeing Jack as if she suspected he might try to sell her something.

The little girl peeked at him as he took out his police ID. "I'm Detective Inspector Jack Anderson of Greater Manchester Police." Seeing Hayley's eyes widen, Jack added, "It's nothing for you to be alarmed about, Miss Bray. I'd like to ask you some questions. If that's OK?"

"What about?"

"Do you mind if we speak inside?"

Hayley hesitated. Her gaze moved past Jack to an old lady walking a dog on the opposite pavement. The lady was eyeing Jack with open curiosity. Hayley waved to her. "Hello, Mrs Madden." She ushered Jack inside, saying matter-of-factly, "That's my neighbour. She's one of the village gossip mafia.

I can do without it getting around that the police have come knocking on my door."

She led Jack along a short hallway cluttered with coats, shoes and wellies. The little girl ran ahead of them into a small living-room furnished with a shabby but comfortable-looking three-piece suite. A circle of dolls and stuffed toys were arranged around a plastic tea set in the middle of the carpet. "Annabelle and I were having a dolls tea party," explained Hayley.

"That tea looks lovely," Jack said, smiling at Annabelle again. "Can I have a cup?"

A gap-toothed smile lighting up her face, Annabelle nodded and set about pouring Jack an imaginary cup of tea. "Thank you," he said as she handed him a plastic cup and saucer. He took a pretend sip. "Mm, delicious. Just what I needed."

"So is this about what happened at Hawkshead Manor?" asked Hayley. "Because I already told the police my family had nothing to do with those people. They came to the house a few times wanting to buy hay, but we had none to spare."

"That's not what I'm here about. I'm looking into the Ridley murders."

Hayley's eyebrows lifted high. "The Ridley murders. That was twenty years ago."

"Murder cases stay open until they're solved."

"If you haven't solved it by now, seems to me it'll stay that way."

"Most likely, but we still follow up any new leads."

"What new leads? And why are Manchester police interested in the case?"

"New leads is perhaps overstating things. As for our interest, the Ridleys lived in Prestwich."

"Oh yes. I forgot." Hayley looked down as Annabelle tugged at her jeans.

"I'm thirsty, Mummy," said the little girl.

"I'd better get this one a drink," Hayley said to Jack. "Would you like a real cup of tea?"

"Please."

Hayley left the room with Annabelle trailing after her. Jack's gaze travelled around the room. A cast-iron mantelpiece was decorated with photos of Annabelle and Hayley. Jack noted there were no photos of anyone who appeared to be Annabelle's dad or of Hayley's parents and brother. A bookcase overloaded with toys, board games and children's books occupied an alcove to the left of the fireplace. Jack approached it and ran a finger over the spines of the books. He turned at the sound of Annabelle entering the room. She was clutching a cup of milk in one hand and a biscuit in the other. She clambered onto the sofa, pointed at Jack and said through a mouthful of biscuit, "Dad."

A sharp pang went through him as he found himself wondering whether he would he ever hear Charlie say that to him.

"That's not your dad, Annabelle," said Hayley, returning with two mugs of tea. "Sorry," she said, handing one to Jack. He waved away her apology as she explained, "Annabelle's going through a phase of calling any man with dark brown hair dad."

"Do you mind me asking where her dad is?"

"He lives in Carlisle. He doesn't bother with Annabelle." Hayley spoke with the fatalistic air of someone used to rolling with whatever life threw at her. It was the same matter-of-factness Pam had displayed when talking about her husband's illness, but without the world-weary resentment.

"Sorry to hear that."

"Don't be. She's better off without him. We were only together a few months. He was working on Shaw Farm over in Wasdale. He took off not long after I got pregnant."

"What's his name?"

"Martin Price. Why?"

"Is he the reason you fell out with your parents?"

Hayley frowned. "How do you know about that?"

"It's like you said, people in villages do a lot of this." Jack made a talk-talk signal.

Hayley stared into her tea for a moment. "Martin was part of the reason."

"Was your dad's illness the other part?"

Hayley looked up, her eyes narrowing. "Who have you been talking to?"

"I spoke to your mum earlier today. Your dad was too ill to get out of bed."

Hayley's annoyance turned to concern. She heaved a sad sigh. "He's been like that on and off for years."

"What's wrong with him?"

"We don't know. He gets pains in his joints. Migraines. Sometimes he's so tired he can't stand up. The doctors did all sorts of tests but couldn't find anything wrong. They wanted to put him on antidepressants, send him to a therapist. Mum refused. Depression's a dirty word to her. She said dad just needed to rest. But resting didn't do him any good. He just got worse and worse. I kept trying to tell her we should do as the doctor said, but..." She faded off with a shake of her head.

Her words transported Jack back to Rebecca, the months she'd spent in bed debilitated by depression. His own eyes had once been haunted by the same hopelessness he now saw in Hayley's. "And how long has this been going on for?"

Hayley puffed her cheeks. "It's difficult to say. I suppose dad first started feeling off about six or seven years ago."

"Was anything going on at the time? Was something stressing him out?"

"Only the usual stress and strains of keeping the farm going." Hayley gave Jack a probing look. "I don't see what any of this has got to do with the murders."

"I'm just trying to look at things from a fresh angle."

"And you think what? That my family might have something to do with what happened?"

"I know it's uncomfortable, Miss Bray, but it's my job to ask these—"

Annabelle interrupted Jack with a high-pitched, "Mummy!" She held up her now empty cup. Its plastic lid had come off and a cushion was spattered with milk.

"How did that happen, Annabelle?" Hayley asked sternly. "Did you take the lid off?"

The girl shook her head.

Sighing, Hayley picked up the cushion. "We'd better get this cleaned up, hadn't we?"

"Yes Mummy."

"Excuse me a moment," Hayley said to Jack. This time, Annabelle remained where she was as her mum left the room with the cushion. The sound of running water came from the kitchen.

"Whoopsie," Jack said to Annabelle.

Wiping a ring of milk from her lips with the back of her hand, the little girl got off the sofa and tottled over to the bookcase. She pulled out a book and turned to give it to Jack. It was a slim hardback with a spine frayed by age and use. On its cover there was an illustration of a smiling gingerbread man running along a winding path. He was being chased by an old man and woman, a horse and a cow.

Jack's smile faded. "Is this your book?" His question was answered by what he saw as he opened the book. 'To Hayley. Love from Mum and Dad' was written on the first page. 'Hayley' had been crossed out and 'Neal' had been inserted in its place. In turn, 'Neal' had also been crossed out and replaced once again with 'Hayley'. This was repeated three times.

Annabelle prodded the book, giving Jack big blue eyes as if she wanted him to read it to her. His gaze skimmed over the text 'Once upon a time a little old woman and a little old man lived in a cottage...' He flicked through well-thumbed pages displaying pictures of the gingerbread man escaping from an oven and jumping out of an open window, then the old woman and man chasing him. They were joined by a pig, then a cow, then a horse. The gingerbread man was smiling until he came to a river. Then his arms were flung up in dismay. In the next picture he was talking to a fox.

Creases of curiosity clustered on Jack's forehead. The text next to the picture had been altered from 'A sly fox came out from behind a tree' to 'Wendy came out from behind a tree'. Likewise the following sentence had been changed to '"I'll help you cross the river," said Wendy.'

Jack looked up as Hayley came back into the room. "Who's Wendy?" he asked, fixing her with an unwavering stare.

She blinked as if taken aback, then made to take the book from him. He drew it away from her reach, rising to his feet and repeating, "Who's Wendy?"

Hayley's eyebrows twitched with annoyance. "I don't know. Now give me that book back."

"I'm afraid I can't do that. This could be evidence."

"Of what?"

Jack wasn't surprised by Hayley's confusion. It had never been made public that the killers taunted Tracy with lines from The Gingerbread Man. The police hadn't wanted to risk spurring them to destroy evidence. "Sit down, Miss Bray."

"No. I've had enough of your insinuations." Hayley stabbed a finger towards the door. "I want you out of my house."

"If that's what you want, I'll leave, but I'll be back and next time I'll have a whole team with me – constables, detectives, Forensic officers. And we'll turn your house upside down while the entire village watches. Is that what you want?"

Hayley's voice rose. "Are you threatening me?"

"I'm simply telling you what will happen. Look, I'm not here to accuse you of anything. I'm here to find out who shot and stabbed to death two adults and a child less than a mile from where you grew up. There are circumstances here you're unaware of. If you'll allow me, I'll explain." Jack motioned for Hayley to sit.

She eyed him uncertainly before stooping to sweep Annabelle into her arms. She sat down on the sofa with the child on her lap as if Annabelle provided a buffer between her and Jack. She stared expectantly at him.

He tapped the book. "When did your parents give you this?"

"It was a birthday present." Hayley thought for a moment, then added, "I think I was six."

"From the inscription in the front, I take it your brother Neal wanted it for himself."

"He loved the pictures. He took the book and wrote his name in it. Mum and Dad made him give it back, but he kept taking it until they got him his own copy."

"If you were six, that would have made Neal what?"

"Eight."

"Eight," echoed Jack. "A bit old for The Gingerbread Man."

"A bit," agreed Hayley. "But then again Neal was always young for his age."

"How do you mean?"

"He was a slow learner. Always bottom of his class. He was small too, at least at that age. People used to think we were twins. All the more so because..." Hayley faded off as if she'd thought better of voicing what was on her mind.

"Because of what?"

Seemingly without realising she was doing it, Hayley stroked Annabelle's shoulder-length wavy hair. "Well because we had the same hair and mum used to dress us in matching clothes."

"What type of clothes?"

"Just *normal* stuff. T-shirts, jeans..."

Jack noted the stress Hayley put on the word 'normal'. In his experience, normal people – whatever that meant – didn't feel the need to emphasise their normality. He opened the book at the picture of the fox and gingerbread man and pointed to the altered text. "Did Neal do that?"

"Yes."

"Why?"

"He had an invisible friend called Wendy. It was just one of those silly childhood things." Hayley gave a little laugh, but Jack saw no amusement in her eyes.

Glancing thoughtfully at the book, he flipped forwards to a picture of the fox with the gingerbread man in its mouth. "The fox promises to help the gingerbread man cross the river and, after doing so, eats him. That doesn't sound like the sort of invisible friend I'd want to have."

"Yes well, Wendy was..." Hayley paused for the right word, "mischievous."

"In what way?"

A rise of irritation came into Hayley's voice again. "Oh I don't know. It was all so long ago. Look, you said you'd explain what these other circumstances are."

"Run, run as fast as you can. Stop. We want to eat you. Are those lines familiar to you?"

Hayley narrowed her eyes as if she suspected Jack was trying to trick her. "Of course they are. They're from the book you're holding."

"When Tracy Ridley was running away from her attackers, they shouted those words at her."

Silence followed this revelation. Jack watched every movement of Hayley's face. He saw nothing but surprise in her eyes.

"Run, run as fast as you can," repeated Annabelle, a broad smile of recognition spreading across her rosy-cheeks. She pointed a chubby finger at the book and, struggling to pronounce the 'g', said, "Innerbread man, Mummy,"

"Yes darling." Hayley's voice was as hollow as an empty coffin. She looked from the book to Jack, her eyes haunted with confusion. "What does it mean?"

"Tell me more about Wendy."

Hayley was silent for another moment as if searching her memory. "Like I said, she was mischievous. When Neal was naughty, she'd get the blame. She liked to play pranks. You know the kind of thing. Salt in your cereal. A spider in your lunchbox. Neal first mentioned her when he was five or six. I think it was because mum was reading Peter Pan to him. That's why Dad got rid of that book."

"Your dad didn't approve of Wendy?"

Hayley huffed through her nostrils as if that was a serious understatement. "He hated her. He said it wasn't normal for Neal to have an invisible friend."

Normal. There was that word again. "Why not? Seems perfectly normal to me. My daughter had one when she was about the same age."

"The problem was, Neal used to dress up as Wendy. He'd put on my dresses and shoes and plait his hair. Dad found him like that one day." Hayley grimaced at the memory. "He flipped out, beat Neal black and blue with a belt. He cut off Neal's plaits and made him promise never to mention Wendy again."

"How old was Neal?"

"Eight. A few weeks later he stole that book from me." Hayley pointed to The Gingerbread Man. "Dad acted angry, but I think it actually pleased him when he saw the changes Neal had made to the book. If Neal thought

Wendy was a sly fox, that was a good thing. It meant she wasn't his friend anymore."

"So that was the end of Wendy?"

Once again, Hayley hesitated to reply. She sucked her lips hard enough to leave them bloodless. Annabelle suddenly wriggled free from her mum's embrace. She plopped down onto the carpet and resumed playing with her tea set.

"Well, was it?" pressed Jack.

Hayley blinked. "Sorry, I was miles away. Yes, yes that was the end of Wendy."

"And what about Neal himself?" Jack asked after a doubtful little pause. "How would you describe him as a child?"

"He was quiet, shy."

"Did he have any real life friends?"

"No. Even if he'd wanted friends, there was no time for them. After school we worked on the farm – feeding the sheep, shearing, lambing and all the rest of it."

"Did Neal enjoy the work?"

Hayley shrugged. "He just got on with it."

"So Neal had difficulty expressing his emotions."

Hayley frowned faintly as if she thought Jack was trying to put words in her mouth. "I suppose you could say that."

"Would he ever get angry? Throw tantrums? Lash out?"

"No never. Even when Dad used to hit him, he'd just stand there and take it."

"What about Wendy? Would she get angry?"

Jack noted the slight hesitation before Hayley replied, "Not really."

He stared at her as if waiting for her to say more.

Looking up from her tea set, Annabelle said, "Pasta, Mummy."

"OK, darling," Hayley replied quickly as if relieved for an excuse to leave the room. "I need to make Annabelle's tea," she said to Jack. "So if you wouldn't mind..." She glanced pointedly towards the door.

Jack remained where he was, subjecting Hayley to the same steady stare. She made to stand, but he motioned for her to stay put.

She sighed sharply. "Look, I don't see what else I can say that could possibly be of any help to you."

Jack decided to chance his arm. "You could tell me the truth, Hayley." A career criminal like Karl Robinson would have laughed in his face at such a direct accusation of dishonesty. Being called a liar was nothing to them, but for 'normal' people it was enough to throw them off balance, make them emotional. And an emotional person was more likely to let slip, if not the truth, then at least something of interest.

Hayley's eyes widened in indignation. "I've told you the truth."

Jack shook his head. "Do you know what the maximum sentence for perverting the course of justice is? Life imprisonment. In a case like this, you might expect to serve two to three years for assisting an offender."

"What are you talking about?" exclaimed Hayley. "Assisting what offender?"

"If you conceal information that could lead to an arrest–"

"This is insane! I'm not concealing anything about Neal."

Jack cocked an eyebrow. "I never said you were."

Confusion vied with Hayley's anger. "Yes you did."

"No. I said I don't think you're telling me the whole truth. You're the one who related that back to Neal. Why is that?"

Hayley's mouth opened and closed silently. Annabelle tugged at her hand, whining, "Pasta, pasta..."

Hayley found her voice. "You're playing mind games with me."

"This isn't a game, Hayley," Jack stated gravely. "People are dead. Other people are still suffering. And somewhere out there are two killers who might one day do the same thing to someone else."

"It's been twenty years."

"It doesn't matter how long it's been. This was an opportunistic crime. Given the opportunity, the killers will do it again. More people will die. More lives will be ruined." Jack made a circular motion. "And so it goes, until something breaks the cycle. I've seen it happen."

"Pasta, pasta..." Annabelle persisted.

Hayley closed her eyes, touching a hand to her forehead in a way that reminded Jack of Butterfly.

"Pasta."

"Alright!" Hayley retorted exasperatedly. "I'll get you your sodding pasta."

The little girl's eyes swelled with tears. Hayley's expression moved swiftly from anger to guilt. "Sorry, Annabelle," she soothed, picking her up and cuddling her. "Mummy shouldn't have shouted at you."

Annabelle pressed her face into her mum's shoulder, her sobs quietening down to snuffles. Hayley gave Jack an almost pleading look. "I need to make her tea."

He motioned towards the door as if to say, *Don't let me stop you.* "I've told you what will happen when I leave here, Hayley. As soon as I'm out of the front door, I'll apply for a search warrant. Whilst I'm waiting for that, I'll speak to your parents and brother. Then I'll speak to any other relatives, family friends, acquaintances, neighbours, the family doctor, people you and your brother went to school with, the postman, the milkman. I'll pull your family's life apart thread by thread. Even if it takes another twenty years, I'll find out what I want to know. And if you've withheld anything from me, you'll be prosecuted and you *will* go to prison." He spoke as if it was an inevitability. From the way Hayley's lips trembled, he knew his words were getting through. He continued to press, "And if social services deem it necessary, Annabelle will be taken into care."

A fierce light flashed in Hayley's eyes. "Over my dead body she will be."

Jack thought about Butterfly again. The way her eyes would flash like a tiger's if anyone or anything threatened Charlie. He softened his voice. "I understand how you feel, Hayley. I have a daughter myself. We do whatever it takes to protect the ones we love."

"I love my brother too. If I've been protecting him for all these years, what makes you think I'll talk to you now?"

"Because children change everything. Nothing brings things into clearer focus than having another life totally dependent on you. You sacrifice everything for them – relationships, ambitions. Nothing else matters."

Tears spilled over Hayley's eyelashes. Silent seconds passed. Jack watched his words sink deeper and deeper into their target. Hayley heaved a sigh that seemed to come from the bottom of her lungs. "I wasn't lying," she said quietly, her eyes dropping away from Jack as if she was ashamed. "Wendy never came back after Dad beat her out of Neal, but someone else took her place. His name was Butch." She gave a nervy laugh. "One day, Neal started speaking in this odd deep voice and walking around with his chest puffed out. We all thought it was funny... at first. Neal started lifting weights to build his muscles. Dad approved because he needed help with all the heavy lifting. Neal was skinny as a rake back then, but he was strong." She grimaced as if at an unpleasant memory.

Picking up on it, Jack asked, "Did your brother ever hurt you?"

"We used to fight sometimes, like all siblings do. One time I walked into his bedroom and he was doing muscle poses in the mirror naked. I couldn't help it, I burst out laughing. Next thing I knew, his hands were around my throat and he was squeezing so hard I couldn't breathe. His face was all twisted out of shape. He looked like a different person. He shouted at me, 'No one laughs at Butch!' I thought I was going to pass out, but he let go and said, 'You mention this to anyone and I'll finish the job.' I ran from his room. I was too scared to say a word to our parents, but a few days later Dad saw the bruises on my neck. When he asked about them I broke down and told him. He went mad. Even madder than when he found Neal dressed as Wendy. He hit Neal and called him a coward for hurting someone weaker than himself."

Jack resisted the urge to point out the inherent hypocrisy in Alistair Bray's accusation. He didn't want to disturb the flow of Hayley's story. She was staring past Annabelle at an indeterminate spot on the carpet, lost in her memories.

"But this time, Neal didn't just stand there and take it," continued Hayley. "He was fourteen. He'd shot up as tall as Dad in the previous year. He hit him back. I can still see the look on Dad's face. Like... Like a hand had reached down from the sky and clocked him one. The two of them stared at each other for a second, then they started swinging like they were trying to knock each other's block off. And every time Neal threw a punch, he'd shout in that same put-on deep voice, 'There's only room for one man in this house!'" She shook her head. "Sounds like a bad joke, doesn't it?"

"No," disagreed Jack. He was thinking about the men who'd attacked the Ridleys. The first had seemed nervous and unsure of what he was doing. The second had been aggressive and dominant. He'd taunted the first man for ejaculating prematurely. But had there really been two attackers? Could it have been one attacker using two voices? According to her statement, Tracy had only heard the second voice after a bag was put over her head. She would have been none the wiser if both attackers were in fact one and the same person – or indeed if that attacker wasn't a man, but a fourteen-year-old boy. Was it possible? Could Neal Bray have murdered the Ridleys, egged on by his invisible friend? "So who won the fight?"

"Neither of them. Mum got between them and put a stop to it. She made Neal apologise and promise never to put his hands on me again."

"And did he keep his promise?"

Hayley nodded. "He also promised to send Butch away like he had Wendy, but Dad wasn't having any of it. He took Neal out of school. Kept him close, working the farm. I think that was when Dad first got depressed. It all just got too much for him."

"I take it then that Neal didn't keep *that* promise."

Hayley pursed her lips as if uncertain how to answer. "Well he did and he didn't. He never let Butch out in front of Dad again, but sometimes when he was speaking to Mum or me – especially if he was angry – his voice would change and we knew it was Butch. Mum made me promise not to tell Dad. She was terrified that if Neal and he had another fight someone would end up seriously hurt. And then there were the other incidents..." She trailed off as if she couldn't bring herself to say any more.

"What other incidents?" prompted Jack.

Hayley chewed her lips. As if sensing her distress, Annabelle reached up to gently touch her mum's face. Hayley smiled at her, tears filling her eyes again. Drawing in a shuddering breath, she went on, "Neal used to spy on me undressing. I caught him at it twice. The second time he was..." She wrinkled her face in distaste. "He was masturbating. I told Mum. She had words with Neal and he never did it again. At least not to my knowledge. I suppose he might have just been sneakier about it. Then there was the thing with the cat. We kept cats to keep the rats and mice down. There was a tabby called Tigger that Dad was fond of. Dad found Tigger in the woods gutted and hanged from a tree. He guessed it was Neal – or Butch – that had done it. He tried to go for Neal, but Mum stopped him. I remember he kept yelling at her, 'He needs help. He's sick in the head.' But she wouldn't hear it. Keep it in the family. That's her motto."

"Tell me what happened on the day of the killings?"

"We were working as usual. Stacking a delivery of hay."

"And?"

"And what?"

"According to you and your parents' statements you were all together at the time of the killings. But that was a lie, wasn't it?"

Hayley's eyes fell away from Jack's again.

"Wasn't it?" Jack repeated forcefully enough to make her flinch.

As if the words were being dragged out of her one at a time, Hayley said, "Neal wasn't at the farm when Tracy Ridley showed up. He'd been out setting snares in the woods. He came back to the house not long before Sergeant Ramsden arrived."

Jack had heard enough. Mental defectiveness, sexual deviancy, violence – Neal had displayed more than enough abnormal traits to place him smack bang at the top of the list of suspects. The police had overlooked him for three reasons. Firstly, they'd been too focused on Beech and Sutton. Secondly, he was only fourteen-years-old at the time. But mainly because of Pam Bray's motto – *Keep it in the family*. That's exactly what the Bray's had done. They'd covered for Neal for twenty years.

Tears spilled from Hayley's eyes as she lifted her gaze to Jack. "I only did as Mum told me, that's all. I'm so sorry. What's going to happen to me?"

"That depends on whether your brother killed the Ridleys."

"He did it."

"How do you know? Did he tell you that he did?"

Hayley shook her head. "Nothing was ever said. Not a word. But we all knew he'd done it. Dad even got rid of the old shotgun he'd taught Neal to shoot with. All these years what Neal did has hung over us, poisoning everything." She hugged an arm across her stomach. "It makes me want to puke just thinking about it."

Frowning disapprovingly, Annabelle touched her Mum's lips as if trying to push them up into a smile. Hayley kissed the toddler's fingers. "It wasn't only because I couldn't stand to see Dad get any worse that I left the farm. I couldn't risk Annabelle being around Neal." She touched her throat. "Every time he looked at her, I felt like I couldn't breathe."

"So you think he's still dangerous?"

"I don't know. I haven't seen Butch in years, but he's still in Neal. I'm certain of it." Hugging Annabelle close, Hayley looked at Jack with eyes that seemed to be pleading for mercy. "So what happens now?"

"I'm going to head over to your parents' farm. You're going to stay here and wait to hear from me. I must ask you not to let your parents know I'm coming. If you do contact them, criminal charges may be made against you further down the line."

"I won't contact them. I know I should have come forward years ago. I can't tell you how many times I've thought about it. I've even picked up the phone to call the police, but..." Hayley exhaled a juddering breath. "I just couldn't bring myself to do it. He's my brother."

"Well let's hope you're wrong about him."

Hayley shook her head as if to say, *I'm not.*

Jack felt a twinge of sympathy. *Keep it in the family.* That motto had ended up costing Hayley the very thing it was supposed to protect. He wondered what he would have done in her situation. He hoped he never had to find out. As he turned to leave, Annabelle gave him a wave. Smiling, he waved back.

CHAPTER 23

Charlie let out a cry, straining against the straps of his seat. With difficulty, Butterfly twisted around so that her head was resting on the seat's padded armrest. An acrid whiff told her that his nappy needed changing. There was nothing she could do about that though. Karl had tied her up expertly. Charlie settled down as she hummed one of his favourite lullabies through the cloth gag. It occurred to her that maybe she should just let him cry. The noise might attract attention from a passer-by. But she couldn't bear to see him in distress. Besides, who would pass by here other than an occasional rabbit?

She crooked her neck to look at the dashboard clock. Karl had been gone for almost half-an-hour. What if he'd been caught? Would he tell the police about her and Charlie? If not, they might be trapped here indefinitely. A bud of panic opened in her chest at the thought. *Stay calm,* she told herself. *No matter what happens to Karl, Jack will come looking for us. He'll find us.*

She jerked her head around at a tap on a window, hoping her prediction had come true. Her eyebrows dropped in disappointment at the sight of Karl's grinning mug. But there was also a small measure of relief in her expression. And not only because she could tend to Charlie. If Karl had been captured, their hunt for the killers would be at an end.

A whole new set of emotions engulfed her as she saw that Karl wasn't alone. A quivering mixture of anxiety and excitement greeted the sight of Phil Beech's long, thin face. The gamekeeper's hands were interlocked across the back of his head. The Glock was pressed into his back. His mouth and eyes were downturned. His chin hung dejectedly against his chest.

Karl opened the door, saying gleefully, "Look which dumb redneck popped out for a sneaky cig."

"Listen, I don't know what–" Phil started to say. He broke off with a grimace as Karl kicked him behind the knee. Another swift kick sent him to his knees.

"You don't speak unless I say so," warned Karl. "Have you fucking got that?"

Phil nodded. Keeping the gun on the gamekeeper, Karl flicked open his knife and reached to cut Butterfly loose. She rubbed the circulation back into her hands, eyeballing Phil with a look of faint revulsion. Another cry from Charlie caused her to turn to him.

"We haven't got much time before those coppers realise this wanker's gone," Karl said as she took Charlie out of his seat.

"His nappy needs changing." Butterfly's tone brooked no argument.

Karl's gaze shifted between Phil and the surrounding trees as Butterfly cleaned Charlie and strapped a fresh nappy around his plump thighs. When she was done, she returned Charlie to his seat and gave him a dummy to keep him occupied. She pulled up the seat's hood so he couldn't see what was going on outside the car.

She turned to look down at Phil. He stared at the ground, his narrow shoulders hunched as if in anticipation of being hit again. A liver-spotted scalp glimmered greasily through his thinning hair. His hollow cheeks were flecked with white stubble. In contrast to his sharp chin and cheekbones, his nose was bulbous and veiny, doubtless as a result of spending most of his free time in The Rose and Crown. He made for a sorry sight, but Butterfly's voice was cold and hard as she said, "Look at me. Who am I?"

Phil lifted his beady eyes to hers. His lips curled contemptuously away from tobacco-stained teeth. "You're one of them nutters from the manor house."

A violent urge to smack the contempt from Phil's face threatened to get the better of Butterfly. How dare this piece of shit judge her! Fear. That was what she wanted from him. Fear and the truth. "You and I have spoken before. A long time ago."

"I don't remember."

"Neither do I."

Phil's forehead wrinkled in confusion. "You're off your bloody rocker."

A razor-thin smile touched Butterfly's lips. "Maybe I am. If someone murders your entire family when you're only eleven, it tends to mess you up."

"I've no idea what you're talking about."

"Let me give you a clue," Karl put in jauntily. "You two first met twenty years ago in The Rose and Crown."

Phil's confusion turned to narrow-eyed realisation. "Tracy Ridley?"

"Ding. Got it in one."

"At least that's who I used to be," corrected Butterfly.

"I didn't kill your family," said Phil.

"Bullshit!" snarled Karl. "Your pal Dale told me the truth. That fat fuck spilled everything, including the contents of his belly," he nodded at Butterfly, "before she put a bullet between his eyes."

Phil's jaw slackened in shock. "Dale... Dale's dead?"

"Ding. Right again. And you're next unless you tell us where the other half of the necklace is."

"What necklace?"

Karl chuckled. "Not a bad actor is he?" he said to Butterfly. "Show him?"

Butterfly withdrew the 'Little Sis' necklace from beneath her vest. Phil squinted up at it. "I've never seen that necklace before. I don't know what Dale told you, but it wasn't true. If you stuck that gun in his face, he would have said anything to save his skin." There was little fear in Phil's voice. He'd swiftly overcome his shock at the news of Dale's death and now his eyes were narrow and calculating again.

"You're lying," said Karl. "It's written all over your ugly fuck face."

Ignoring him, Phil fixed Butterfly with a steady look. "Yeah, I was in the Rose and Crown that day and yeah I thought you were a cheeky little bugger who needed a good hiding. But I didn't kill your family. Like I told the police, after I finished my drink I–"

Karl stabbed the gun into the back of Phil's head, silencing him. He turned bright, eager eyes to Butterfly. "It's time to do this."

Her forehead twitched. A familiar *thud, thud* was beating at her brain. "I want to see the necklace."

"I don't have it," said Phil. "Go ahead shoot me, but you'll be killing an innocent man."

"Innocent?" scowled Butterfly, the drum upping its volume. "Your best mate was a child molester."

"Dale made mistakes. We all make mistakes."

"Mistakes?" Now it was Butterfly's lips that peeled back in contempt. "Is that what you call raping a schoolgirl?"

"Dale didn't rape that girl. The little slut knew exactly what she was doing."

"She was fourteen!" exploded Butterfly.

Karl glanced around uneasily at her raised voice, but he didn't try to quieten her. His eyes glowed with anticipation as he watched her anger swelling.

"But that doesn't matter to men like you, does it?" she continued, a vein pulsing on her forehead. "All that matters is getting what you want. Fuck everyone else."

"I'm not like Dale."

"We've seen your computer and box of tissues," leered Karl. "I bet if the coppers had a look at your hard-drive you'd be in deep shit."

Pushing his chin out defiantly, Phil retorted, "I'm not the criminal here."

Karl whipped his hand out, slamming the Glock into Phil's jaw. The gamekeeper toppled sideways, spitting blood and shattered teeth. Karl caught hold of Butterfly's hand and pulled it towards the pistol. Pressing his hands over hers, he took aim at Phil's head. "Do it," he urged.

The drum battered Butterfly's brain as she stared into Phil's face. She still saw no fear in his eyes. Why wasn't the bastard scared? He should be grovelling, begging for mercy. She found herself thinking about Tracy's police statement. The first man to appear from the woods – the one everyone believed was Phil – had been shaky-voiced with nerves. The second man – who, it followed, had to be Dale – had been much more sure of himself. But now the roles were reversed – Dale had fallen to pieces the instant the gun was pointed in his face, Phil was the one with nerves of steel.

"The necklace." Butterfly's voice was an insistent hiss.

"Forget the necklace," said Karl. "We don't have time to find it now."

"I need to see it."

"No you don't. You need to do what you should have done years ago – kill this fucker. Finish this!"

Thud, thud, THUD... Butterfly ran a bone-dry tongue over her lips. Her finger touched the trigger.

"What are you waiting for?" urged Karl. "You know what he is. You said it yourself. He takes what he wants and fuck everyone else. Fuck your sister, fuck your parents, fuck you, fuck the entire world just so long as he gets his kicks."

Butterfly grimaced. The drum was getting louder and faster. Her gaze moved over Beech. Six foot or more and thin. That was the description of the killer and that was Beech's description. Louder and faster... *Dale didn't rape that girl. The little slut knew exactly what she was doing.* Louder and faster... *So what if he's not nervous? It was him. He did it. You don't need the necklace. Do it. Pull the trigger!* Her finger tightened. Another sound vibrated painfully against her eardrums. She turned to look into the car. Charlie was crying again. Suddenly she couldn't hear the drum. All she could hear were Charlie's high-pitched wails.

Her finger slackened. "If I take his life, I'm no different to him."

"Listen to me, Io," Karl said loudly as if trying to make himself heard to someone a long way off. "This is your chance to make everything right. You won't get another one."

"I keep telling you, Karl. Io's gone and she's not coming back."

He shook his head hard. "No. I saw her."

"I don't care what you saw and I don't care what you say. I won't do this."

Karl's face seemed to crumple beneath the resolve in Butterfly's voice. He lowered his head. With a flicker of sympathy in her eyes, Butterfly rested a hand on his shoulder.

He jerked his head up at her touch. "Io!" he shouted, his voice shrill with desperation. "This is for you!"

He thrust a finger through the trigger-guard and squeezed against Butterfly's finger. The trigger clicked. The muzzle flashed. Pain raced through Butterfly's wrist as the gun recoiled. A swirl of crows fled the treetops as the gunshot echoed through the woods. Butterfly wrenched her hand away from the Glock, stumbling and falling to her backside. Her eyes bulged at Phil. The gamekeeper was lying on his back, clutching his chest. Blood was welling between his fingers. His breath was rattling like an empty spray paint can. His lips were working like a fish out of water. There was more than enough fear in his eyes now.

Karl stared at the wounded man as if mesmerised. Butterfly's fingers closed around a tennis-ball sized stone. Almost before she realised what she was doing, she was springing to her feet and swinging her hand at Karl. The stone connected with the side of his head. His eyes widening in pain and surprise, he staggered and fell on top of Phil. He tried to get up, but Phil's hands were suddenly on his throat, squeezing. Karl thrust the Glock up under Phil's chin and pulled the trigger again. Phil's head jerked back against the ground, a torrent of blood gushing from his nostrils.

Butterfly didn't wait around to see what happened next. She dashed around to the far side of the car, jerked the door open and fumbled at the straps securing Charlie. For a second that seemed like an eternity, the straps refused to click loose. Then, almost sobbing with relief, she was lifting Charlie into her arms, turning and fleeing through the farm gate.

"Io!" Karl's voice rang out behind her.

She didn't look back to see if he was chasing her. She concentrated on running and not tripping over. A footpath climbed a grassy slope, veering rightwards towards a line of trees. Upon reaching the trees, she saw another open expanse of grass beyond them. She left the track, working her way uphill, using the trees for cover. Charlie squirmed and cried in her arms.

"Shh," she soothed breathlessly.

Sweat was stinging her eyes and her lungs were burning by the time she reached the brow of the hill. The trees led to a hawthorn hedge, beyond which there was a gravel farm track. Shielding Charlie from the thorns, she squirmed on her elbows and knees through a hole in the hedge.

"Io!" Karl's voice echoed again, sounding farther away, but nowhere near far enough.

Butterfly peered through the hedge. Her heart kicked hard as she caught sight of him staggering through the trees. One side of his face was streaked with blood. Staying hunched low, she ran along a lane that cut a straight line between fields of grazing sheep. She'd gone maybe eighty metres when she came to a farm gate on her left. Karl would be in the lane any second now. She clambered over the gate and made her way along the inside of the hedge.

Charlie let out another wail. Butterfly shushed him, but it was too late.

"Io stop!" yelled Karl, leaping over the gate. "I love you."

Butterfly desperately scanned her surroundings. Fifty or sixty metres away, trees marched along the far side of the field. It looked to be the edge of a larger wood. If she could make it there, maybe she could lose Karl. Fighting for oxygen, she put on a burst of speed. Halfway across the field, she threw a glance over her shoulder. Karl was about twenty metres behind her and, unburdened by a ten-month-old child, gaining fast.

Panic pounding in her chest, Butterfly veered towards a hedge on her right. She aimed for a gap, spotting at the last instant that it was filled by a sagging barbed wire fence. She scissored her legs over the wire, twisting an ankle and falling. The breath whooshed from her lungs as she landed on her back in the lane. She lay too winded to move. As Karl tried to hurdle the wire, his jeans snagged on a barb. He grimaced, exclaiming, "Fuck."

Charlie kicked his legs, bawling at the top of his lungs. The sound crackled through Butterfly like an electric current, giving her the strength to clamber to her feet. Pain speared her ankle as she set off in a limping run. The lane curved towards a farm gate that led to a dusty, mud-encrusted farmyard. A tractor and a Landrover were parked between a white farmhouse and a stone barn with a sagging slate roof. A sense of déjà vu struck Butterfly so powerfully that it almost stopped her in her tracks. She'd been here before. She knew it with absolute certainty.

The next second she saw the sign on the gate – 'Bray Farm'. A gasp of relief escaped her. It seemed the Brays were destined to always be her saviours.

She pulled a loop of rope up over the gatepost, shoved the gate open and ran for the farmhouse. A collie dog nosed open the front door. Was it the same dog that had run out to greet Tracy? No, that dog would have died years ago. The dog skittered off to one side as Butterfly staggered into the house. She slammed the door behind herself, frantically looking for a key. There was a bolt! She slapped it into place and allowed herself a second to haul in a ragged breath and shush Charlie. She flinched as the collie jumped up to press its nose against a window, barking furiously.

She turned and found herself in a kitchen with a rectangular scarred wooden table surrounded by four mismatched chairs at its centre. The table was laid with cutlery and plates for two. Wellies were lined up on the flagstones next to the door. Flames flickered in a stone fireplace. Logs were stacked in a wicker basket on the sooty hearth. A threadbare armchair and a dog basket were drawn up to the fireplace. Clothes hung drying from a ceiling airer above the mantelpiece. Dozens of red-white-and-blue rosettes were pinned to the ceiling beams. Pans of vegetables and potatoes bubbled atop a big old Rayburn. The sweet aroma of roasting lamb filled the air.

"Hello," shouted Butterfly, heading for a door at the far side of the kitchen. "Is anyone here?"

The question met with silence.

The door led to a gloomy hallway wallpapered with more rosettes and photos of prize-winning sheep and lambs. To Butterfly's left, uncarpeted stairs rose into gloom. To her right was a closed door. Ahead, an open door looked onto a living-room with a beamed ceiling. A shabby three-piece-suite strewn with multi-coloured woollen blankets faced an ancient-looking television. The late afternoon sun slanted into the room through small windows deeply recessed in thick exposed stone walls.

Butterfly tried the closed door. A breath of cold, damp air caressed her face. The door opened onto steep stone steps leading down into a dark basement. Her eyes darting around in search of a phone, she went into the living-room. Her gaze lingered on a mug of steaming tea balanced on an arm of the sofa. Someone had recently been in the room.

"Hello," she shouted again, turning to climb the stairs. The thick walls seemed to swallow her voice.

The stairs led to a rectangular landing with five doors. Two were open. She glanced into a dated but clean bathroom with a deep cast-iron bath, a ceramic sink and a toilet with a high-flush cistern. Beyond the second open door was an unused-looking bedroom – metal-framed single bed with a bare mattress, blank bookshelves and an empty dressing table. There were faint, dusty outlines where pictures had been removed from the white plaster walls. It was as if the room had been stripped of every trace of occupation after someone died in there.

Butterfly opened the neighbouring door and squinted into a darkened room. Sunlight probed at the edges of closed curtains, dimly illuminating floorboards partially covered by a sheepskin rug. The room was stuffily warm. Embers glowed in a cast-iron fireplace. In front of the fireplace was a double bed draped with blankets and a pink eiderdown.

Butterfly's heart gave a lurch. There was someone in the bed! The shape of their body moulded beneath the sheets was visible, but their head was hidden from view.

"I'm sorry to come into your house like this," she said, stepping into the room, "but I need to phone the po–" She broke off, her forehead furrowing.

She recognised the man in the bed from the case file photos, but only just barely. The years had not been kind to Alistair Bray. His once dark hair was now grey. His hollow, clean-shaven cheeks were almost as ashen as his hair. His eyes were so sunken that Butterfly thought at first that they were closed. As she neared the bed, she saw that he was staring at the ceiling. His pupils were so blank that she might have mistaken him for a corpse if not for the faint rise and fall of his chest.

"Mr Bray." She spoke quietly, like someone at a dying man's bedside.

He showed no sign of having heard. She moved her hands over his eyes. He didn't blink. His pupils remained fixed on the ceiling or, perhaps like her grandma's, on some place that only he could see. She stared down at the catatonic man, wondering what had done this to him. A stroke? Some sort of breakdown? Her gaze travelled around the room – no phone – before coming to land on Alistair again. Sadness glimmered in her eyes for the man who had once helped her.

She left the room, crossing the landing to open one of the final two doors. Her forehead creased again, this time with bemusement. A single bed was made up with a faded Transformers duvet and pillowcase. A gang of worn-out teddy bears occupied the pillow. The walls were plastered with posters of muscular action heroes – Rambo, Rocky, Conan the Barbarian – and cartoons – Duck Tales, Rugrats, The Simpsons. Occupying pride of position above the bedhead was a picture of a pointy-hatted silhouette flying through a moonlit sky. 'Never Grow Up' was emblazoned across a huge moon.

In contrast to the childish décor, the clothes strewn over the bed and floorboards appeared to belong to an adult male – long-legged jeans, XX-sized chequered shirts. Butterfly almost tripped over a set of dumbbells as she approached a dark wood wardrobe. She opened the wardrobe. It too contained a man's clothes.

It was as if the room was simultaneously occupied by a young child, a teenager and an adult.

Her gaze shifted to a bookshelf. Books on sheep farming – 'The Veterinary Book for Sheep Farmers', 'Sheep Farming for Meat & Wool' – were mixed in with children's books – 'The Wind in the Willows', 'Winnie the Pooh', 'The Tale of Peter Rabbit'.

Her eyes stopped on a well-read book. The lines on her forehead intensified. Slowly, almost reverently, she traced a finger down the book's cracked spine. She withdrew it and looked at the picture of the running gingerbread man on its cover. Something fell out from between the book's pages and landed with a metallic clatter on the floorboards. Nestling Charlie against her hip, she crouched to retrieve the object. Her eyes grew as big as the moon on the poster. In her palm lay a silver necklace with a jigsaw piece shaped pendant on it. 'Big Sis' was engraved into the pendant.

Her fingers cold with sweat, Butterfly took out her 'Little Sis' pendant and put the two puzzle pieces together. They fitted perfectly!

Her head snapped around at the sound of a floorboard creaking. Before she could see who was creeping up on her, something slammed into her head. Pain exploded in her temples. Then she was collapsing down into darkness as deep as a mineshaft.

CHAPTER 24

"They're just dragging the bottom of the pond," Eric informed Jack upon picking up the phone. "Nothing to report as yet."

"That's not why I'm calling," said Jack. "I'm on my way to Bray Farm. I need you to meet me there ASAP."

"Why?"

"I think it was Neal."

"Neal?" A rise of comprehension came into Eric's voice. "You don't mean—"

"That's exactly what I mean," broke in Jack, shoving the car into gear and speeding away from Hayley's house.

"What makes you think that? Has Hayley—"

"I'll explain when I see you," Jack interrupted again, racing towards the edge of the village. Hayley's fear of the consequences of letting her parents know he was on his way would only temporarily hold her in check. Sooner or later, the family loyalty that had kept her quiet all these years would compel her to reach for the phone.

"OK Jack. I'm on my way. Just you make sure you wait for me."

Jack hung up and focused on pushing his speed as high as possible. The river sparkled amongst the trees to his right. His tyres screeched as he careered across the humpback bridge. He shifted to a lower gear as the road ascended Leagate Brow. Not far beyond the brow of the slope, he turned onto the stony track that led to Bray Farm. The sheep in the fields to either side scattered away from the roar of his engine.

He made a sharp right onto an even narrower track with grass running down its centre. Moments later he was pulling up at the entrance to the farmyard. The front gate was open. The collie dog raced through it barking.

There was no sight of Pam or Neal. Jack eyed the farmhouse and adjoining barn. Apart from the dog, it was a peaceful scene.

As Jack got out of the car, the dog retreated, baring its teeth and growling.

"It's OK boy." Jack tried to sound non-threatening, but the dog bristled and barked again. Jack frowned. The collie wasn't simply saying hello. Something had got it spooked. His phone rang. Eric's voice came apprehensively through the receiver.

"They just pulled Dale's body out of the pond."

Jack squeezed his eyes shut as if blocking out a sight he couldn't bear to see. "Jesus."

"There's something else. I've been on to my guys at Phil Beech's cottage. Phil's gone."

"What? How?"

"Buggered if I know. I'm heading over there. The AFOs are with me. We're about ten minutes away."

"I'll see you there."

Jack pocketed the phone, whirling to duck back into the car. The Brays had kept their secret for twenty years. Another few hours wouldn't make any difference. Even if Hayley contacted her parents, the Brays weren't going anywhere. Alistair was bedridden. And Neal wouldn't last five minutes in the world outside the farm.

He stopped as a sound reached him from the farmhouse. He cocked his head, listening. There it was again – a high-pitched cry, like a baby in distress.

The collie heard it too and raced back towards the farmhouse. Jack sprinted after it with one name ringing in his mind – *Charlie*!

CHAPTER 25

"Why did you hit her?"

The voice found its way past Butterfly's veil of unconsciousness. It belonged to a woman with a thick local accent. It sounded anxious and angry.

Butterfly was lying flat on her back on a surface as cold and hard as a mortuary slab. The bedroom floor? She doubted it. The air had a mildewy odour.

"She found the necklace."

The second voice was male with the same accent. It simply sounded anxious.

"What necklace?"

"*The* necklace. The one Butch took from them."

"You mean those people he–" The woman fell silent as if she couldn't bring herself to say any more.

Butterfly cracked her eyelids. The glare from a bare bulb dangling overhead brought a sheen of tears to her eyes. She was in what appeared to be a basement. Black mould mottled a low, arched ceiling of flaking white paint. Rabbits, hares and squirrels were strung from hooks on the ceiling. The animals had been slit open and gutted, but not skinned. The air was musky with their scent. She was on a stone table. To her left was another such table piled with coils of wire, balls of twine, sharpened sticks, pliers and other equipment for making snares. At the far end of the basement, next to the stone stairs was a chest freezer.

The woman was walking back and forth in front of the freezer. She had bobbed brown hair and a ruddy, weathered face. A striped apron was strung over her sturdy shoulders and large, saggy breasts. Butterfly recognised Pam Bray the same way she had Alistair. Pam had aged better than her husband, although the stoop in her shoulders and the bags under her eyes suggested the years had taken their toll on her too.

A warbling cry pulled Butterfly's gaze away from Pam to a tall, thirty-something man whose muscular frame filled out jeans and a chequered shirt. Dark wavy hair dangled over the man's eyes as he looked at the baby he was holding awkwardly in his arms. Charlie let out another shrill wail. Butterfly resisted an almost overwhelming urge to jump up and snatch him away from the man.

"Here, Neal, give him to me," said Pam. She took Charlie from Neal. Charlie quietened down as she expertly cradled and rocked him. She angled him so that he could see Butterfly. "Look, there's your mum. There, there, no need to cry, little one."

Butterfly lay statue-still, hardly daring to breathe. Her mind was racing. Neal was one of the killers. That much she was sure of. Who was Butch? A friend of his? An older mentor? She thrust the question aside. It didn't matter right then. What mattered was getting Charlie away from Pam. First she would have to deal with Neal. But how the hell was she supposed to do that? He looked strong enough to pick her up and break her in two. *Think,* she commanded herself. A name sprang into her mind – *Karl*! A bolted door wouldn't keep Karl out of the house for long. He would find a way in.

Butterfly resisted a fresh impulse to spring into action as Pam pressed her nose against Charlie's hair. "It never ends," Pam murmured, her eyes racked with exhaustion.

Neal looked at her sheepishly from under his floppy fringe. "I'm sorry, Mum."

She swatted his words away. "What are we going to do?" she asked, seemingly speaking as much to Charlie as Neal.

Neal's eyes lit up as if he'd had an idea. "Why don't we ask Butch? He'll know what to do."

"No," Pam shot back. "Not him."

"We have to. What other choice do we have?"

Shaking her head, Pam resumed pacing to and fro. "There's no end to it." Her voice was clogged with sorrow. "No end."

"Yes there is." Neal pointed at Butterfly. "Don't you realise who she is? She's Tracy Ridley."

Deep creases spread from the corners of Pam's eyes as she squinted at Butterfly. "The little girl who came to us for help? No. It can't be."

"It is. She had this." Neal showed his mum the 'Little Sis' necklace.

Pam reached for it, but snatched her hand back as if it might be cursed. "How?" she murmured. "How could she have known?"

"It doesn't matter how she knows." A tremor of nervous excitement came into Neal's voice. "What matters is that no one else knows."

Pam threw her son a scathing look. "Have you forgotten about those policemen that were here earlier?"

Neal's head shrunk between his shoulders like a scolded dog's. "Of course not, but they don't know. Otherwise they'd have arrested us, wouldn't they?"

Pam's face softened with thought. "You may well be right, son, but that doesn't mean they don't suspect us." She glanced at Butterfly. "And if they find her here, it really will all be over."

"Then we have to make sure they don't find her."

Pam's gaze slid from Butterfly to Charlie, riven with uncertainty. "And what about this little one?"

"We'll take him into Wasdale, leave him somewhere where he'll be found."

Pam stopped pacing. As if she didn't want Charlie to hear, she mouthed, "Tell Butch to do what needs to be done fast. I don't want him doing anything..." she sought the right word, "unnecessary to that girl. Do you hear me?"

"Yes Mum."

She turned to ascend the steps. Butterfly felt a wrenching in her gut as Pam disappeared from sight with Charlie. There was a squeak of ill-oiled hinges as the basement door was opened and closed. Then Butterfly was alone with Neal. *Where the fuck are you, Karl?* she wondered. Wherever he was, there was no time to wait and hope. If she was going to act, she had to do so before Butch got here. She'd spotted a pair of heavy-looking pliers on the other table. If she could get her hands on them, maybe she could overpower Neal. It wasn't much of a chance, but it was all she had.

As she tensed in readiness to make a grab for the pliers, she heard a voice that seemed to reach out from some subconscious nightmare. "You can stop pretending," the deep voice said. "I know you're awake."

Butterfly's heart hammered against her ribs. She held herself still. Was this Butch? How had he got here so fast?

There was a gravelly chuckle. "If you don't open your eyes, I'll cut your eyelids off. You've got three seconds. One... two..."

Butterfly opened her eyes and, in that instant, she understood. The figure at the end of the table was Neal, but at the same time it wasn't Neal. A crooked, leering grin had twisted Neal's face out of shape. There was no nervousness in his eyes, only cruel amusement. His hair had been combed back into straight lines. He loomed over her, somehow seeming to have grown several inches.

"Butch." Butterfly's voice scraped out.

"At your service, madam," Butch said with a little flourish and half-bow.

"It was you who killed my family."

Butch's grin rose even higher. "Course it was me. You didn't think that little pussy, Neal, could have done that, did you? That clown's about as much use as a limp dick in a brothel." He let out a booming laugh at his joke and ran his tongue over his lips as if tasting something sweet. "I'll tell you this, my dick was anything but limp when I saw what your sister had under her t-shirt."

Butterfly's eyes gleamed with the desire to grab the pliers and smash Butch's skull like a boiled egg.

He chuckled again. "Hell hath no fury, eh? No need to feel left out, sweet cheeks. You were a bit young for my tastes back then, but you've done a lot of growing since in all the right places." He laid a sandpaper-rough hand on Butterfly's leg and ran it up to her inner thigh.

"Take your fucking hand off me." Butterfly's voice was like a knife being sharpened.

"I see you haven't changed in other ways. Still a fighter. Good, that's just how I like them."

Butch dug his powerful fingers into Butterfly's thigh. Wincing, she kicked out at his face. He dodged aside, bringing his fist down like a hammer against her chest. All the air whistled from her lungs. She flung up her hands as he raised his fist to hit her again.

Like a projector slide being changed, Butch's smile vanished and Neal's anxious, almost apologetic expression took its place. His voice jumping up several octaves, he said, "No Butch. I told Mum we wouldn't do this to her."

Butch's sneering smile returned. "What's wrong with having some fun?"

His face an assortment of tortured twitches, Neal shook his head. "Mum said just do what needs to be done and get rid of her."

"Your mum doesn't tell me what to do," scowled Butch. "No one does. Now keep your gob shut, unless you want me to leave and let you deal with her." There was a second of silence, then Butch added, "Yeah, that's what I thought." He jerked his chin at Butterfly. "Just because you're scared shitless of what's under her clothes."

"That's not true," Neal retorted, his cheeks reddening.

"Isn't it? Then prove it."

"I don't need to. I've been with women."

Butch let out another boom of laughter. "Oh yeah, what were their names? Wait, don't tell me. There was Flossie and Baa-bara—"

"Shut up!"

"Only if you do what you couldn't do back in '98."

"OK, I will!"

Neal grabbed at Butterfly. Gasping, she tried to push him away. He swatted her hands aside and ripped open her vest. His eyes expanded at the sight of breasts still swollen from having breast-fed Charlie for the first eight months of his life. Neal's hands trembled as he made to pull down her bra. Her nails flashed out, drawing four crimson streaks down his cheek. His fist thundered into the side of her head. Pain radiated inwards all the way to the deep place where the bullet was lodged. Butterfly's eyes rolled like a slot machine as she fought not to lose consciousness again.

"I... I'm sorry," stammered Neal.

"What are you apologising for?" growled his alter ego. "Stop messing around and show me you're finally a man."

Thick fingers fumbled at Butterfly's belt. She tried to roll off the table, but shovel-sized hands pinned her in place. "Stop!" she cried as her jeans were yanked down around her knees.

As if doing as he was told, Neal stopped just as his fingers were finding their way into her underpants. "Oh no." His voice thickened. His eyes squeezed together. "No, no, no." He pressed his hands to his groin, a shudder running through him. The flush on his cheeks deepened to a blazing red.

Thunderous laughter burst from him as Butch took control. "I knew it! I knew you'd blow your wad before you could get your cock out, just like last time. Now stand back, little boy, and let me show you how a real man does it."

He clambered onto the table, prising Butterfly's legs apart with one hand. His other hand clamped onto her throat, squeezing hard enough to make her bladder spasm and try to release its contents. "You won't escape this time," he bellowed, his face so swollen with blood and hate as to be almost unrecognisable.

Do something, Butterfly's mind screamed. She futilely attempted to pry Butch's hand off her throat. *His eyes! Go for his eyes!* She stabbed her fingers at the huge black pools of his eyes, forcing him to abandon trying to tear off her underpants. Seizing hold of her fingers, he bent them back so forcefully that there was a crunch of snapping bones. A hoarse scream pushed its way up her constricted windpipe. She bucked and twisted, seeking to drive her knees into his groin. He lay on her like a concrete blanket, crushing the last precious gasps of oxygen from her. She could feel his erection prodding her thigh. His hand returned to her underwear, but he snatched it away again as she released a hot gush of urine.

"You dirty bitch!" he roared, locking both hands onto her throat.

He's right, Butterfly thought. *This time you're not going to escape.* As she felt herself inexorably slipping back into unconsciousness, one thought comforted her – Charlie would live. She was thankful that she could die knowing that. In some ways maybe her dying was the best thing that could happen. Charlie wouldn't remember any of this. He would grow up unencumbered by her emotional baggage. He would be whoever he wanted to be.

She felt the fear flowing out of her. Her arms dropped limply to her sides. She stared up at Butch, her eyes as calm as his were maniacal. The pain in her throat and lungs was as hot as a blowtorch, but it wouldn't last much longer. Soon she would feel no more and know no more.

Goodbye Charlie, goodbye my beautiful little boy, she thought as blackness descended over her. But then the pressure on her windpipe was slackening and a great gulp of air was rushing into her lungs. The face looming over her washed back into focus. Only it wasn't Butch's face. Nor was it Neal's. This face was open-mouthed and wide-eyed with concern.

"Oh thank god. I thought you were dead." The voice was comically high-pitched. It abruptly dropped to a rumble of fury. "Wendy, you bitch!" Then it jumped back up again. "You leave her alone, you evil brute."

Just how many other personalities does this schizo have? wondered Butterfly, heaving in more oxygen as Wendy climbed off her. Her thoughts returned to the Peter Pan poster in Neal's bedroom. Was that where Wendy came from?

Wendy's gaze darted around the basement as if she expected someone to pounce from the shadows. "Quick." She tugged at Butterfly's hand. "You have to get out of here before he comes back."

Butterfly managed to lift herself a few trembling centimetres before collapsing back against the table. Her limbs felt as if they'd been pumped full of cement.

Wendy's face spasmed. She clenched her teeth as if battling terrible pain. "I can't hold him—"

She broke off as Butch burst to the surface. "You already ruined his life once," he scowled. "I won't let you do it again, you little bitch."

Wendy fought her way back into view. "You're the one who ruined his life, not me. Neal hates you. He wants you to go away and never come back."

"Go away and never come back?" Butch's laughter bounced off the walls. "That big sissy wouldn't last five minutes without me."

"He's not a sissy."

"Yes he is."

"Not."

"Is!"

"Not!"

Neal was flicking back and forth between alter egos so fast that Butterfly couldn't tell which was which. He clutched his hands to his head as if to stop it from splitting apart. He staggered against the adjacent table, scattering bundles of wire and twine.

"Bitch," roared Butch.

"Monster," retorted Wendy. "I'll kill you before I ever let you hurt anyone again." She grabbed the pliers and made as if to bash Neal's head in with them.

"Hey!" put in a voice that belonged to neither Wendy nor Butch.

The sound of it gave Butterfly the strength to lift her head. She gave a sob of relief. Karl was descending the stairs. Blood glistened on his face. There was blood on his leg too where the barbed wire had torn his jeans and the flesh beneath.

"Move away from her." Karl motioned with the Glock.

Neal stepped away from Butterfly. The nervous expression was back. "Where's my Mum?"

"I'm the one asking the questions. You've got about ten seconds to tell me what's going on here before I paint the walls with your brains."

"No," croaked Butterfly. "Don't shoot him."

She looked at Neal, her eyes reflecting his uncertainty. She didn't know what to feel. Should she hate him? Pity him? All she knew for sure was that he had to live. And not only because he had to face justice, but because they might need him to leverage Charlie away from Pam.

Her gaze returned to Karl. "His mum's got Charlie."

"Then let's go get–"

Karl broke off as, with surprising speed for a big man, Neal flung the pliers at him. Karl swayed sideways like a boxer slipping a jab. The pliers glanced off his shoulder and clattered against the wall behind him. It was enough to give Neal the chance to leap towards Butterfly and coil his muscular arms around her. She groaned as he bear-hugged her.

Karl levelled the Glock at him again. "Put her down or you're a dead man." His voice was icy, but there was a shimmer of fear in his eyes.

Wendy's shrill voice piped from Neal's mouth. "Do as he says!"

"No, don't," interjected Butch. "He won't risk shooting." A taunting grin spread over his face. "He luuurves her."

Karl's face creased in confusion. "What the fuck is this?"

"Wendy." Butterfly's voice grated out as Butch's arms compressed her ribs. "He's hurting me. Please tell him to stop."

"Stop!" demanded Wendy. "Stop hurting her."

Butch laughed. "I'll do more than hurt her if this pretty boy doesn't put down his gun."

Butterfly groaned again as the pressure intensified.

"OK, OK," said Karl, stooping to place the Glock on the floor. He kicked the pistol underneath the freezer.

At the same instant, Butch tossed Butterfly aside and charged at Karl. Butterfly thudded into a wall and crumpled like a doll to the floor. As Butch bore down on him, Karl's hand darted into his pocket and emerged with his knife. In a single fluid motion, he flicked it open and deftly sidestepped Butch. The three-inch blade darted out. Butch grunted as it sank into his stomach just below his ribs. He threw a looping punch that would have taken Karl's head off if he hadn't bobbed under it. The blade flashed towards Butch again, slicing shallowly across his neck. With a bellow of pain and fury, Butch made a grab for Karl. The smaller man danced out of Butch's reach.

The combatants faced each other for a heartbeat. Butch's barrel chest was heaving. His eyes were ablaze with murderous rage.

"The bigger they are..." taunted Karl, grinning wolfishly.

Butch touched a hand to the blood blotting his shirt. The flames in his eyes leapt higher. Fists flexing convulsively, he charged again. Karl thrust the knife at his chest. Butch shoved out a hand. The blade pierced his palm, the bloody point emerging between the fine bones on the back of his hand. Instead of snatching his hand away from the knife, Butch closed his fist around it. A look of savage triumph spread over Butch's face as Karl futilely tried to yank the blade free. With his other hand, Butch threw a thundering punch. Karl slipped away from it. Another punch skimmed past Karl, and another, and another. The men reeled around the basement, neither relinquishing their grip on the knife.

Butch's fist clipped Karl's forehead. It was only a glancing blow, but it was sufficient to open a gash above Karl's eyebrow. His eyes expanding as if he couldn't believe how powerful the punch was, Karl lurched sideways with fresh blood streaming down his face. He managed to keep hold of the knife's handle, but only for a second. Another punch connected, crushing his nose, sending him sprawling against the freezer. Blood spattered the flagstones as Karl thrust a hand under the freezer and groped about for the Glock.

As if it was nothing more than a thorn, Butch pulled the knife out of his palm and flung it aside. He grabbed Karl's legs, dragged him into the centre of the room and rolled him over. Karl's fist lashed Butch's face. Butch grinned as if Karl had caressed his cheek. He unleashed a barrage of hammer fists that mashed up Karl's lips and mangled his cheekbones.

As Butterfly watched Butch pulverising Karl, she felt something she'd never expected to feel – a surge of protectiveness towards her ex-lover. She dragged her jeans up over her thighs and fought her way upright. There was a bundle of sticks that had been sharpened ready to be thrust into the earth. Grabbing a stick with her good hand, she staggered towards Butch. With every scrap of strength she had, she drove it into Butch's back. Bellowing like a castrated bull, he jerked an elbow into her midriff. She doubled over with air whistling between her teeth.

Butch reached back to yank the stick loose before grabbing Butterfly's throat once again. As his fingers closed over her windpipe, she cried out, "Wendy! Help me, Wendy!"

The words got through. The fingers uncurled. Wendy's high-pitched voice rang out, "Run, Tracy. Run!"

Butterfly's gaze moved to Karl. Blood was bubbling between his pulped lips, but he was conscious. When she reached for him, he caught hold of her hand and used it to haul himself onto his knees. She hooked an arm under his armpit and pulled him towards the stairs.

"My gun," he burbled through broken teeth.

"Forget your gun."

Leaning into each other like drunken old friends, Butterfly and Karl clambered up the stairs. Butch's voice boomed out behind them, "You little bitch, they're getting away."

"Good," Wendy shot back. "Serves you right."

"Neal," roared Butch. "You big sissy, you mummy's boy. Are you going to let her do this?"

Neal's trembling, aggrieved voice joined the party. "I'm not a mummy's boy."

"Then stop them. Kill them!"

Butterfly and Karl glanced back as a loud crash echoed around the basement. Neal had upended the freezer and was bending to retrieve the Glock. As fast as their unsteady legs would allow, they climbed the final few steps, shoved open the basement door and fell into the hallway. Butterfly kicked the door shut and looked around for something to wedge against it. Her eyes stopped dead on the kitchen. Her breath stopped on her lips. For a second, everything seemed to stop.

CHAPTER 26

The collie scrabbled at the backdoor, whining to be let in. Jack tried the handle. The door was locked. He peered through an adjacent window into a kitchen. Pans were bubbling on a Rayburn and the table was set for a meal, but there was no one to be seen. Another high-pitched cry rang out from inside the house, louder now. Jack's eyebrows dipped into a troubled V. There was a baby in the house. Of that he was sure. The question was – whose baby was it? Neal was a loner with severe mental health issues and Pam was in her sixties with a chronically depressed husband. It was a sure bet that the baby wasn't theirs.

Jack pressed his ear to the window. There was something heart-wrenchingly familiar about the cry. It reminded him of one that had woken him up countless times over the past ten months. Could it be Charlie? Had Butterfly and Karl somehow come to entertain the same suspicions as himself? His eyes flitted around the farmyard. Butterfly's car was nowhere to be seen.

His frown intensified as the crying turned up a notch. If it *was* Charlie, he sounded distressed.

Jack warily made his way around the side of the house. He found what he was looking for – an open ground-floor window. As he peeked into a living-room, the crying stopped. The sudden silence only heightened his anxiety. Had someone tended to the baby's needs? Or...

He didn't allow his thoughts to travel any further down that line. He couldn't permit fear to take control. He needed to stay focused.

Hooking a leg over the windowsill, he manoeuvred himself through the window. Quickly and quietly, he lowered himself to the flagstone floor and padded past a sofa with a steaming mug on its arm. The scent of roasting meat filled his nostrils as he stepped into a hallway.

He came to an abrupt halt at a muffled roar of unmistakable anger and pain. The sound had come from beneath the floor. His gaze moved to a closed door. Did it lead to a basement? Another roar rang out. It sounded like there was an enraged bull on the rampage down there.

His heart gave a sickening lurch as an image sprang into his mind of Neal pummelling Butterfly with his ham-sized fists. Forgetting his caution, he darted towards the door. He stopped again as a familiar, heavily accented female voice demanded to know, "What the hell are you doing in my house?"

Jack jerked towards the stairs. Pam Bray was standing halfway down them, clasping a bundle of blankets to her chest. Her dark eyes were wide with indignant surprise.

"I heard someone shouting."

"That was Neal."

"Why was he shouting?"

"We had an argument."

Another bellow shivered the closed door. "He sounds in pain," said Jack.

"He gets like that when we argue. That's why he goes down to the basement. Not that it's any of your bloody business. You've no right to be in here."

"I'd like to talk to him."

"Well you can't. And if you don't leave right away, I'll have you done for breaking into my house." Pam advanced down the stairs. Thrusting out a hand calloused by years of caring for a farm and a family, she ushered Jack into the kitchen.

"I heard a baby crying."

"I'm looking after my granddaughter."

Jack turned to look Pam in the eyes. "I've just come from your daughter's house. Annabelle was there."

"Did I say my granddaughter?" she shot back quick as a flash. "I meant my niece."

Jack held her gaze, his eyes steady and probing. "You're lying."

Pam didn't blink, but pale blotches appeared on her cheeks. "I don't care if you think I'm lying." She pointed to the backdoor. "I want you out of my house."

The bundle of blankets in her arms stirred. A little hand emerged from the folds of material. A tiny, tremulous voice followed it. "M…m…"

Jack would have known that voice anywhere. "Charlie!" he gasped, reaching for the bundle.

Pam backed away, bumping up against the work surface. She snatched up a vegetable knife from a chopping board and thrust the blade out in front of her.

Jack's eyes darted between the knife and the blankets. Could he disarm Pam before she had a chance to hurt Charlie? Possibly, but he couldn't take the risk. There would soon be a unit of AFOs less than a mile away. They could be at the farmhouse within minutes. Surely Pam and Neal would realise the futility of their situation once the farmhouse was surrounded by armed police.

Jack put up his hands. "There's no need for the knife. I'm leaving."

"It's too late for that." Pam's voice quavered between anger and tears. "Why did you have to come here? Why can't you all just leave us alone?"

She flinched at a floor-shuddering bang from the basement. An instant later, two figures fell into view in the hallway.

Karl looked like he'd done twelve rounds with Mike Tyson. One of his eyes was swollen shut. Blood oozed from his caved-in nose and deep cuts on his eyebrows and lips. If it hadn't been for the butterfly tattoo, Jack would have struggled to recognise him.

Butterfly looked to be in better shape, although her face was as pale as milk. She kicked out and there was the sound of a door slamming shut. Her eyes darted around, passing over Jack before coming to rest on Pam.

Hope and fear mingled in her eyes as she clambered to her feet. Karl staggered groggily after her as she hastened into the kitchen.

Pam's panicked eyes danced between the newcomers and Jack.

"Charlie." Butterfly said the name in a choked whisper.

At his mum's voice, Charlie pushed at the blankets again and they fell away from his rosy-cheeked face.

"Stay back," exclaimed Pam, the knife shaking so hard that it looked like she was on the verge of having some sort of fit. "What have you done to Neal?"

As if in answer, the basement door slammed open and a hulking figure stepped into view. Pam gave out a low cry at the sight of the blood on her son's shirt, neck and hands. Neal's chest was heaving as if he'd run a marathon. His dark hair was plastered to his forehead with sweat. His eyes flitted from Jack to Butterfly and Karl. The pistol in his hand followed suit as if he was uncertain who to aim it at.

"Easy Neal," said Jack. "Don't do anything foolish. Armed police are on their way."

"You're lying," countered Pam. "You wouldn't have broken in here if other police were on their way."

Jack's eyes appealed for her to come to her senses. "Eric Ramsden knows I'm here. When I don't report in, he'll come looking for me. Listen to me, Pam. It's over."

"It's over." She repeated his words slowly as if struggling to make sense of them. A sudden look of comprehension flooded her face. "He's right, Neal." Her voice was full of sadness, but also agonisingly deep relief. "It's over. It's finally over."

She lowered the knife and held out Charlie. Butterfly moved swiftly to take him. She hugged him to her chest, eyeing Neal warily.

"Now you, Neal," said Jack. "Put down the gun."

Neal looked at his mum as if seeking guidance. She nodded, saying softly, "Put it down, son."

He heaved a great shuddering breath. His hand started to drop, but then his face twitched and contorted like a rubber mask. His lips stretched into a maniacal grin. His eyes bulged as if something was pushing from behind them.

"It's not over until that bitch is dead," exploded Butch, jerking the Glock towards Butterfly.

She pivoted around to shield Charlie with her body. The ear-splitting retort of the gun reverberated around the kitchen. She tensed, expecting to feel a bullet tearing through her flesh and bone. But there was nothing. No punch of impact. No pain. Just the zingy metallic odour of gunpowder. Turning, she saw that Karl was standing between her and Butch. A rose of blood was flowering where the bullet had penetrated Karl's chest. He looked at her, wide-eyed. They held each other's gaze for a heartbeat, then his knees buckled.

As Karl collapsed, Jack ran at Butch. Grabbing the gun with one hand and Butch's wrist with the other, he pushed downwards and twisted. Butch grimaced as his trigger finger was bent backwards. He brought his fist down on the top of Jack's head as if trying to hammer him into the floor. The blow sent a jolt of pain along Jack's spine. He twisted the gun further, forcing Butch to let go to prevent his finger from being broken.

Butch shoved Jack aside and ran for the door. He'd pulled the bolt and was out of the door before Jack could regain his balance.

"Neal!" cried Pam, running after him.

Jack looked to make sure Butterfly and Charlie were OK. Butterfly was staring at Karl over Charlie's shoulder. There were tears in her eyes. The reservoir of blood pooling on Karl's chest suggested the bullet had hit one of the major arteries that flanked his spine. If that was the case, he didn't have long left. He stretched a hand up towards Butterfly, mouthing, "I... I..."

"I know you love me," she mouthed back, taking his hand.

Karl shook his head. His face contorting with the effort, he forced out his words in a rasp. "I killed Beech and Sutton." His eyes rolled towards Jack. "Do you hear?"

Jack nodded.

A choking sob that was as much sorrow as relief rose up Butterfly's throat. She summoned a sad smile for Karl. "Thank you."

Jack gave her his phone. "Call an ambulance and put pressure on the wound."

As Butterfly grabbed a tea towel, Jack pocketed the Glock and went after Pam and Neal.

Neal was already out of sight. Pam was running arthritically towards the lane. Jack caught her up easily. "Stop," he ordered her.

He didn't wait around to see if she obeyed. Catching sight of Neal fifty or sixty metres up ahead, he increased his speed.

Neal was lumbering along like a wounded grizzly with his arms dangling at his sides. Glancing over his shoulder, he called to Jack in a singsong voice, "Run, run as fast as you can. You can't catch me I'm the gingerbread man!"

His tree-trunk legs ate up the ground, increasing the distance between the two men. Jack knew it wouldn't last long. Neal had been gasping for breath even before he ran out of the house. His heavy muscles would rapidly fill with lactic acid and begin to feel like lead weights.

Where the farm track met the lane that branched off Wasdale Road, Neal turned right. When Jack reached the T-junction, Neal was nowhere to be seen. Peering over the hedges to either side, he spotted him in the field that sloped down towards the trees bordering the River Bleng. As Jack ducked through a hole in the hedge, Neal's voice drifted back to him again, "I've run away from a little old woman and a little old man and I can run away from you, I can!"

Jack sprinted down the slope, taking care not to trip over the numerous mole hills dotting the field. Neal was clutching his blood-soaked side. Even going downhill, his speed had noticeably slowed. Centimetre by centimetre, Jack was gaining on him.

Coming to another hedge, Neal threw up his hands and burst through it. The foliage sprang back upright and Jack lost sight of him again. Jack made for a gap in the hedge a few metres off to the left. A strange childlike laugh came from beyond the hedge. Jack jumped through the gap and saw that Neal had extended his lead once more.

Jack began to reel the metres back in. Neal was running with an increasingly pronounced stagger. Several times, he stumbled and almost fell. By the time he reached the trees, he was only ten or fifteen metres ahead of Jack. Neal weaved through the trees, thrusting aside low-hanging branches. Sunlight sparkled on water up ahead.

"The gingerbread man came to a river," Neal called out breathlessly. "'Oh no!' he cried because he couldn't swim."

Now I've got you, thought Jack. Despite their size difference, he was confident that this time he would be able to restrain Neal. The bigger man looked almost out on his feet. His head was drooping and he sounded as if there was barely any breath left in his lungs.

The trees opened up and the river came into full view. A grassy bank shelved towards a pebbly shoreline. The channel of sun-splashed water was only about ten metres wide. As Neal ran down the bank, Jack wondered whether it was shallow enough to wade across. Calling on his muscles to give an extra ounce of speed, he dived to tackle Neal around the waist.

Neal stumbled but didn't go down. He twisted to clamp his hands onto Jack's head. Jack realised that he'd badly miscalculated. An insane strength pulsed through Neal's hands. The pressure on Jack's skull was so intense

228

that he feared his head would be crushed like a melon in a vice. His fingers sought the wound in Neal's side and pressed into the warm, sticky laceration. Grimacing, Neal thrust Jack to the ground.

Neal turned to wade into the water. It was deceptively deep. Within a few paces, it was up to his thighs. "Oh dear, I'm a quarter gone," he said in that same chanting voice. Another couple of steps and the water was past his waist. "Oh I'm half gone." The water rose to his shoulders. "I'm three-quarters gone." Gurgling as the water filled his mouth, Neal exclaimed, "I'm all gone!"

As the water closed over Neal's head, Jack scrambled to his feet and plunged into the river. It shelved steeply beneath his feet, cold enough to snatch his breath away. Struggling to get enough oxygen into his lungs, he ducked under the surface. A vague shape was visible through the dark water a metre or two down. Jack dove towards it, stretching out a hand. He caught hold of Neal's arm and attempted to pull him upwards. Neal prised his hand away. Jack returned to the surface, sucked in air and dove again. This time, Neal grabbed Jack and pulled him so close that their eyes were centimetres apart. He held Jack there for a moment, then shoved him away. Jack broke the surface with a gasp. He didn't dive again. He'd read the warning in Neal's tortured eyes – *Leave me alone, unless you want to die with me.*

Jack waded to the shore and dropped panting to the smooth pebbles. He watched the water. A few bubbles burst on the surface above Neal, then there was nothing. The river flowed on. He heaved a sigh.

"Jack!"

He turned at the familiar voice. Eric was running through the trees accompanied by officers sporting semi-automatic rifles.

"We saw you coming down the hill," said Eric. "Where's Neal?"

Jack pointed towards the river. "In there."

Eric's eyebrows lifted. "Bloody hell. How long's he been under?"

"Too long."

"Are you sure?"

Jack nodded. "I tried to pull him out but..." He trailed off into another heavy sigh.

"Where are his mother and father?"

"Back at the farm, along with Butterfly, Charlie and Karl."

"Bloody hell," Eric exclaimed again. "We found Phil Beech, shot dead."

Nodding as if he'd expected to hear as much, Jack handed Eric the Glock. "I took that from Neal after he put a bullet in Karl."

Jack's words prompted a third, "Bloody hell," from Eric. "I'd better call an ambulance."

"Butterfly's already called for one. Not that it'll do much good."

As Jack rose to his feet, Eric suggested, "We'll head up to the farm in my car."

They made their way along the riverbank, emerging from the trees at a lane that had already been cordoned off by police tape in readiness for scene of the crime officers.

Eric's Landrover was parked on the wooden bridge. They set off in it, followed by the AFOs in a BMW with red 'armed response vehicle' stars in the windows.

They found Pam at the farmyard gate holding her head in her hands as if she already knew Neal's fate. She said nothing, avoiding eye contact as Eric cuffed her wrists.

The AFOs went into the house, shouting, "Armed police!"

They re-emerged with Butterfly and Charlie. Jack didn't need to ask about Karl's condition. Butterfly's grim face said it all. She hurried across to him. He enveloped her and Charlie in a hug, kissing them. "Oh Jack, I..." Butterfly trailed off as if she didn't know what to say.

"It's OK," he said softly.

"I didn't know if I'd ever see you again."

He smiled. "You won't get away from me that easily."

"I don't ever want to be away from…" Butterfly's voice faltered. "I don't ever want…" she repeated, wrinkling her forehead as if her mind had suddenly gone blank. She swayed on her feet.

Jack caught her. "What's wrong?"

Butterfly didn't hear him. The drum was beating in her head like a panicked heart. She felt as if she was on a roundabout, spinning faster and faster. The world was blurring. As her body went limp, she pushed Charlie into Jack's arms and slipped through his hands like cooked spaghetti.

"Butterfly," he exclaimed as her eyes rolled back in their sockets.

She tried to speak, but all that came out was a garbled, "Tfggn ohfg Chgliee." She felt a stab of frustration. *Take care of Charlie.* That was all she wanted to say. Why wouldn't the words come?

The world wobbled back into focus. Jack was looking away from her, his mouth opening and closing frantically. Charlie was staring at her with his big blue-grey eyes. He looked as placid as a Buddha. She held onto his gaze with everything she had, but it wasn't enough. The drumming swept her up and carried her away to some unremembered place.

CHAPTER 27

She could hear voices, but they were so faint she couldn't make out what they were saying. Like a fish swimming against a strong current, she edged towards the voices. Slowly, ever so slowly, they grew loud enough that she could identify an occasional word – *well... expected... how...longer... not...*

She clung to the words, using them to pull herself forwards fraction by fraction. She could see a light now, as if she was approaching the end of a tunnel. The light was growing brighter. Suddenly she found herself squinting up into a man's face. He had worried brown eyes. He was wearing a baggy sweatshirt and tracksuit bottoms. At his side was a bespectacled, suited man whose expression was both concerned and curious. They were in a white room of humming, beeping machines.

"Welcome back," said the bespectacled man. "How are you feeling?"

"How am I feeling?" she murmured, forming each word tentatively like someone testing out a new language.

"Any pain?"

She replied with the slightest shake of her head. Her body felt warm and floaty.

The other man took her hand in his. His fingers were clammy. "Butterfly," he said, his voice edged with anxiety and hope.

"Butterfly," she echoed. Then, as if the word had pierced a membrane in her mind, it all came rushing back. A small smile found its way onto her lips. "Hi Jack."

Heaving a breath of relief, Jack broke into a smile too.

"Where am I?" asked Butterfly.

"Cumberland Infirmary in Carlisle," the bespectacled man informed her.

Butterfly's bleary gaze shifted to him. "Hello Doctor Summers."

"So you remember our names. That's very good," said the doctor. "What else do you remember?"

Butterfly's eyebrows pinched together as an image of Karl's lifeless face flashed through her mind. For a moment, she couldn't bring herself to speak. Then she asked, "Where's Charlie?"

"He's with Laura and Naomi," said Jack.

"I want to see him."

"You will do soon," said Doctor Summers. "Right now you need to rest. You've been through a long operation."

"The bullet," Butterfly murmured with sudden realisation. Trembling with the effort, she lifted a hand to her bandaged head.

"We removed it."

Her eyes danced between the doctor and Jack as if she couldn't believe her ears. "It's out?"

"That's right," smiled Jack.

She released a shuddering breath. *It's out!* her mind exclaimed. *And you're still here. You're still Butterfly.* She wasn't sure whether to laugh, cry or do both.

Jack's smiled wavered. As if he could hardly bring himself to say it, he began hesitantly, "Karl said he killed Sutton and Beech. That's right, isn't it? He killed them both?"

Butterfly's gaze drifted off, a cleft forming between her eyebrows again. Had Karl killed Sutton or had he said he did to protect her?

"I'm not sure you should be asking those types of questions now," said Doctor Summers.

"You're right. I'm sorry." Jack's gaze sought out Butterfly's. "And anyway, I already know the answer."

Her haunted eyes met his. "Do you?"

Recovering his smile, he nodded. "Now close your eyes. Get some sleep. I'll be here when you wake up."

"You promise?"

Jack gently squeezed her hand. "I promise."

With a shudder, Butterfly allowed her eyelids to slide down. Another image flashed into her mind. She saw herself standing over a lifeless body as fat as an old pig. She was holding the Glock. A bullet had already torn away part of Dale's skull, splattering chunks of bone and brain over the rug. But that didn't stop her from pulling the trigger again and again and again, until his babyishly smooth face had been all but obliterated. As the echo of the final bullet faded away, she stared at him with cold nothing in her eyes.

CHAPTER 28

Jack lifted Charlie out of his car seat. Butterfly was still too unsteady on her feet to carry him. The operation had played havoc with her balance. The tablets Doctor Summers had prescribed only partially alleviated the dizziness that washed over her every time she stood up. She adjusted her bobble hat in the mirror before getting out of the car. It was an unseasonably warm September day, but her hair had not yet grown back enough to conceal the curving Frankenstein scar on the lower left side of her skull. Not that she felt particularly self-conscious about the scar. Much like with the tattoo, it was simply easier not to have to answer the questions it prompted.

With Charlie nestled in the crook of his arm, Jack took hold of Butterfly's uninjured hand. The fingers Butch had broken were still bandaged and splinted. "We can't stay long," he reminded her.

They had an appointment at Greater Manchester Police Headquarters that afternoon. Ostensibly it was to go over Butterfly's statement, but Jack had been given a heads up as to the real reason. Despite having Sutton's blood on her clothes, her fingerprints being on the Glock and a gunpowder residue test showing she'd been within close proximity of the pistol when it was discharged, Butterfly was to be officially informed that no charges would be laid against her. Jack had heard Karl's dying confession. The ligature marks where Karl had tied Butterfly's wrists and ankles confirmed that she'd been with him under duress. Beech's bloody fingerprints had been found on Karl's throat. Footprints with tread patterns matching Karl's trainers had been found at the edge of the pond where Sutton's corpse was dumped. All of it added together was seemingly enough to put Butterfly in the clear.

Jack pressed a buzzer, and a nurse came to the door. "How is she today?" Butterfly asked as they signed-in.

"Same as usual," answered the nurse.

Same as usual. In other words, away with the fairies. Butterfly sighed.

"It'll brighten her up seeing Charlie," Jack tried to reassure her.

She pursed her lips doubtfully, recalling her previous visit. She stopped outside her grandma's room and said to Jack, "Do you mind if I talk to her alone for a moment?"

"Of course not," he said, looking askance at her.

Without replying to the question in his eyes, she went into the room. Shirley was laid in bed, staring off into space. Butterfly searched her face. It was like looking at a blank page. She rested a hand on her grandma's spindly arm. "Hello Grandma, it's me."

It's me. It was such a vague way to identify herself, but there seemed little point saying, *It's Butterfly,* when Shirley would have known her as Tracy. Removing the bullet hadn't brought Tracy back. Or Io. Those parts of her remained cloaked in darkness.

Not that it would have made any difference if she'd called herself Tracy. Shirley continued to stare obliviously at the ceiling.

Butterfly stooped closer, so close that Shirley's frizzy grey hair tickled her eyes. "We got him, Grandma," she whispered into Shirley's ear. "The man who murdered Mum, Dad and Charlie is dead."

She drew back to look in Shirley's eyes. Nothing. Not even the faintest flicker of awareness. Tears threatened to fill Butterfly's eyes. She fought them back, remonstrating with herself, *What did you expect? You're about ten years too late.*

Before turning to leave, she kissed her grandma's forehead and murmured, "I'm sorry."

"What's going on?" asked Jack, catching hold of Butterfly's hand as she passed him.

"I'm sorry," she apologised again. "You were right. We shouldn't have come here today."

Jack gave her a look that suggested he understood completely why she'd needed to make the trip.

"I still don't know whether to hate or pity Neal," she said.

"You don't need to feel anything for him anymore. He can't ever harm you again."

Charlie stretched his hands towards her, mumbling, "M...m..."

As always, Butterfly found a smile for him. Keeping a tight hold of her hand, Jack headed for the car.

As they left behind Rochdale, Butterfly stared silently out of the window. A short while later they were passing through the outskirts of Manchester. She drew in an apprehensive breath when the glass and concrete box of GMP HQ came into view.

"Remember what we discussed," said Jack. "Keep it simple."

Butterfly nodded. They'd been over and over what she should say, especially where Dale Sutton was concerned. "When I passed out, Dale was still alive. And when I regained consciousness, I was back in the car."

"And that's *all* you need to say."

Butterfly turned to Jack, her eyes tormented with the question – *Is it?* "I had the dream again last night. Karl was trying to make me shoot Dale. That sound, that drum was banging in my head. I fell to the floor and everything went black. But this time I regained consciousness in the bungalow and said to Karl, 'Give me the gun.'" Her voice quickened. "And he gave me it and I pointed it at Dale's head and–"

"You've got to stop this, Butterfly," cut in Jack. "It was only a dream."

"But what if it's not just a dream?"

"It is. So stop torturing yourself. Do you hear?" When Butterfly didn't reply, he repeated, "Do you hear?"

She gave a little nod, tentatively lifting a hand to her forehead as if afraid of what she might find. "It's strange, even though the bullet's gone, I can still feel it in there sometimes. I can feel Tracy and Io too, even though I can't remember them."

"Doctor Summers said that if your memory hasn't returned by now, it most likely never will."

"I don't care what he says. They're in there."

A barrier lifted and Jack pulled into the carpark. "We shouldn't be talking about this. Let's just concentrate on getting through the next hour. OK?"

"M...m...m..." Charlie chirped up.

Butterfly glanced at him. She gave another more determined nod. "When I passed out, Dale was still alive. And when I regained consciousness, I was back in the car," she repeated. "Karl told me he'd shot Dale. I tried to run away with Charlie. That's when he tied me up..." she trailed off with a shake of her head.

"I know you hate lying, Butterfly, but ask yourself this – what would telling the truth achieve?" Jack stooped his head to catch her eyes. "Besides, Karl *did* shoot Sutton. All that crap about Io coming back was just him trying to manipulate you. The fact that you refused to shoot Beech proves what I'm saying." He cupped Butterfly's chin, angling it towards him. "You can do this. Tell them what they need to hear, then we can go home and get on with being a family. That's what you want, isn't it?"

"More than anything." For the first time, there was genuine conviction in Butterfly's voice. "But it's not just the lying. It's..." Once again, she faded off into a troubled silence.

"It's what? You think Io will come back and hurt someone? That's not going to happen, and I'll tell you why. Karl's gone. Neal's gone. There's no reason for Io to come back."

Karl's gone. The words sent a sharp little pain through Butterfly's heart. She glanced at herself in the wing mirror. The tattoo's colours somehow seemed to have lost their lustre since his death. "There's no reason for Io to come back," she echoed.

"That's right. Now come on, let's get this over with."

They got out of the car. Jack lifted Charlie from his seat. Pressing her nose to Charlie's head, Butterfly inhaled deeply as if seeking to draw strength from him.

They headed into the building. Jack nodded hello to his colleagues as they made their way along a corridor. They caught a lift up to the Serious Crime Division's floor.

They were met by Steve. An angry red indent above Steve's right eye lingered from his fight with Karl. "You're looking a lot better," he said to Butterfly.

She smiled. "No I'm not, but thanks anyway."

Steve broke into his usual cheeky-chappie grin as he turned to Charlie. "Bloody hell, Charlie boy, you get bigger every time I see you."

Butterfly felt another squeeze in her chest. *Charlie boy.* That was what Karl had called Charlie.

"No need to look so worried," Steve said to her. "This is just a formality. The DCI's waiting in interview room two."

They made their way to a claustrophobically windowless little room with a table and three chairs in it. The table was cluttered with recording equipment, case files and mugs of coffee. Two of the chairs were already occupied. Detective Chief Inspector Paul Gunn – a mid-forties man with grizzled hair and a face almost as crumpled as his suit – rose to shake Jack and Butterfly's hand. He introduced the other attendee – a late middle-aged woman with broad angular features that made Butterfly think of the Brays. "This is Detective Inspector Alice Hayton of Cumbria CID."

A frown tugged at Jack's eyebrows. "No one mentioned that a detective from Cumbria would be present."

"This is a joint investigation between Cumbria Constabulary and Greater Manchester Police. It's standard procedure. You know that, Detective

Anderson," pointed out Paul. "Now if we could get cracking. Time's ticking on."

Paul's impatience reassured Jack that there was nothing to worry about. Paul was fighting a constant battle against his workload. Like a hamster on a wheel, he only slowed down when something out of the ordinary caused him to stop and take a closer look. Nothing in his manner suggested that was the case.

Butterfly gave Jack a tense smile. "I'll see you soon."

"I'll be just outside if you need me." He put his hand on her arm for a moment as if to steady her, before stepping from the room.

Steve closed the door on his way out. Paul and Alice sat back down. Paul motioned for Butterfly to do likewise, saying, "I must inform you that we're being filmed." He pointed to the recording equipment. "We will also be making an audio recording of today's interview. My name is Detective Chief Inspector Paul Gunn." He motioned to Alice. "And this is Detective Inspector Alice Hayton. The time by my watch is three thirty PM, and the date is the twenty eighth of September 2018. The place is Greater Manchester Police Headquarters. For the purpose of this interview, could you please tell me your full name?"

"My name is Butterfly–"

"You legal name," interrupted Paul.

A faint frown touched Butterfly's forehead. She was still going through the process of changing her name by deed poll. A shiver ran down her spine, like someone had stepped on her grave, as she said, "My name is Tracy Ridley."

"And your date of birth?"

"Tenth of the fifth, 1986."

"And your home address?"

Butterfly gave her address and Paul continued, "Although you're attending this interview voluntarily and are not under caution, I'm still obliged to advise you of your rights."

He went through the same procedure as on the previous occasions Butterfly had been interviewed, advising her that she had the right to remain silent and that anything she said might be used against her in a court of law. Lastly, he handed her a document to sign declaring that 'I do not want a solicitor present at this time. My decision to answer questions without having a solicitor present is free and voluntary.'

"OK, Tracy, I'd like to talk to you about the events that occurred in Gosforth, Seascale and at Bray Farm on August twentieth 2018." Paul removed a sheath of papers from a folder and placed them in front of Butterfly. "This is a transcript of the statement you gave on the twenty second of August in Cumberland Infirmary. Could you please read it through and confirm that all the details are correct?"

Sweat prickled on Butterfly's palms as she read through the statement. It was all in there – Karl kidnapping her and Charlie, Phil Beech's death, Neal Bray's insanity. The only thing missing was Karl's claim that she – or rather Io – had shot Dale Sutton. Reliving that day made her feel angry, queasy, sad and other things she dare not allow herself to acknowledge in that room with two detectives staring at her. Upon coming to the end of the statement, she said in a low voice, "Yes, it's correct."

"Could you please speak clearly into the microphone?"

Forcing herself to meet Paul's gaze, Butterfly repeated, "It's correct."

"Are you positive about that?" Detective Hayton asked, watching Butterfly through spectacles that magnified her unblinking blue eyes.

"Yes, why do you ask?" Even as the words were leaving her mouth, Butterfly wanted to kick herself. Jack had told her time and again to say only what was absolutely necessary.

"Dale Sutton."

Butterfly's heart palpitated at the name. *Did they know something about his death that she didn't?* DI Hayton's next words seemed to suggest otherwise, "You say your ex-boyfriend, Karl Robinson, tried to force you to shoot Dale. Is that correct?"

"Yes."

"So the Glock was in your hand?"

"That's correct."

"Why didn't you turn it on Karl?"

"I couldn't. His hand was over mine." Butterfly recited the words Jack had drummed into her, "When I passed out, Dale was still alive. And when I regained consciousness, I was back in–"

"Mm-hmm," DI Hayton broke in. "Yes, that's what your statement says." With a seemingly casual motion, she flipped open a folder revealing a post-mortem photo of Dale's face. "And while you lay unconscious, your lover – sorry, ex-lover – put five bullets into Dale. Five," she repeated the number as if it held some special significance.

There was an extended silence. Butterfly was no longer looking DI Hayton. She was looking at the photo. It was the first time she'd seen it. Arrows and numbers indicated the entry wounds. One bullet had destroyed Dale's nose. Another had torn open his left cheek, exposing a row of uneven teeth. A third had left a gaping cavity in place of his right eye. A fourth and fifth had combined to shear off the upper left quarter of his skull. What little remained looked like a horribly disfigured waxwork.

Butterfly's clammy hands gripped the table as she leant closer to the photo. She wanted to look away, but her eyes were welded to Dale's face. It was as if someone had reached into her dream and pulled the grisly death mask from it.

It wasn't just a nightmare, she said to herself. *You did it. Oh Christ, oh god. You killed him!*

SHE IS GONE

"Five bullets," DI Hayton said again. "All to the face and head. Seems like overkill, don't you think?"

"I–" Butterfly's voice snagged in her throat.

"Are you OK?" asked Paul. "Would you like a glass of water?"

Before Butterfly could reply, DI Hayton pressed on, "One or two bullets would have been enough to do the job. But five... That suggests to me that Dale's killer was venting a deep-seated rage on him. I'm not sure Karl had that kind of emotional investment in his death."

Just tell the truth. Tell them you killed him.

Butterfly put a hand to her head. There was a strange shifting sensation inside her skull, a feeling of something worming its way up through the layers of mental soil. She winced as pressure built behind her forehead.

Paul threw his colleague a disapproving glance. "I wasn't aware that Detective Hayton intended to pursue this line of questioning. If you'd like to stop or take a–"

"Thank you but there's no need," Butterfly interrupted. Her voice was even and composed. Her eyes fell to the photo again. There was no flicker of emotion in them. She might have been looking at a picture in a clothing catalogue.

"Why do you think Karl felt the need to put five bullets in Dale?" asked DI Hayton.

"Because he loved me," Butterfly stated simply, meeting the detective's eyes.

They held each other's gaze for a moment. Then, nodding as if satisfied by the answer, DI Hayton flipped the folder shut.

The rest of the interview went smoothly. DI Hayton asked a few questions about Phil Beech's death that Butterfly answered without hesitation. Paul wrapped the interview up by asking Butterfly if she had anything she wanted to say.

"No," she replied.

99

"And do you have any complaints about the way you've been treated today?"

"No."

"OK. The time is four fifteen PM. This is Detective Chief Inspector Paul Gunn."

Paul switched off the recording equipment. "I'd like to apologise. There was no need for you to see that photo."

"Please accept my apologies too. I didn't mean to upset you," DI Hayton said disingenuously. With a shake of her head, she glanced at the folder containing Dale's photo. "The things we do for love, eh?"

She stared at Butterfly as if waiting for a reply. *Not one more word than necessary.* Butterfly's internal voice was cold and calm now. Her face as unreadable as her grandma's, she turned her back on DI Hayton and left the room.

Jack hurried to her with Charlie in his arms. "How did it go?"

"Fine."

He frowned as if he was unsure what to make of her flat response.

"M...m..." Charlie burbled, wriggling to get to Butterfly. She looked at him, blank-faced.

"Are you sure?" asked Jack.

"Why do you keep asking?"

"Well, it's just you don't..." He trailed off as if thinking better of finishing the sentence.

"Don't what?" There was a knowing glimmer in Butterfly's eyes. "Don't seem like myself?"

Jack's frown deepened. "What happened in there? Has something upset you?"

"You've seen it, haven't you?"

"Seen what?"

244

Leaning in as if to kiss Jack, Butterfly murmured, "The photo. Five bullets. You know I killed him."

His eyes darting towards the interview room, Jack took hold of Butterfly's arm and drew her along the corridor. His voice dropped. "I'll tell you what I know." He made a circular motion to Charlie, Butterfly and himself. "This is what matters. The rest of it... well it can go to hell along with Dale Sutton."

"You should have told me."

Jack blinked away from Butterfly. "Maybe but..." His eyes returned to hers. "I can't lose you, Butterfly."

They stared at each other, Jack's eyes intense with hope, Butterfly's strangely empty.

Charlie grabbed hold of her sleeve. Pressing his lips into a flat line, he suddenly said, "Mama."

Like a damn bursting, the expression flooded back into Butterfly's face. "Did you hear that?" she said, smiling in astonishment.

Jack's face mirrored hers. "I heard it."

Butterfly plucked Charlie from Jack's arms. "Say it again, Charlie. Say mama."

Charlie obligingly chanted, "Mama, Mama, Mama."

Butterfly laughed. "Well done, Charlie!"

Jack gave her an apologetic look. "You're right, I should have told you." He sighed. "I just want everything to be OK."

"You're not going to lose me, Jack." She leaned in and this time she kissed him before tenderly drawing his head onto her shoulder. She repeated DI Hayton's parting words under her breath. "The things we do for love."

"What did you say?"

"I said I love you." Butterfly took Jack's hand. "Let's go home and get on with being a family."

ABOUT THE AUTHOR

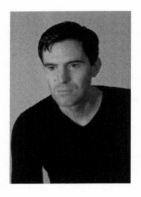

Ben is an award winning writer and Pushcart Prize nominee with a passion for gritty crime fiction. His short stories have been widely published in the UK, US and Australia. In 2011 he self-published Blood Guilt. The novel went on to reach no.2 in the national e-book download chart, selling well over 150000 copies. In 2012 it was picked up for publication by Head of Zeus. Since then, Head of Zeus has published three more of Ben's novels – Angel of Death, Justice for the Damned and Spider's Web. In 2016 his novel The Lost Ones was published by Thomas & Mercer.

Ben lives in Sheffield, England, where – when he's not chasing around after his son, Alex – he spends most of his time shut away in his study racking his brain for the next paragraph, the next sentence, the next word...

If you'd like to learn more about Ben or get in touch, you can do so at www.bencheetham.com

OTHER BOOKS BY THE AUTHOR

Now She's Dead

(Jack Anderson Book 1)

What happens when the watcher becomes the watched?

Jack has it all – a beautiful wife and daughter, a home, a career. Then his wife, Rebecca, plunges to her death from the Sussex coast cliffs. Was it an accident or did she jump? He moves to Manchester with his daughter, Naomi, to start afresh, but things don't go as planned. He didn't think life could get any worse...

Jack sees a woman in a window who is the image of Rebecca. Attraction turns into obsession as he returns to the window night after night. But he isn't the only one watching her...

Jack is about to be drawn into a deadly game. The woman lies dead. The latest victim in a series of savage murders. Someone is going to go down for the crimes. If Jack doesn't find out who the killer is, that 'someone' may well be him.

Who Is She?

(Jack Anderson Book 2)

A woman with no memory.
A question no one seems able to answer.

Her eyes pop open like someone surfacing from a nightmare. Shreds of moonlight glimmer through a woodland canopy. How did she get here? A thousand bells seem to be clanging in her ears. There is a strange, terrible smell. Both sweet and bitter. Like burnt meat. Her senses scream that something is very, very wrong. Then she sees it. A hole in the ground. Deep and rectangular. Like a grave...

After the death of his wife, Jack is starting to get his life back on track. But things are about to get complicated.

A woman lies in a hospital bed, clinging to life after being shot in the head. She remembers nothing, not even her own name. Who is she? That is the question Jack must answer. All he has to go on is a mysterious facial tattoo.

Damaged kindred spirits, Jack and the nameless woman quickly form a bond. But he can't afford to fall for someone who might put his family at risk. People are dying. Their deaths appear to be connected to the woman. What if she isn't really the victim? What if she's just as bad as the 'Unspeakable Monsters' who put her in hospital?

Don't Look Back

What really haunts Fenton House?

Adam's eyes swelled in horror at the sight that confronted him. Henry was standing with his back against the front door, pale and rigid, his left hand pressed to his neck. Blood was seeping between his fingers, running down his wrist and dripping from his elbow onto the back of Jacob's head. Jacob was facedown on the tiled floor, arms outstretched to either side with blood pooling around his wrists. There was a faintly metallic butcher's shop smell in the air...

After the tragic death of their eleven-year-old son, Adam and Ella are fighting to keep their family from falling apart. Then comes an opportunity that seems too good to be true. They win a competition to live for free in a breathtakingly beautiful mansion on the Cornish Lizard Peninsula. There's just one catch – the house is supposedly haunted.

Mystery has always swirled around Fenton House. In 1920 the house's original owner, reclusive industrialist Walter Lewarne, hanged himself from its highest turret. In 1996, the then inhabitants, George Trehearne, his wife Sofia and their young daughter Heloise disappeared without a trace. Neither mystery was ever solved.

Adam is not the type to believe in ghosts. As far as he's concerned, ghosts are simply memories. Everywhere he looks in their cramped London home he sees his dead son. Despite misgivings, the chance to start afresh is too tempting to pass up. Adam, Ella and their surviving son Henry move into Fenton House. At first, the change of scenery gives them all a new lease of life. But as the house starts to reveal its secrets, they come to suspect that they may not be alone after all…

The Lost Ones

The truth can be more dangerous than lies...

July 1972

The Ingham household. Upstairs, sisters Rachel and Mary are sleeping peacefully. Downstairs, blood is pooling around the shattered skull of their mother, Joanna, and a figure is creeping up behind their father, Elijah. A hammer comes crashing down again and again...

July 2016

The Jackson household. This is going to be the day when Tom Jackson's hard work finally pays off. He kisses his wife Amanda and their children, Jake and Erin, goodbye and heads out dreaming of a better life for them all. But just hours later he finds himself plunged into a nightmare...

Erin is missing. She was hiking with her mum in Harwood Forest. Amanda turned her back for a moment. That was all it took for Erin to vanish. Has she simply wandered off? Or does the blood-stained rock found where she was last seen point to something sinister? The police and volunteers who set out to search the sprawling forest are determined to find out. Meanwhile, Jake launches an investigation of his own – one that will expose past secrets and present betrayals.

Is Erin's disappearance somehow connected to the unsolved murders of Elijah and Joanna Ingham? Does it have something to do with the ragtag army of eco-warriors besieging Tom's controversial quarry development? Or is it related to the fraught phone call that distracted Amanda at the time of Erin's disappearance?

So many questions. No one seems to have the answers and time is running out. Tom, Amanda and Jake must get to the truth to save Erin, though in doing so they may well end up destroying themselves.

Blood Guilt

(Steel City Thrillers 1)

Can you ever really atone for killing someone?

After the death of his son in a freak accident, DI Harlan Miller's life is spiralling out of control. He's drinking too much. His marriage and career are on the rocks. But things are about to get even worse. A booze-soaked night out and a single wild punch leave a man dead and Harlan facing a manslaughter charge.

Fast-forward four years. Harlan's prison term is up, but life on the outside holds little promise. Divorced, alone, consumed by guilt, he thinks of nothing beyond atoning for the death he caused. But how do you make up for depriving a wife of her husband and two young boys of their father? Then something happens, something terrible, yet something that holds out a twisted kind of hope for Harlan – the dead man's youngest son is abducted.

From that moment Harlan's life has only one purpose – finding the boy. So begins a frantic race against time that leads him to a place darker than anything he experienced as a detective and a stark moral choice that compels him to question the law he once enforced.

Angel Of Death

(Steel City Thrillers Book 2)

They thought she was dead. They were wrong.

Fifteen-year-old Grace Kirby kisses her mum and heads off to school. It's a day like any other day, except that Grace will never return home.

Fifteen years have passed since Grace went missing. In that time, Stephen Baxley has made millions. And now he's lost millions. Suicide seems like the only option. But Stephen has no intention of leaving behind his wife, son and daughter. He wants them all to be together forever, in this world or the next.

Angel is on the brink of suicide too. Then she hears a name on the news that transports her back to a windowless basement. Something terrible happened in that basement. Something Angel has been running from most of her life. But the time for running is over. Now is the time to start fighting back.

At the scene of a fatal shooting, DI Jim Monahan finds evidence of a sickening crime linked to a missing girl. Then more people start turning up dead. Who is the killer? Are the victims also linked to the girl? Who will be next to die? The answers will test to breaking-point Jim's faith in the law he's spent his life upholding.

Justice For The Damned

(Steel City Thrillers Book 3)

They said there was no serial killer. They lied.

Melinda has been missing for weeks. The police would normally be all over it, but Melinda is a prostitute. Women in that line of work change addresses like they change lipstick. She probably just moved on.

Staci is determined not to let Melinda become just another statistic added to the long list of girls who've gone missing over the years. Staci is also a prostitute – although not for much longer if DI Reece Geary has anything to do with it. Reece will do anything to win Staci's love. If that means putting his job on the line by launching an unofficial investigation, then so be it.

DI Jim Monahan is driven by his own dangerous obsession. He's on the trail of a psychopath hiding behind a facade of respectability. Jim's investigation has already taken him down a rabbit hole of corruption and depravity. He's about to discover that the hole goes deeper still. Much, much deeper...

Spider's Web

(Steel City Thrillers Book 4)

**'So he wove a subtle web, in a little corner sly...
And merrily did sing, "Come hither, hither, pretty fly..."'**

A trip to the cinema turns into a nightmare for Anna and her little sister Jessica, when two men throw thirteen-year-old Jessica into the back of a van and speed away.

The years tick by... Tick, tick... The police fail to find Jessica and her name fades from the public consciousness... Tick, tick... But every time Anna closes her eyes she's back in that terrible moment, lurching towards Jessica, grabbing for her. So close. So agonisingly close... Tick, tick... Now in her thirties, Anna has no career, no relationship, no children. She's consumed by one purpose – finding Jessica, dead or alive.

DI Jim Monahan has a little black book with forty-two names in it. Jim's determined to put every one of those names behind bars, but his investigation is going nowhere fast. Then a twenty-year-old clue brings Jim and Anna together in search of a shadowy figure known as Spider. Who is Spider? Where is Spider? Does Spider have the answers they want? The only thing Jim and Anna know is that the victims Spider entices into his web have a habit of ending up missing or dead.

Mr Moonlight

Close your eyes. He's waiting for you.

There's a darkness lurking under the surface of Julian Harris. Every night in his dreams, he becomes a different person, a monster capable of evil beyond comprehension. Sometimes he feels like *something* is trying to get inside him. Or maybe it's already in him, just waiting for the chance to escape into the waking world.

There's a darkness lurking under the surface of Julian's picture-postcard hometown too. Fifteen years ago, five girls disappeared from the streets of Godthorne. Now it's happening again. A schoolgirl has gone missing, stirring up memories of that terrible time. But the man who abducted those other girls is long dead. Is there a copycat at work? Or is something much, much stranger going on?

Drawn by the same sinister force that haunts his dreams, Julian returns to Godthorne for the first time in years. Finding himself mixed up in the mystery of the missing girl, he realises that to unearth the truth about the present he must confront the ghosts of his past.

Somewhere amidst the sprawling tangle of trees that surrounds Godthorne are the answers he so desperately seeks. But the forest does not relinquish its secrets easily.